THROUGH TIME *AND* CONFLICT

THE MAX TRILOGY

Contents

Foreword	VI
Copyrights	IX
Max: Not So Quiet On The Western Front	
Contents	3
1. Into the Depths	5
2. The Shadow of War	15
3. The Calm Before the Storm	22
4. Shattered Silence	30
5. Reflections of Change	38
6. A Place to Call Home	48
7. Echoes of the Past	58
8. The Empire Picture House	62
9. The Man Behind the Lens	66
10. Arthur and Violet	72
11. New Beginnings	80
Max: Escape From Berlin	
Contents	85
1. Shadows over Berlin	86

2.	The Descent	92
3.	A Flicker in the Darkness	99
4.	The Phoney War	106
5.	The Escape	113
6.	A Fragile Dawn	119
7.	The Unseen Enemy	126
8.	Road to the Maginot Line	131
9.	The Perilous Crossing	136
10.	An Ominous Reckoning	143
11.	Betrayal at Longuyon	149
12.	Ghosts in the Mist	161
13.	The Call for Help	166
14.	Fires in the Square	171
15.	A Path Less Taken	177
16.	Crossing the Divide	185
17.	A Haunting Horizon	190
18.	Epilogue: After the Storm	199

Max: The Heat of the Cold War

	Contents	205
1.	Beneath the Red Banner	207
2.	Family Threads	211
3.	Turning Pages	216
4.	Waves and Skyscrapers	224

5. Into the Shadows	231
6. Castro's Catch	241
7. The Long Road North	252
8. Cranes Over London	257
9. Footsteps in the Gallery	262
10. A Life of Books and Tea	268

Foreword
The Max Trilogy

While researching our dog's family tree, we managed to trace his lineage back to the early twentieth century. Along the way, we found an extraordinary line of whippets, all named Max, who took part in remarkable adventures tied to significant moments in history

The earliest Max we found (Max I) was a gift from the Mackenzies of Dundee to Lord and Lady Ryecroft. After Lord Ryecroft's untimely death, Max was taken under the care of Albert, Ryecroft's young valet and butler.

In 1914, Albert and Max were sent to France, but they returned home shortly after due to a catastrophic explosion that left Albert with life-changing injuries. Max became his steadfast companion as they started anew in the North of England. During the war's final years and into the

1920s, they faced navigating a post-war society that wanted to brush aside all memories of The Great War and look to the future.

The second Max (Max II) belonged to Charles Sterling , a British diplomat living with his family in Berlin before World War II. Following a street attack, Charles was imprisoned. He kept his true identity hidden, but on his release, he discovered that his family and all other British diplomats had been evacuated from Germany. As he returned to his deserted home, he saw that his pet dog, Max, was being cared for by their next-door neighbours. Charles planned his escape from Berlin by stealing a car, only to find that Max had crept into the vehicle with him. While hiding in a forest, they spotted German soldiers and tanks heading towards the Ardennes forest. The British and French High Command had previously believed an invasion through this route was impossible. Charles and Max raced against time to warn the Allies and attempt to return home themselves.

Max's great-grandson (Max III) was given to Charles's youngest son Edward, who, against all the rules, took him to Oxford University in 1959 to study modern languages. After graduating, Edward worked in a bookshop for a time. One day, his father, Charles, called to inform him of an opening for a junior admin clerk position in Washington, D.C., for 12 months. Edward and Max reluctantly set sail, leaving Edward's fiancée behind in England.

The job was rather mundane until one day, Edward's boss tasked him with a secret mission to Cuba. The Americans, Cubans, and Russians were not being truthful about the situation on the island, and his boss believed a man with a pet dog who was fluent in Spanish would raise no suspicions. As soon as they arrived under the cover of darkness, they spotted suspicious activity along the waterfront in Havana. The following day, Max barked a warning of danger on the quay, leading to an evacuation just before an explosion that could have killed or injured dozens, including someone very important.

Charles and Max returned to England, only to discover that Guy McClean, someone he knew at university, and someone he suspected might be a traitor, was working in Buckingham Palace overseeing the Queen's collection of paintings. They warned the government that he could be a spy passing secrets to the Soviet Union. In turn, the government suspected Edward of being the spy. Following a dramatic showdown in which Max chased Guy across Hampstead Heath, McClean escaped, only to resurface in Russia two months later. Despite McClean's escape, Max received a certificate of bravery from Buckingham Palace to accompany his Medal of Honour from the Cuban government.

Edward married his fiancée in 1963, and they settled down to run their own bookshop, continuing the legacy of adventure that began with the first Max.

Copyright © 2024 by John Woods.

All rights reserved.

No part of this publication may be reproduced, distributed, or transmitted in any form or by any means, including photocopying, recording, or other electronic or mechanical methods, without the prior written permission of the publisher, except as permitted by copyright law.

The story, all names, characters, and incidents portrayed in this production are fictitious. No identification with actual persons (living or deceased), places, buildings, and products is intended or should be inferred.

1st edition 2024

MAX: NOT SO QUIET *ON* THE WESTERN FRONT

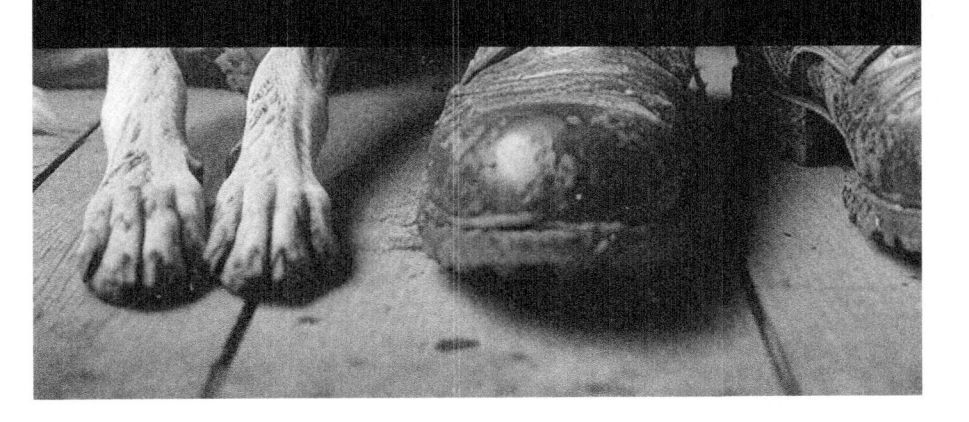

Contents

1. Into the Depths — 5
2. The Shadow of War — 15
3. The Calm Before the Storm — 22
4. Shattered Silence — 30
5. Reflections of Change — 38
6. A Place to Call Home — 48
7. Echoes of the Past — 58
8. The Empire Picture House — 62
9. The Man Behind the Lens — 66
10. Arthur and Violet — 72
11. New Beginnings — 80

Chapter One

INTO THE DEPTHS

MAY 1915. EUROPE WAS ablaze with war. The Great War, as they were already calling it, had cast a shadow over the continent, drawing men and nations into a conflict that seemed to have no end in sight. Yet, far from the trenches and battlefields, the *RMS Lusitania* cut across the Atlantic Ocean, its bow slicing through the waters as it made its way from New York to Liverpool. Onboard were hundreds of passengers, some on business, and some simply returning home. Among them were Lord Ryecroft, a distinguished Englishman, his valet Albert, and Max, the sleek, elegant whippet who never strayed far from Albert's side.

The voyage had been largely uneventful, despite the lurking danger posed by German U-boats prowling the waters. The deadly game of war had recently turned the seas into a perilous place, targeting civilian ships. But the Lusitania was a grand and powerful vessel, and many onboard believed it was untouchable—too large and too important to be a target.

Albert, though vigilant, tried not to let the war cloud his mind. He had his duties to Lord Ryecroft, a man of unwavering routine, who had taken Albert and Max with him on a brief but important business trip to America. The trip had gone smoothly, and they were now on their way home, crossing the great expanse of the Atlantic. Max, ever the faithful companion, rested by Albert's feet, his smooth coat gleaming in the soft light of the ship's interior. The dog's calm presence was a comfort, a reminder that life aboard the ship was still tranquil, at least for now.

As the Lusitania drew closer to the Irish coast, the mood onboard shifted. The air felt heavier, as though the ship itself carried the struggles of the war-torn world beyond the horizon. Passengers gathered on deck, straining their eyes to catch the first glimpse of land, eager to reach the safety of home. It was a cool afternoon, and the sea stretched out before them, dark and vast, the wind whipping up small waves that lapped against the ship's hull.

Albert stood near the railing with Max at his side, Lord Ryecroft a few steps behind, gazing thoughtfully towards the distant horizon. The wind tousled his greying hair as he surveyed the sea with the composed demeanour he always carried. Albert watched him for a moment, his thoughts drifting back to their time in New York. The business trip had been successful—Lord Ryecroft had met with several influential figures and secured a new deal that promised to strengthen his already formidable standing back in England.

As Albert turned his gaze back to the sea, a murmur ran through the crowd on deck. People were pointing, their voices rising in confusion and fear. Albert followed their eyes and saw it—a dark shape cutting through the water. For a moment, it seemed innocuous - just another wave cresting in the distance. But then, as the shape grew clearer, a chill ran down his spine. It was a periscope, unmistakably protruding from the sea like the sharp fin of a predator.

"It's a U-boat," someone whispered, their voice trembling.

The realisation spread quickly through the passengers, and the murmurs turned to shouts of alarm. The German U-boat surfaced, its menacing presence fully revealed, and before anyone could react, the torpedo fired. It shot across the water in a streak of white foam, closing the distance between the U-boat and the Lusitania in mere moments.

Then came the explosion.

The impact was deafening, a roar that tore through the ship with brutal force. The deck beneath Albert's feet trembled violently, and for a heart-stopping moment, everything seemed to freeze. The torpedo had struck the ship on the starboard side, and smoke billowed into the air, mingling with the screams of terror from passengers and crew alike.

Albert instinctively reached for Max, pulling the frightened whippet closer to him as chaos erupted around them. A second explosion followed, louder and more violent than the first. The ship groaned, its massive frame shuddering as power flickered and died. The Lusitania began to list to the starboard, the angle of the deck growing more severe with each passing second. Panic swept through the passengers like wildfire.

Below deck, many were trapped in the lifts, their escape routes cut off by the ship's failing power. Above, lifeboats were being hastily lowered into the sea, but in the confusion, many overturned before they even hit the water. Some lifeboats spilt their passengers into the freezing ocean, while others crashed down onto the deck, crushing those unfortunate enough to be beneath them.

Amid the screaming and shouting, the great ship was sinking. In less than eighteen minutes, the mighty Lusitania would be swallowed by the sea. Albert knew he had to act quickly. He scanned the deck for Lord Ryecroft but couldn't see him in the confusion. Panic tightened in his chest, but he forced himself to focus. Max was whimpering at his side, his slim body shaking with fear.

Albert spotted a lifeboat being lowered nearby, though it was already half-filled with passengers. Without hesitation, he scooped Max into his arms and rushed towards it. He reached the boat just as it was about to be lowered into the water. There was no room for him, but he could save Max.

"Take him!" Albert shouted over the din, thrusting the trembling dog into the arms of a woman already seated in the boat. She nodded, her face pale with fear, and cradled Max in her lap as the lifeboat descended towards the churning sea below.

Albert was not so fortunate. The lifeboat was full, and he was left standing on the deck as the ship tilted further, the angle now so steep that it was nearly impossible to stand. The Lusitania was sinking fast, and Albert knew he had little time. He scrambled towards the railing and, with a final glance at the surrounding chaos, threw himself into the water.

The cold hit him like a punch to the gut, stealing the breath from his lungs. For a moment, Albert was disoriented, floundering in the icy sea as waves crashed over his head. He struggled to stay afloat, his limbs heavy with exhaustion and shock. Around him, other passengers were in the water, some clinging to debris, others swimming desperately to the lifeboats. But many were already succumbing to the cold, their cries for help growing weaker with each passing moment.

The Lusitania continued to sink, the great ship groaning as it was pulled into the depths. Albert could see it, its massive hull slipping beneath the waves, creating whirlpools that dragged down anyone too close. He kicked his legs furiously, trying to distance himself from the ship's deadly pull. The lifeboat carrying Max was not far off, and Albert paddled towards it, his muscles screaming in protest.

Suddenly, the ship's final plunge created a massive wave – a wall of water that surged towards the lifeboat. Albert watched in horror as the wave lifted him and slammed into the small craft. The lifeboat rocked violently, nearly capsizing, but the passengers inside clung to the sides, their knuckles white as they fought to stay inside. Max yelped in fear, but the woman holding him gripped him tighter, her arms wrapped around the whippet in a protective embrace. Water splashed over the sides of the boat, drenching everyone, but miraculously, the lifeboat stayed afloat.

Albert, still struggling in the water, clung to a piece of debris floating nearby. His body was numb from the cold, his muscles aching with the effort to stay above the surface. He could barely feel his hands any more, and every kick sent a jolt of pain through his legs. But he had to stay focused. The ship was gone now, swallowed by the sea, and the cries of those left in the water were growing fainter.

The moments dragged on, every second an eternity. The fishermen of Queenstown on the Irish coast had seen the disaster from the shore, but it would take hours for their boats to arrive, even though they were mere miles from safety. Undaunted, the men leapt in their boats and set out to sea.

Albert's thoughts were a jumble of desperation and determination. He kept his eyes on the lifeboat, on Max, willing himself to survive long enough to reach it. Every so often, the woman in the lifeboat glanced at him, her face pale and stricken, but she held Max securely in her lap, her lips moving in what appeared to be a prayer.

And on the shore of Queenstown, they prayed, too.

The women had gathered on the quayside as soon as word of the sinking reached them, their shawls wrapped tightly against the biting wind. They stood in clusters, silent but for the soft murmur of their prayers. Rosary beads slipped through their fingers as they whispered words of comfort and supplication, their eyes fixed on the distant horizon where the lifeboats were drifting. Mothers, wives, and daughters of sailors and fishermen who knew all too well the dangers of the sea. They prayed for the souls of the lost and for those still fighting to survive.

The sound of the waves lapping against the shore was the only accompaniment to their prayers, a rhythmic pulse that echoed the sorrow in their hearts. They had seen the smoke rising from the sea, and now they waited, hoping against hope that the fishing boats would return with survivors. Some held candles, the flickering flames casting a soft glow in the growing twilight as they prayed fervently for a miracle.

Albert, unaware of the scene unfolding on the shore, was in his own battle for survival. His limbs felt like lead, and he could barely keep his head above water. The icy waves crashed over him again and again, each one threatening to pull him under for good. His breath came in ragged gasps, his strength all but gone. But in the distance, he could hear something—a low, steady sound. It was a boat engine. The fishing boats had arrived.

With what little strength he had left, Albert turned his head and saw them—small, sturdy boats cutting through the water, their lights bobbing in the darkness as they made their way towards the scattered lifeboats and debris. Shouts carried over the waves as the fishermen began their desperate work, pulling survivors from the water and hauling them into their boats.

One of the fishing boats pulled alongside the lifeboat that carried Max. The crew quickly tossed ropes to the passengers, who grasped them with shaking hands. The woman with Max was one of the first to be helped aboard. A fisherman reached down, gently lifting Max from her lap and passing the trembling dog to another crewman. Max, though soaked and terrified, was alive. The whippet was placed in the arms of another woman, who cradled him with the same care and reverence as she might have held a child.

Albert, still floating in the water, felt his body growing heavier, the cold seeping into his bones. But then he felt hands grab him—strong, calloused hands that pulled him up and into the fishing boat. He collapsed onto the wooden deck, gasping for breath, his vision blurred by exhaustion and saltwater. The cold seemed to cling to his skin, even as he was covered with a rough woollen blanket.

He lay there for a long moment, his body shaking uncontrollably, but then he felt something warm and familiar at his side. Max had found him. The whippet, trembling but alive, nosed Albert's cheek, his tail wagging faintly despite the trauma they had both endured. Albert managed a weak smile and reached out to stroke the dog's wet fur, feeling the warmth of his small body.

The fishing boat turned towards the shore, its engine humming steadily as it navigated through the wreckage-strewn waters. Around them, other boats were pulling survivors from the sea, their crews working tirelessly as the last light of day faded into night. The rescue had begun, but for many, it was too late.

As the boat neared the shore, the glow of candles and lanterns became visible through the mist. The women of Queenstown stood on the quayside, their prayers still rising into the evening air, mingling with the soft murmur of the sea.

When the boat reached the dock, Albert and Max were helped ashore, their bodies weak but intact. As Albert stumbled onto solid ground, the sound of whispered prayers reached his ears. He looked up and saw the women of Queenstown standing together, their hands clasped in prayer, their faces etched with both sorrow and hope. One of them, a woman with kind eyes and a shawl wrapped around her shoulders, stepped forward and placed a hand on Albert's arm.

"You've made it, thank God," she said softly, her voice thick with relief.

Albert nodded, too exhausted to speak. He glanced down at Max, who was now sitting at his feet, his head resting on Albert's leg. The warmth of the woman's hand and the sight of the praying women offered a small comfort amid the devastation.

As the fishing boats continued to bring more survivors ashore, the women of Queenstown kept praying. For the lost, for the living, for the souls still adrift. The war had reached their shores in the most brutal way, but for now, there was a fragile peace in their prayers.

Albert stood motionless at the edge of the rocky shore, his feet sinking slightly into the wet sand as the cold waters of the Celtic Sea lapped at his boots. Max stood beside him, his sleek body quivering slightly, his brown eyes wide with confusion. The wind howled around them, carrying with it the scent of salt and brine, the distant echo of chaos from the wreckage of the RMS *Lusitania* still haunting the air. But all Albert could focus on was the absence—the unbearable truth that Lord Ryecroft had been swallowed by the sea, lost to the cold depths forever.

For a long moment, Albert simply stared out at the water, watching as the waves rolled in and out with a rhythm that felt indifferent to the human lives it had just consumed. The sea, vast and endless, had taken his master, his employer, the man whose life had intertwined with his in ways Albert had never fully acknowledged. And now that bond was severed by the cruel hand of fate. His heart pounded in his chest, his hands clenched into fists at his sides as a wave of helplessness washed over him. How could this be the end for a man like Lord Ryecroft? A man so full of life, of stories, of experiences? To die not in the halls of his estate, surrounded by family and the grandeur of his title, but here—alone, in the cold, dark sea.

Max whimpered softly, his muzzle brushing against Albert's leg, as if sensing the heavy grief radiating from his companion. The dog had been restless ever since they reached the shore, his gaze darting back and forth as though searching for his missing master. Max had been loyal to Lord Ryecroft, too—his silent, devoted shadow, always at his side during long walks across the estate or quiet evenings in front of the fireplace. Now, with no scent to follow and no familiar face to look to, Max was lost in his own way, the instincts that guided him failing in the face of this cruel reality. Albert knelt beside the dog, his trembling hand resting on Max's head.

His voice, when it came, was hoarse and barely above a whisper. "He's gone, lad... he's gone." The words felt foreign in his mouth, as though saying them would somehow make them real, but the truth was undeniable. Lord Ryecroft was dead, drowned in the icy waters. For years, Albert had served Lord Ryecroft as a valet, tending to his every need and following him across the world on his travels, and now all of that was over. Gone, like the man himself, sinking to the bottom of the ocean where no one could reach him. Max whined again, his nose nudging against Albert's chest, as if urging him to do something – to act. But what could be done? The sea was a grave now, and Lord Ryecroft was buried beneath its surface, never to be retrieved. Albert's grief felt as vast as the ocean before him – an overwhelming emptiness that left him numb.

Ryecroft had stood tall, a man of privilege untouched by the chaos that raged around them. Now, that illusion was shattered. How many times had Lord Ryecroft laughed in the face of danger, brushing off the risks of war and travel as though they were mere inconveniences? How many times had he said, "Don't worry, Albert, the world's a dangerous place, but we'll manage: we always do"? Those words, once spoken with such confidence, now rang hollow in Albert's ears.

The wind picked up again, tugging at Albert's coat, and for a brief moment, he closed his eyes, letting the cold air sting his cheeks. There was no way to turn back time, no way to change what had happened. The sea had claimed Lord Ryecroft, and there was nothing left for Albert to do but mourn. Yet even in his sorrow, a question began to form in his mind—what now? What was to become of him without his master? Without the man who had been his employer, his companion, and, in many ways, his protector? What was he without Lord Ryecroft?

Albert rose to his feet slowly, feeling the exhaustion in his bones, the grief weighing him down. Max followed his lead, standing beside him, ever the faithful companion. For a moment, they stood together in silence, looking out at the expanse of water where Lord Ryecroft had vanished. It felt like the end of an era; a chapter of his life closed forever in the most brutal of ways. There was nothing more to do here—nothing more to say. "We'd best be going, Max," Albert muttered quietly, his voice thick with emotion. "There's no sense in standing here any longer."

Max looked up at him, his eyes still full of confusion, but he obeyed, staying close to Albert's side as they turned away from the shore. They began to walk, their footsteps slow and heavy. The wind continued to howl around them, the waves crashing behind them as if to remind them of the loss that now lingered in the air. The sinking of the *Lusitania* had claimed hundreds of lives, but for Albert, the loss of Lord Ryecroft felt like the collapse of an entire world.

Max pressed against his leg, offering what comfort he could, and Albert reached down to scratch the dog behind the ears. "We'll get through this, Max," he whispered, though the words felt empty. They had to—there was no other choice.

Chapter Two
The Shadow of War

It had been months since the tragedy aboard the *RMS Lusitania,* but the grief still hung thick over Ryecroft Manor. The estate, a sprawling testament to centuries of wealth and nobility, now belonged to Edgar, Lord Ryecroft's eldest son. He had inherited the title, the wealth, and the responsibility, but none of the wisdom or temperament that had once defined his father. The manor itself, usually a place of quiet dignity, now felt suffocated by unspoken resentment and a profound sense of loss.

Albert, the loyal valet who had served Lord Ryecroft for years, had returned from the doomed voyage across the Atlantic, haunted by the memory of the sinking ship. Max, the family's sleek and graceful whippet, had survived too, but Lord Ryecroft had been claimed by the icy depths of the Irish Sea. The household mourned, yet Edgar's simmering anger remained an unshakable presence. heavy presence. He had kept Albert on, but the unspoken accusation lingered between them: why had Albert survived when his father had not? Max, now Albert's sole responsibility, had sensed the changes too. The dog had become Albert's shadow, following him through the manor, providing silent companionship where words would have failed. The two had formed a bond stronger than before, linked by the shared trauma of their narrow escape. Life at Ryecroft Manor carried on, but beneath the surface, everything was different.

The war in Europe had raged on for over a year. The initial fervour, the naive belief that it would be over by Christmas, had faded. The newspapers were filled with stories of endless battles, trenches filled with mud and blood, and the mounting list of dead and wounded. But for Edgar and his friends, the war still held a strange allure—a chance to prove themselves, to be heroes.

In the drawing room, Edgar sat reading the latest reports from the front lines. His sharp features, so similar to his father's, were twisted in thought. He glanced up as Albert entered the room, carrying a tray of tea and biscuits. Max followed quietly, his soft eyes watching Edgar warily.

"I've made my decision," Edgar said suddenly, not looking up from his newspaper.

Albert placed the tray on the table, a knot tightening in his stomach. He had been expecting this. Edgar had spoken of little else since the war began. It was only a matter of time before the young lord decided he, too, would go to fight.

"I'll be joining the army," Edgar continued, his voice carrying the certainty of a man who had never doubted his own importance. "It's time I did my part. I can't sit here while the rest of the country fights the Germans."

Albert stood silently, his hands clasped behind his back. It wasn't his place to argue, but the dread he felt was palpable. "I'm taking the horses to France," Edgar added, glancing at Albert as if this were the most obvious thing in the world. "I'll need someone to care for them. You'll come with me, of course." Albert's heart sank further. He had no choice. As Edgar's valet, his duty was to follow, to serve. But the thought of the trenches, the war-torn fields of France, filled him with a cold, creeping fear. "And Max will come too," Edgar said, his gaze falling briefly on the whippet. "He can help with the rats. They say the trenches are full of them, and I can't have the horses frightened by vermin."

Albert stifled a bitter smile. Max, the delicate whippet, was as afraid of rats as Edgar's pampered horses would be. But he said nothing. There was no point in arguing. Edgar had made up his mind. "As you wish, sir," Albert replied quietly. Edgar's eyes narrowed slightly, sensing Albert's hesitation, but he said nothing. Instead, he turned back to his newspaper, already lost in thoughts of glory and adventure.

That evening, Edgar's closest friend, Charley Fox, arrived at Ryecroft Manor. Charley, like Edgar, was the son of privilege, and he carried himself with the same air of entitlement that came with being born into the upper class. He bounded into the drawing room with all the enthusiasm of a schoolboy on holiday, his broad grin and sparkling eyes betraying none of the gravity of the situation. "Well, old chap, are you ready for the adventure of a lifetime?" Charley asked, clapping Edgar on the back. Edgar grinned in return, the two young men buzzing with excitement. They spoke of the war as if it were a game, a thrilling challenge that would end with parades and medals. "I've already arranged for my horses," Edgar said proudly. "We'll be off to France within the week. You should see the lads down at the regiment, Charley. They're all eager to get to the front. We'll show the Germans what for, eh? " Charley laughed, shaking his head. "Can't wait. It'll be over before Christmas this year, mark my words. We'll be back in time for a proper New Year's ball."

Albert, standing just outside the door, overheard their conversation. He had seen the realities of death and destruction first hand. The sinking of the Lusitania had shattered any illusions he might have had about the nobility of war. But Edgar and Charley were blind to it, caught up in their youthful exuberance, their fantasies of glory. The sound of footsteps interrupted their conversation as Lady Ryecroft and Julia entered the room. Lady Ryecroft, still draped in the mourning clothes she had worn since her husband's death, carried herself with quiet dignity. Julia, barely twenty and already weary of the war, looked at her brother with a mixture of fear and admiration. "Edgar, must you go?" Lady Ryecroft asked softly, her voice tinged with worry. "I can't stay here, Mother," Edgar replied, his tone firm. "It's my duty. Father would have wanted me to go. I can't let the country down." "But you're all we have left," Julia said, her voice trembling. "Father's gone, and now you want to leave us too?" Edgar's expression softened slightly, but his resolve remained unchanged. "I'll be back before you know it. The war won't last forever. We'll beat the Germans, and I'll return. You'll see." Lady Ryecroft pursed her lips. "I've already lost my husband," she whispered. "Must I risk losing my son as well?"

Edgar sighed, frustrated by their reluctance to understand. "This is bigger than us, Mother. Bigger than the estate. If we don't fight, who will?" Julia's eyes filled with tears, but she said nothing more. An intense stillness settled over the room, leaving everyone silent. Charley, sensing the shift in mood, stood up and clapped his hands together. "Well, we'll make sure Edgar comes back in one piece, won't we, Albert?" He said, glancing towards the valet with a forced grin. Albert nodded, though he didn't believe it for a second. He had seen what the sea and what war could do. And now he would be going to face it all again—this time, in the mud and blood of France.

But it wasn't just Edgar who had been swept up by the call to arms. Conscription didn't come into force until 1916, and in the autumn of 1915, the excitement of young men, eager to enlist, had spread like wildfire. Albert could see it in the way they talked about duty, bravery, and adventure, as though the war was some grand quest, a test of their manhood.

Yet, to Albert, these sentiments felt hollow—echoes of the idealism he had once seen and heard before his time serving Lord Ryecroft. And now, as he watched Edgar pack his things and prepare for what he saw as the adventure of a lifetime, Albert couldn't shake a deep sense of foreboding.

One rainy evening, as the fireplace crackled at Ryecroft Manor, Julia had asked Albert to intervene. "You must talk some sense into him, Albert," she'd said, her voice trembling as she gripped her teacup tightly. "I can't lose him too. He's already speaking of charging into battle like it's some grand adventure, but you know better. You've *seen* what happens out there." She paused, looking down at her hands. "Please... you have to stop him." Albert had always respected Julia's strength, but now, sitting in the candlelit parlour, she seemed more fragile than ever, her father's death still fresh in her heart. Her fear for Edgar was palpable, and Albert understood it well. But even as he sat listening, a conflict began to churn inside him. He knew that the difference between life and death could just be the toss of a . He was far removed from the romanticised view of war that Edgar now eagerly sought. But at the same time, how could Albert deny the young man his sense of duty? It wasn't for *glory* or *adventure*, but for a cause bigger than oneself. "I'll talk to him," Albert had promised Julia. "But I can't force him to stay. The decision is his."

Later that evening, he found Edgar alone. Max, picking up on the charged atmosphere, stayed close by Albert's side, his dark eyes alert and full of understanding. "May I speak with you, sir? " Albert said quietly, his voice steady but serious. Edgar turned, his youthful enthusiasm evident in the gleam of his eyes.

"Is it about the war?" Edgar grinned, clearly eager to share his plans. "I've decided, Albert. I'm going. It's what Father would have wanted, isn't it? He always spoke of duty and honour, and now it's my turn."

Albert bit back a sigh. "Your father knew the responsibility those words held, Edgar. Duty and honour are more than just words. They come with a price—one you might not fully understand yet." "I know it won't be easy," Edgar countered, frowning slightly. "But I'm not afraid. I'll fight for England, for all of us." As they parted ways that evening, Albert couldn't shake the unease gnawing at him. He had done what Julia asked—spoken to Edgar, tried to temper his youthful excitement—but he knew that Edgar would still go. And while he admired the young man's sense of duty, he dreaded what the war would do to him.

The days passed quickly, preparations for the journey consuming every waking moment. Edgar's horses were groomed and packed, their gear meticulously prepared. The manor buzzed with the activity of servants and stable hands, all working to ensure that everything was in place for Edgar's departure. Albert, though silent in his duties, felt the burden of the coming journey pressing down on him. Max, ever the faithful companion, stayed close by, sensing the unease that radiated from his master.

On the day of their departure, the docks on the south coast were a hive of activity. Ships were being loaded with munitions, supplies, and horses. The air was thick with the smell of coal smoke and saltwater, and the sound of shouting men filled the air as soldiers prepared to board.

Edgar and Charley arrived in high spirits, their excitement palpable. Charley, ever the showman, had driven his brand-new motorcar down to the docks, showing it off to anyone who would listen. The sleek black car gleamed in the sunlight as Charley honked the horn, waving to Edgar with a wide grin. "Look at this beauty!" Charley shouted, beaming as he parked the car near the dock. "We'll be the envy of the regiment!" Edgar laughed, clearly impressed. "I can't wait to take it for a spin in Belgium. The roads will be clear once we've beaten the Germans back."

Albert, standing beside Max at the edge of the dock, watched the scene unfold with a sinking heart. The excitement of the young men around him, the cheers and laughter, felt hollow. He couldn't shake the sense of impending doom. The war wasn't going to be over by Christmas. It wouldn't be over for a long time, if ever. Max whined softly, pulling at his leash, as if sensing Albert's unease. Albert knelt down and stroked the dog's head, whispering a soft reassurance, though his own heart was filled with dread. "It'll be alright, boy," he muttered, though he wasn't sure he believed it.

As the ship towered before them, its great steel hull casting a shadow over the dock, Albert felt a cold chill run down his spine. The last time he had boarded a ship, it had ended in disaster. And now, here he was again, about to cross the sea—this time to face war, death, and the unknown. Edgar and Charley boarded the ship with their usual bravado. Albert followed behind, Max at his side. As they stepped onto the gangplank, Albert glanced back at the English shore, knowing that when they returned, nothing would ever be the same. The ship set sail, carrying them towards France, towards the trenches, and towards a war that would test them all in ways they could never have imagined.

Chapter Three

The Calm Before the Storm

The parade ground outside Armentières was a hive of activity. Soldiers in crisp uniforms marched in rows, their boots drumming against the packed earth. Everywhere Albert looked, men were setting up tents, hoisting supplies, or laughing with each other as they jostled for space in the growing camp. The smell of boiled beef wafted from a massive catering tent, mingling with the scent of horses and freshly turned earth. The air was thick with excitement and nerves. Edgar stood at the edge of the chaos, hands on his hips, surveying the scene with a satisfied smile. "Quite the spectacle, isn't it?" he said. "We're really in it now. I've not slept in a tent since school, but I imagine this will be fun."

Charley, leaning against his motorcar with a smirk, shook his head. "Fun, you say? You've lost your mind. I've booked the honeymoon suite at the Hôtel de Ville for myself." His voice carried an air of smugness. "Why on earth would I sleep on the ground when I could have velvet curtains and a real bed? " Edgar raised an eyebrow. "You scoundrel! The honeymoon suite, no less? " Charley laughed. "Of course. I planned ahead. Who knows how long we'll be stuck out here? Might as well enjoy some luxury while I can." Howard, a gangly young officer, and a friend to them both, had been listening quietly, grinned and nudged Charley. "Might be the best idea you've had. I'm not keen on this camping business either." Edgar glanced between the two, his smile fading just a little. "We'll see who's laughing when you're dragging yourselves back here in a day or two. But fine—enjoy your fancy hotel." Charley gave a mock bow. "Don't mind if I do...Let's see if there are some rooms left." The three of them shared a chuckle before climbing into Charley's motorcar. The engine roared to life, and with a final wave, they sped off towards the city, leaving Albert and Max alone in the middle of the bustling camp. Max sat beside Albert, his ears twitching at the unfamiliar sounds. Albert watched the car disappear into the distance.

The drive into Armentières was far from quiet. Charley was at the wheel, his confident grip on the steering wheel mirroring the playful banter that filled the car. Edgar sat in the front, a smirk pulling at the corner of his mouth, while Howard lounged in the back, his boots up on the seat. "Well, boys, get ready to live like kings tonight!" Charley shouted above the noise of the engine. He was always one for luxury and excess, and his gleeful anticipation only heightened as the narrow streets of Armentières appeared before them. The town was bustling with soldiers and civilians alike, the war making its presence felt in every corner, yet life carried on. They pulled up in front of the Hôtel de Ville, an impressive building with its grand facade still retaining an air of faded elegance despite the strain of wartime. Charley stepped out of the car first, his eyes scanning the hotel with a satisfied nod. "Right then," he said, adjusting his jacket as Edgar and Howard followed suit. "I've already got the honeymoon suite." He gave Edgar a wink. "Now, let's see what they've got left for you two."

The three of them strode through the hotel's grand entrance, their muddy boots leaving faint traces on the marble floor as they made their way to the reception desk. The lobby was dimly lit, a chandelier swaying slightly overhead, casting long shadows on the walls. At the far end of the room, the bar gleamed under the low lights, but the receptionist at the desk barely glanced up from his ledger as the men approached. Edgar leaned forward on the counter, tapping it impatiently. "We need two rooms," he said, his tone clipped. "We're here on military business, so see to it that we're taken care of." The receptionist, a pale, wiry man with a tired expression, looked up slowly, his eyes flitting between Edgar and Howard before returning to his book. "I'm afraid we only have one room left, monsieur. The hotel is nearly full." Howard's brow furrowed, and he exchanged a glance with Edgar. "One room? " he scoffed. "You must be joking."

The receptionist shook his head politely but firmly. "Non, monsieur. Only one." Edgar, his patience already thin, leaned across the desk and grabbed the guest book, pulling it towards him. "Well then, let's see who's staying here, shall we? " He flipped through the pages, his eyes scanning the names written neatly in the ledger. Howard stood beside him, chuckling under his breath. "We'll find someone to turf out," Howard said, his voice a low mutter. "This place is crawling with second-rate officers." The receptionist looked on, clearly displeased but too accustomed to such behaviour to protest openly. Edgar grinned as he ran his finger down the list of guests, a cruel satisfaction building as he eyed potential targets.

Meanwhile, Charley, uninterested in the squabbling, wandered off to the bar. As he strolled into the dimly lit lounge area, his eyes caught sight of a distinguished-looking man seated at a table, a glass of whisky in one hand and a deck of cards being shuffled idly in the other. The man's finely tailored suit set him apart from the usual hotel patrons, and his well-groomed appearance spoke of someone who took care to hide his vices. Charley recognised him — an American journalist, Edward Miller, presumably sent over to cover the war for his New York newspaper.

Charley had met Miller years ago in London at one of those high-society soirées where the wine flowed as easily as the gossip. Miller had been in the city covering a political story for the paper, and Charley, back then a fresh-faced young man with a penchant for mischief, had been taken with the sharp-tongued American. Charley slid into the chair next to him, nodding to the bartender before turning his attention to the journalist. "Afternoon," he said with a casual smile. "Care for a game? " Miller looked up, his eyes glassy but alert. "Do I know you ?" He asked, his voice slurring just slightly. His eyes were fixed on Charley, a faint smirk playing about his lips. A wave of recognition came over his face, "London was it? That night at The Savoy? "Charley chuckled, cutting the deck with practised ease. "You've got a good memory for someone who drinks as much as you do." "Don't we all? " Miller replied and raised his glass in a mock toast.

Miller gave Charley a slow, measured glance, his fingers drumming lightly on the deck of cards. "What's the stake? " he asked, his voice smooth, but with just a hint of a slur—a subtle giveaway from years of practiced drinking. Charley's smirk widened as he leaned back in his chair. "How about this? " he said, reaching into his coat and pulling out his revolver, placing it on the table with a soft clink. Miller barely blinked, dismissing the offer with a wave of his hand. "I've no use for a revolver." Charley raised an eyebrow, then shrugged. "Alright, something more enticing. How about an exclusive tour of the British military camps? Off-limits to your lot. You'd have the story of a lifetime." He paused for effect. "For your room here at the hotel." Miller's eyebrow shot up, a flicker of hesitation crossing his face. The offer was tempting, and Charley knew it. After a moment's pause, the thrill of the gamble got the better of Miller. He placed the deck down in front of Charley and gave a tight smile. "Deal."

The game began with quiet intensity. The other military men in the bar, sensing the stakes, gathered around the table, their drinks in hand, as they watched the cards fall. Charley dealt with swift, practiced hands, his eyes never leaving the cards, while Miller kept his focus sharp, trying to outplay the young officer who clearly had a cocky swagger about him. As the game progressed, it became clear that Miller, despite his confidence, was losing ground. Charley played with the casual grace of someone who knew exactly what he was doing. He made it look effortless, never revealing just how much he was manipulating the deck.

The final hand was dealt. Miller, sweat beading on his forehead, stared at his cards. His hand trembled slightly as he placed them down on the table. Charley, with a grin that spread slowly across his face, revealed his cards—a winning hand. The bar erupted in laughter and applause. The guests were amused by the spectacle, their cheers ringing out as Miller's face paled. Charley leaned forward, his grin widening. "Looks like you'll be needing a new place to stay, old boy." Miller sat back, disbelief flickering across his features before resignation settled in. His hand clenched around his glass of whisky, but he forced a tight smile. "Looks like I will," he muttered, pushing back his chair and standing up, his movements stiff.

The crowd parted as he made his way towards the door, his head held high despite the humiliation. "Enjoy the room," Miller said with a forced laugh, though the bitterness was clear. "I hear the smaller hotel down the street's just as fine." Charley raised his glass in a return mock toast, watching with satisfaction as the American settled his bill at the reception. The crowd began to disperse, still chuckling at the spectacle, and Charley turned back to the bar, where Edgar and Howard were now joining him, looking impressed. "Well, gentlemen," Charley said, clapping his hands together, "looks like I've solved our little room problem." Edgar and Howard exchanged glances, both smirking. "Nicely done," Edgar said, patting Charley on the back.

With Edgar gone, there wasn't much for Albert and Max to do except find their tent and make some sense of the surrounding chaos. "Well, Max, looks like it's just us," he said, scratching the dog behind the ears. Max glanced up, his brown eyes alert, and let out a quiet huff, as if agreeing. Together, they moved through the rows of tents, weaving between soldiers and piles of gear.

The camp buzzed with the sound of soldiers pitching tents, laughing, and swapping stories about what they imagined the war would be like. Talk of a swift victory filled the air—how they'd give the Germans a good thrashing. It would certainly be over by Christmas. Nobody seemed to acknowledge that the war had dragged on for over a year with little to show but mounting casualties. It was the same chatter Albert had heard since they'd left England, but a heavy feeling gnawed at him. He couldn't shake the sense that what lay ahead would be far worse than any of them expected.

After some time, they finally found their assigned tent, a small, sagging canvas structure that looked about as welcoming as a cold stone bench. Inside, there was little more than a bedroll and a blanket, but it would have to do. Albert set down his belongings and glanced at Max, who was already sniffing around the cramped space. Max settled in quickly, curling up on the bedroll with a contented sigh. Albert's stomach, however, growled loudly, reminding him that it had been hours since they'd eaten. "Come on, boy. Let's find something to eat," Albert said, pulling the tent flap aside and stepping back into the noisy camp. Max trotted beside him as they headed towards the catering tent, where a line of soldiers had already formed, waiting for their evening rations. The smell of food was stronger here, though it wasn't exactly appetizing. The soldiers in line muttered about the quality of the rations, exchanging jokes about how it looked worse than anything they'd ever eaten back home. When Albert reached the front of the queue, the chef—a burly, red-faced man with a thick moustache—scooped a ladle of stew onto Albert's plate without even looking up. "There you go. Next! " Before Albert could step aside, the chef's eyes fell on Max, who was sitting obediently at his feet. The chef's face brightened immediately. "Well, would you look at that? Now there's a fine-looking dog," the chef said, leaning down to give Max a scratch behind the ears. "What's his name?" "Max," Albert replied. The chef nodded approvingly. "Max, eh? A good name for a good dog." He rummaged around under the counter and pulled out a fat sausage. "Here, this is for him. Don't want a dog like that eating the same slop as you lot." He winked and tossed the sausage to Max, who caught it mid-air and wolfed it down in seconds. Albert grinned. "Thanks." "No problem," the chef said, his grin fading as he returned to dishing out the stew to the next soldier in line.

Albert found a spot on the ground among a group of young soldiers, their faces still full of excitement as they talked about the war ahead. Max sat beside him, licking his lips in satisfaction from the sausage. The contrast between Max's feast and the pale, unappetising stew on Albert's plate wasn't lost on either of them. Max looked at Albert with what could only be described as mild guilt, but Albert just chuckled and gave the dog a reassuring pat. Around them, the chatter of soldiers filled the air. They boasted about the medals they'd win and about the quick and decisive victory they were sure awaited them. They spoke as though the Germans were a mere formality, an obstacle to be cleared before they could return home with tales of bravery. "Won't be long now," one soldier said confidently. "The Germans don't stand a chance." Albert listened quietly, his spoon stirring the stew but never quite bringing it to his lips. These men had no idea what awaited them. Albert had seen the fear, the panic, the death. He knew what war looked like when the veil of glory was ripped away. Max rested his head on Albert's lap, offering silent comfort. Albert absent-mindedly stroked the dog's fur, finding a small measure of peace in his steady presence. The night was settling in now, the noise of the camp slowly fading as soldiers began retreating to their tents. "Come on, Max," Albert said, rising to his feet. "Time to get some sleep."

Back in their tent, Max curled up beside Albert, the dog's warmth a welcome shield against the cold air that seeped in through the canvas. Albert lay on the bedroll, staring up at the sagging roof, his mind filled with the noise of the camp and the knowledge that soon the real war would begin. Sleep came slowly, and when it did, it was restless, filled with dreams of the Lusitania's sinking and the chaos that had followed. Even in his sleep, Albert couldn't shake the feeling that this war would be nothing like the young soldiers expected.

Morning arrived, and the camp roared back to life again. Albert and Max emerged from their tent into the cool morning air, and while others hurried to their duties, Albert went to find and see to Edgar's horses, ensuring everything was in order. Edgar, Charley, and Howard were still absent. Max stayed close by, his alert eyes constantly scanning their surroundings. Albert appreciated the dog's company more than ever now. As the day wore on, the air seemed to grow heavier with the knowledge that soon, the real war would come for them all.

Chapter Four
SHATTERED SILENCE

As the day drew on, the British army camp buzzed with frenetic activity. Rows of soldiers marched in tight formations, their boots drumming in perfect unison against the hard-packed earth. The rhythmic thud echoed through the camp, mingling with the sharp bark of commands from drill sergeants, the clattering of weapons being checked and rechecked, and the grunts of men engaged in vigorous exercises. Nearby, groups of soldiers worked to erect more tents, hammering stakes into the ground and tugging on ropes, while others laughed and chatted, the pressures of war momentarily eased by the camaraderie of shared tasks. The smell of dirt, sweat, and freshly churned mud filled the air. Albert stood on the edge of it all, watching the scene unfold from a distance. Max stood beside him, the dog's lean body alert and tense, his ears flicking at every loud sound. Albert had been in this camp for two days, but it felt like an eternity.

The chaos of constant motion surrounded him, yet he remained apart from it, a solitary figure in a sea of purpose. Edgar, his only commanding officer, had disappeared without a word, and without Edgar's orders, Albert had found himself adrift. The few soldiers who acknowledged him had been friendly enough—some had even stopped to scratch Max behind the ears—but no one had any real direction to offer. They were too busy with their own duties. Albert had tried to pitch in where he could, but without clear instructions, there was little for him to do. Someone had handed him a sack of potatoes to peel at one point, and though he had spent an hour dutifully working on them, it hadn't felt like enough. The burden of inaction gnawed at him. He needed a purpose, something to fill the emptiness that had settled into his bones. As the sun climbed higher in the morning sky, bathing the camp in a harsh, unforgiving light, Albert resolved to take matters into his own hands. He couldn't stand by idly any longer. Edgar had to be somewhere, and if no one could tell him where, he'd find him himself.

"Come on, Max," Albert said quietly, his voice steady with determination. "We're going into town." He gathered his few belongings, slinging a battered rucksack over his shoulder. The road to Armentières stretched out ahead, a dusty path cutting through the fields that surrounded the camp. No one noticed as Albert and Max slipped away from the camp's edge. They were too preoccupied with the constant churn of preparation and routine. Max trotted by his side, his nose twitching as he sniffed the air, picking up on the unfamiliar scents of war and men. After a short while, Albert heard the familiar rumble of an engine approaching from behind. Turning, he saw a military truck bouncing over the uneven ground. The vehicle slowed as it drew closer, the driver leaning out of the window. He was a broad-shouldered man with a grimy cap pulled low over his eyes and a thick coat that looked like it had seen more than its fair share of mud and rain.

"Going somewhere, mate?" The driver called out, his voice rough but friendly. Albert nodded, stopping to let the truck pull up beside him. "Looking for my officer, Lord Ryecroft. Haven't seen him in days.

Thought I'd try the hotels in Armentières." The driver, who introduced himself as Frank, chuckled. "Lord Ryecroft, huh? Officers like him always find themselves in the fanciest spots. You sure he's not just sipping tea in some cushy room?" Albert gave a wry smile, glancing down at Max, who was watching the exchange with keen eyes. "Wouldn't know. But I've got to find him." Frank sized them up for a moment before jerking his thumb towards the back of the truck. "Hop in. I'm not heading all the way into Armentières, but I can get you close enough." With a nod of thanks, Albert and Max climbed into the back. The truck's engine roared to life, and they jolted forward, bouncing along the bumpy road. The ride was rough, but Max curled up beside Albert, his tail twitching as he adjusted to the rhythm of the journey. Albert leaned back, feeling the tension in his shoulders ease slightly with the movement.

After a while, the grand silhouette of the Hôtel de Ville came into view. The truck rolled to a stop a short distance from the imposing building. Its towering stone facade stood in marked contrast to the dusty, makeshift camp they had left behind. The gleaming windows, reflecting the midday sun, gave off a sense of wealth and power that felt almost improper amidst the devastation of war. Frank turned in his seat to glance back at Albert. "This is as far as I go. Good luck finding your officer." Albert nodded gratefully. "Thanks for the lift." He jumped down from the truck, Max trotting obediently beside him, and made his way to the hotel entrance. The scene inside the hotel lobby was surreal. British officers lounged in plush armchairs, sipping drinks and reading newspapers, as if the war was something happening far away from here. Laughter echoed through the foyer, and Albert couldn't help but feel a surge of irritation as he watched a group of officers clinking glasses at the bar.

Swallowing his frustration, Albert approached the first officer he saw—a stout man with ruddy cheeks who appeared to carry some authority. "Excuse me, sir," Albert began, trying to keep his tone respectful but firm. "I'm looking for Lord Ryecroft. Have you seen him?" The officer glanced at Albert, his expression darkening almost immediately. "Who do you think you are, talking to me like that?" he snapped, his voice loud enough to turn heads. Before Albert could respond, the officer shoved him backward, sending him stumbling. "Get out of here, and take that mangy dog with you!" Max, sensing Albert's distress, bristled but remained at his side, his eyes locked on the officer. Frank, who had slipped inside through the kitchen, reappeared just in time to catch the scene. He quickly moved to Albert's side, muttering under his breath. "Leave it to me. Let's get out of here." He guided Albert out of the hotel and into a side alley. "Wait here," Frank instructed before disappearing into the building again.

Minutes passed as Albert waited in the alleyway, his frustration growing. Max sat at his feet. Eventually, Frank re-emerged, his face grim. "No sign of Lord Ryecroft," Frank said, wiping his brow. "Asked around—seems he and a couple of other officers headed out, chasing rumours of German soldiers about 20 miles east". "That's impossible. There aren't any Germans that close to us." Albert replied. Frank shrugged. "Word is, they went back to the camp, took their horses, and went anyway. Want to check it out?" Albert hesitated only briefly before nodding. "Sure, let's go."

Back in the truck, they set off to the east, the landscape becoming more open and rolling as they left Armentières behind. After about forty minutes of driving, they spotted three riders silhouetted on the horizon, their horses standing still against the ridge. Albert squinted, recognising the figures. "That's them," he said quietly. Frank brought the truck to a halt, and Albert climbed out, Max by his side, as they began to walk up the sloping hill to the men in the distance. Charley spotted them first. "Isn't that your man in the distance, Edgar?" Charley called out, his voice echoing across the field. Edgar turned in his saddle, surprise flickering across his face. "Albert, what are you doing here?" He bellowed, "I came to find you," Albert shouted. "There aren't any Germans near here, sir." Edgar dismissed the comment with a wave of his hand. "Look down there. You'll see for yourself." Albert followed Edgar's gaze but saw nothing—just rolling fields and distant trees. He was about to say as much when a sharp whistle pierced the air. Then, the world exploded.

The sharp whistle was the only warning. Before Albert could react, the world erupted in a deafening explosion. The ground beneath them shook violently, and a blast of heat seared his skin. He was thrown backward as if struck by an invisible force, hitting the earth hard. For a moment, the noise of the explosion drowned out all other sounds—everything was a blur of dust, fire, and chaos. Albert lay on the ground, dazed, his vision swimming. He could feel the heat from the blast radiating off the scorched earth, the acrid smell of smoke filling his lungs. His ears rang painfully, and it took a few moments before he could gather his bearings. He tried to push himself up, but a sharp pain lanced through his body, forcing him to stay down. He blinked through the dust and debris, desperately searching for Max. The dog had bolted at the sound of the explosion, disappearing into the haze. Albert felt a surge of despair as he scanned the wreckage. The horses were down, their bodies twisted in unnatural angles, their coats matted with dust and dark streaks of blood, and then—he saw them. Edgar, Charley, and the Howard lay still, their bodies crumpled and motionless. Edgar's arm was flung out, his fingers frozen mid-reach, while Charley's face was partially buried in the dirt, a scarlet stain spreading beneath his head. Howard's legs were tangled beneath him, his chest unmoving. Blood soaked the surrounding dirt; the scene was grotesque and horrifying. It was a tableau of violence and death.

"Albert!" Frank shouted from the distance as he sprinted from the van to the spot where they had gathered. "...!" Without pausing for breath, Frank dropped to his knees beside Albert, quickly assessing the situation. His eyes darted around the scene, taking in the devastation. Albert was the only one alive. "Stay with me," he muttered, shaking Albert's shoulder. "We need to get you out of here." Albert began to drift in and out of consciousness.

Frank dragged him back to the truck and hoisted him into the back as quick as he could. Neither of them noticed the small shadow that crept quietly alongside. Max, ever loyal, had kept his distance after the blast, terrified by the explosion and chaos. But as he saw Frank helping Albert, his instincts drew him closer. Max slunk low to the ground, his slender body moving stealthily towards the truck, unnoticed in the confusion. Albert groaned as Frank settled him onto the hard surface in the back of the lorry, his body wracked with pain. His head felt like it was on fire. He was barely able to focus as Frank climbed into the driver's seat. The engine roared to life, jolting the truck forward down the bumpy road. Max, still unseen, seized the opportunity and leaped silently into the back, curling himself into the corner behind some supplies, hidden from view.

The ride was rough, each bump in the road sending a fresh wave of agony through Albert's battered body. His breathing was shallow. The truck rattled along the uneven path, bouncing over rocks and potholes as it sped towards Armentières. Frank glanced back over his shoulder a few times, his eyes filled with concern for his wounded passenger. He muttered words of encouragement to Albert, though he seemed barely conscious, lost in a haze of pain. He had no idea that Max had jumped aboard. As the truck neared the outskirts of Armentières, the town's landscape came into view. Frank manoeuvred the vehicle through the narrow streets, weaving around other military transports and pedestrians. The hospital stood ahead—a large Neo-Classical building with a makeshift military medical centre attached to it. The area was bustling with activity, soldiers, and darting about as casualties continued to arrive from the front lines. The truck skidded to a halt near the entrance, and Frank jumped out, shouting for help. The medics rushed over, lifting Albert gently from the back. They hurried him inside, assessing his wounds as they moved. Only then did Max finally make his presence known, he slipped out of his hiding place. One of the medics spotted Max. "Oi, where did this dog come from ?" he muttered. Frank turned around, startled. "Max? How did you...?" His voice trailed off, realising that the loyal whippet must have sneaked into the truck while no one was watching. Max padded softly after the medics, his eyes fixed on Albert, who was now being whisked away into the hospital. Frank scratched his head, still stunned by Max's silent stowaway act. "Well, I'll be... he's a clever one, isn't he?" he murmured. A small smile tugged at the corner of his mouth, though it faded quickly as the seriousness of Albert's condition returned to his thoughts. One of the orderlies came over, gently taking Max by the collar. "Sorry, mate, you can't follow him inside. We'll take care of your dog for now," he said, leading Max to a nearby caretaker's room where he could stay until Albert was well enough to be reunited with him. Max, reluctant to be separated from his master, hesitated for a moment before allowing the orderly to guide him away. His eyes stayed fixed on the hospital entrance until Albert disappeared.

The reports in the newspapers days later hailed it as a tale of bravery and triumph. Headlines declared that three British officers had fallen heroically in the line of duty, leading a bold attack on an enemy position and capturing numerous German prisoners. The stories painted a picture of valour, their sacrifice celebrated by a nation starved for victories.

But none of it was true.

There had been no enemy position, no Germans in the area at all. The three officers weren't felled by an act of heroism—they had been killed by a stray British shell, fired accidentally during some practice drill. Their deaths, tragic and senseless, were spun into a narrative of glory that bore no resemblance to the grim reality of the battlefield.

The truth had been buried beneath layers of propaganda, smothered by the need for stories of courage to boost morale. The tragedy of friendly fire was erased, replaced by a sanitised version of events that would never reach the families waiting at home.

Chapter Five

REFLECTIONS OF CHANGE

The time in recovery was an agonising blur for Albert. The hospital room, with its sterile scent and muted colours, had become his prison. Time passed in an eerie rhythm, broken only by the shuffling of nurses' feet and the soft groans of other wounded soldiers. His world had shrunk to the four walls around him and the persistent ache of his injuries. Each day, he could feel the constriction of the bandages, the rough material pressing against his skin, hiding the unknown beneath.

Eating became a struggle in those first few weeks. With his mouth barely able to move, the nurses brought him nothing but thin soups, sliding the spoon gently between the small gaps in his bandages. The warm liquid barely satisfied his hunger, and the act of swallowing was painful, as though every part of his body was resisting the simple task of nourishment. He longed for something solid, something to remind him that he was still alive and human, but each attempt at eating left him exhausted, the small effort taking all the strength he had.

The cries of his fellow soldiers often filled the room day and night, sometimes piercing, sometimes soft, but always present. There were men who had lost limbs, others whose minds had been shattered by the horrors of war. Their pain echoed in Albert's ears, mingling with his own torment, creating a symphony of despair. Occasionally, he would hear a nurse speaking softly in French, trying to comfort one of the men; her was voice calm but tinged with helplessness. They were doing all they could, these French nurses, but there was only so much anyone could do.

The sheets on Albert's bed were stiff with starch, crisp, and clean, but their rough texture irritated his skin, adding to his discomfort. The nights were the worst. Sleep was elusive, and when it came, it brought nightmares— the deafening sound of explosions and the ground shaking beneath his feet. He would wake with a start, his breath coming in shallow gasps, only to be met by the unchanging reality of the hospital room, the bandages still tightly wound around his face.

It was several days before they allowed him even the smallest glimpse of his healing. One morning, after what felt like an eternity of darkness, a nurse carefully unwound the bandages from his eyes. The light was blinding at first, in contrast to the dim, gauzy world he had grown used to. He blinked rapidly, his vision swimming as his eyes struggled to adjust. the explosion, he thought he might be blind. His pulse quickened, panic rising as he tried to focus on the nurse's face, but slowly, the blur began to clear. Relief washed over him as he realised he could still see. His eyes, at least, had been spared.

"C'est bon, Monsieur," the nurse said gently, her French accent soft as she smiled down at him. "Vos yeux... they are good. You can see."

The realisation brought a flood of emotions—relief, gratitude, and fear. He could see, but what would he look like? What had the explosion done to him? The nurse carefully re-bandaged his eyes, leaving them exposed now, but the rest of his face remained hidden, and with it, the full extent of his injuries.

Days blurred into weeks as he waited for the inevitable moment when the bandages would come off. He could hear the nurses speaking softly to each other, discussing the severity of the wounds, but they never told him exactly what to expect. It was as if they, too, were afraid of what lay beneath the gauze. All the while, the hospital continued its routine. The smell of antiseptic lingered in the air, mingling with the faint, earthy scent of boiled vegetables. Nurses bustled about, offering comfort where they could, their faces lined with exhaustion. They worked tirelessly, changing dressings, soothing the wounded, their hands deft and practiced, though the sheer number of injured men meant they could only do so much.

Finally, the day arrived when he was allowed to remove the bandages. A wave of anxiety swept over him as the nurse approached, mirror in hand. His pulse quickened, and dread pooled in his stomach, heavier than the bandages that had cocooned his face for what felt like a lifetime. He could hear the soft rasp of the fabric as it was carefully unwound, layer by layer. His skin, exposed to the air for the first time in weeks, felt foreign, tight, and sensitive.

The nurse's hands trembled slightly as she handed him the mirror. Albert hesitated, gripping it tightly, his knuckles white. His breath came shallow and uneven as he lifted the reflective glass to his face, bracing himself for what he might see. The moment felt suspended in time—every groan, every shuffle of feet, every distant cry from the other soldiers faded into the background as he stared into the mirror. What stared back at him was a stranger.

His face was a patchwork of scars, angry red lines criss-crossing his features, some deep and jagged, others thin and delicate. Parts of his skin were stretched unnaturally tight, while other areas were swollen and discoloured. His lips, once full and expressive, were now twisted into a lopsided grimace. He barely recognised himself.

As Albert gazed into the mirror, horror surged through him, cold and paralysing. His reflection was barely recognisable, scarred and disfigured. His hand trembled violently, and before he could stop himself, the mirror slipped from his grasp, clattering to the floor beside him. He didn't move to retrieve it. Instead, he buried his face in his hands, his shoulders shaking with deep, uncontrollable sobs. Tears poured down his cheeks. It wasn't just the physical transformation that tormented him. He was grieving for the life he had once known—the man he had been. His disfigurement was more than skin deep; it was as if his entire identity had been irreparably altered, and he feared this despair might swallow him whole, leaving nothing left of him.

The hospital staff, though caring, were, at this point in the war, ill-equipped to handle the depth of emotional trauma the soldiers endured. The war had brought a tidal wave of injuries, both visible and invisible, and their training focused on the physical wounds. Few were trained in the intricacies of trauma therapy, and they struggled to find the right balance. Some left patients like Albert to sit in silence, overwhelmed by their pain. Others, in well-meaning but misguided attempts, tried to put on a brave face, offering cheerful words and empty reassurances.

After several days, the hospital staff decided he needed fresh air and, on an overcast winter morning, wheeled his bed out into a small garden area. He was lost in thought when he heard a familiar sound—the excited barks of a dog. Max! The little whippet raced towards him, his tail wagging furiously. Max had been under the care of several members of staff and had waited patiently for today to arrive. The dog leaped onto the bed, nuzzling Albert's hand with an enthusiasm that ignited a spark of joy in his heart. He hadn't realised how much he missed Max until that moment. The dog's non-judgemental gaze and the warmth of his presence filled Albert with a glimmer of hope. For the first time since the explosion, he felt a sense of connection to the world around him.

As soon as they had settled into a routine of healing together, Albert and Max were moved back to England to St. Thomas' Hospital in London to continue their recovery. The new hospital was larger and filled with many injured soldiers, some of whom were severely disfigured; some, like him were still covered in bandages. He was greeted on his arrival by Dr MacGregor, the director of the hospital.

MacGregor stood tall, his presence commanding any room he was in. He was a man of imposing stature, with broad shoulders and a straight-backed posture that spoke of confidence and authority. His thick handlebar moustache curled meticulously at the ends, giving his stern face a distinguished air, while his horn-rimmed glasses perched precisely on the bridge of his nose. His eyes, sharp and intelligent behind the lenses, missed nothing, yet there was a warmth to them that softened his otherwise serious demeanour. His neatly combed dark hair, streaked with grey at the temples, hinted at years of experience, and the way he carried himself suggested both the precision of a surgeon and the compassion of a man who had seen more than his fair share of suffering.

On his appointment to St. Thomas' a year earlier, Doctor MacGregor had been surprised to discover that a significant number of his war-wounded patients were illiterate. For a man who spent Sunday mornings reading the papers and occasionally penning articles for medical journals, the war had introduced him to a different kind of patient—men who moved in circles far removed from his own. Almost as soon as he was appointed, MacGregor had successfully petitioned the government to provide literacy lessons in the hospital for those soldiers who could neither read nor write. His reasoning was simple: after the surgeons had done all they could, the men should at least have a new skill that might help them in whatever future lay ahead. He also believed that it was far better for them to bury themselves in a good book than in the black hole of depression their injuries might dig for them.

Unfortunately, after six months, the funding for these lessons was cut. The decision likely came from some bureaucrat trying to save a few pennies here and there. "Hospitals are hospitals, and schools are schools," was the essence of the letter Dr. MacGregor received. However, by the time Albert and Max arrived at St. Thomas', the nurses had been trained to identify illiterate patients and, when possible, provide discreet, one-on-one literacy lessons at their bedsides. It wasn't a formal program any more, but the staff found small ways to help the men gain a skill that might brighten their future, even amidst the shadows of their suffering.

One morning, Albert received a letter from Julia, Lord Ryecroft's only daughter and his former employer. He stared at the envelope, his hands trembling as he clutched it. Though he couldn't read the words inside, he could guess their contents. Julia had always been kind, but he dreaded the thought of being asked to return to a life where people might see him with pity or disgust. With a heavy heart, he handed the letter to Nurse Catherine, his voice tight.

"Can you... read it to me?" He asked quietly.

Nurse Catherine nodded and sat beside him, carefully opening the letter. She read aloud Julia's gentle words, offering him his old job back at the Ryecroft estate. As the words filled the air, a wave of embarrassment swept over Albert. He couldn't bear the idea of returning to a world where everyone would look at him differently. His fingers traced the scarred skin on his face, and he felt that familiar sting of shame. When Nurse Catherine finished, she looked at him expectantly. "Shall I help you write a reply?" She asked softly. Albert swallowed hard. "I… I don't know what to say."

Together, they worked on his response. Albert struggled to find the words, but with Catherine's patient guidance, he managed to express his feelings. He told Julia he couldn't carry out any duties and that he wasn't the man he once was. He dictated the words with tears brimming in his eyes, and Catherine wrote them down with quiet compassion. Once the letter was finished, she sealed the envelope and took it to the hospital postroom. Max, sensing his distress, nuzzled his master's leg, his warm eyes full of concern.

Weeks passed, and as more injured soldiers filled the hospital, it became clear that Albert's recovery had reached its limit. One afternoon, Nurse Catherine approached with news. "Albert, they'll be discharging you soon. The hospital's overcrowded, and you're well enough to continue your recovery away from here." Albert felt a strange mixture of relief and dread. The hospital, though filled with pain, had become a refuge. Outside, the world seemed uncertain and frightening. What would life be like without the daily care and protection of these walls? Nurse Catherine placed a stack of forms in front of him. "We need to fill these out for your war disability pension," she said, sitting by his side. Albert stared at the paperwork – the lines of text and official stamps a foreign language to him. "I... I can't read any of this." Catherine smiled kindly. "It's alright; I'll help you. Let's go through it together."

She began reading each question aloud, patiently explaining what the forms were asking. Albert nodded along, his throat tight as he answered. "Describe the nature of your injury." How could he put into words the explosion that had ripped his life apart? "Explain how it occurred." He recounted the chaos of the blast that took the men and horses and left him scarred. "Detail the extent of your disability." He spoke quietly of the burns, the damage to his face, and the deep wounds to his spirit. Once the forms were complete, Nurse Catherine tried to comfort him. "You're not alone, Albert. Many men struggle with these forms. You're doing the best you can."

Days later, another letter arrived from Julia. Nurse Catherine sat down to read it to him again. Julia's words were kind and full of warmth. She and her mother had come into possession of a small house in the north of England for him and Max. It had belonged to a former employee of Lord Ryecroft, now empty for some years, and it would be a new start for him. As Nurse Catherine read the letter, Albert felt a flicker of hope. A house of his own. A place away from the stares and whispers. He smiled for the first time in weeks. "Would you like me to help you write a reply? " Nurse Catherine asked, her tone gentle. Albert nodded gratefully. Together, they crafted a response. He thanked Julia, accepting her generous offer and expressing his gratitude. After just 4 months in St. Thomas', Albert and Max prepared to leave.

Dr. MacGregor's efforts may not have been fully realised, but they weren't entirely in vain. For men like Albert, the kindness and patience of the nurses, particularly Nurse Catherine, had made a world of difference. A positive, at least, from his time in the hospital was that he'd gone from being illiterate to semi-literate, thanks to the dedication of the staff and Nurse Catherine. It was a small step, but a significant one all the same. In a world that had stripped him of so much, this newfound ability felt like a quiet victory—one that gave him a glimmer of hope for whatever future lay ahead. Max, as if understanding the shift in his master's mood, wagged his tail and rested his head on Albert's knee, as though the future ahead of them wasn't as bleak as it had once seemed.

The day finally arrived for Albert and Max to leave the hospital. As he prepared to go, he covered his face with a large scarf, a makeshift shield against the world that felt too harsh for his disfigured features. The staff had bought Max a new collar and lead, and the little dog pranced beside him. As they stepped out of the hospital, the staff gathered to wave goodbye, their wellwishes echoing in the air. They walked the short distance to Waterloo Station and took the underground train to Kings Cross before the short walk to St. Pancras. Albert looked at himself in the reflection of the train window, and for a moment, he couldn't help but chuckle at the absurdity of his appearance. With the scarf wrapped tightly around his face, he felt like a bank robber on the run. But he didn't care. He had Max by his side, and perhaps, just perhaps, there was a chance for a new life waiting for him in that small house in the north of England. As the steam train rolled away from the station, Albert felt the eyes of the other passengers upon him. Some stared openly, their gazes lingering on the scarf that concealed most of his face, while others quickly turned away, as if they couldn't bear to look. Albert tried to ignore their stares, focusing instead on the rhythmic chug of the train as it carried him farther away from the life he had known. Max lay curled up at his feet. He thought about the house Julia had mentioned, picturing it in his mind. Would it feel like home? Would he ever feel comfortable enough to step outside without a scarf? The questions swirled in his head, leaving him feeling restless and anxious.

But deep down, a flicker of hope burnt, urging him to look forward to the life that lay ahead.

When the train finally came to a halt, Albert took a deep breath and adjusted the scarf around his face. He stood, steadying himself as he prepared to step onto the platform. The air was crisp, and the scent of fresh earth filled his lungs as he disembarked. Max followed closely, his tail wagging as he took in the new surroundings. He stepped outside, squinting against the sunlight. He took the handwritten address out of his pocket and followed the directions. Finally finding his bearings, he spotted the small house in the middle of the street. It stood quietly, waiting for him, and he felt an unexpected rush of warmth at the thought of finally having a place to call his own.

Chapter Six

A Place to Call Home

Albert's new home was nestled in a small village in the north of England, far removed from the stately grandeur of Ryecroft Manor. The landscape was marked by chimneys billowing smoke into the air, casting a grey hue over the soot-stained buildings that lined the cobbled streets. The village, with its unassuming charm, offered a striking contrast to the opulence of the manor, where high ceilings and ornate chandeliers had once welcomed guests in style.

As they approached the weathered door of their new house, Albert rummaged through his pocket for the key, his fingers trembling slightly as they brushed against the cool metal. He found the key and inserted it into the lock with a small click, pushing the door open to reveal a dimly lit hallway. A cardboard box sat on the doorstep, its contents spilling slightly. Curiosity piqued; he brought it inside, placing it on the worn wooden floor. Inside the box were flowers—wilted but beautiful in their own way—alongside a bottle of whisky and a note from Julia.

Albert set the box down and took a moment to absorb his surroundings. The house had an air of neglect, the kind that comes from years of abandonment. The walls, once painted a bright cream, had dulled with time, now faded and yellowing in places. The furniture, still in place from the last occupant, was coated in a thick layer of dust that made the air heavy and musty. The scent of old wood and damp lingered, mixed with the faint, sour smell of stale air that hadn't been disturbed in years. It was the kind of smell that clung to everything—a mixture of mildew, aged fabric, and the earthy undertones of a house long forgotten. As he walked through the rooms, the smell of dust intensified, along with a slight hint of mothballs, likely from some forgotten drawer or old cupboard. In the corners of the room, cobwebs hung thick like threads from the ceiling, and the small windows, fogged with grime, let in only a fraction of the light from outside. Despite the gloom, there was a quiet stillness in the house, a silence that felt moderately comforting. Max padded softly behind him, sniffing the air. Even the whippet seemed unsure, his nose twitching at the unfamiliar scent. For all its neglect, the house was his now, and Albert saw in it the potential for something new—a place where he could start again.

After slowly reading Julia's note, which offered words of comfort and encouragement, he sat down in an old armchair, only to stand up again moments later. His gaze fell upon the mirror hanging above the fireplace, and a wave of trepidation washed over him. With a deep breath, he reached up and removed the mirror from its hook, turned it around, and rested it on the floor. He unscrewed the cap of the whisky and poured a generous glass, contemplating whether to down it in one swift motion or to savour the taste. In the end, he took a sip, letting the warmth of the spirit wash over him, providing a fleeting comfort. Max jumped onto his lap, his presence grounding Albert in the chaos of his thoughts. He stroked the whippet's soft fur, letting out a deep sigh as he began to process the enormity of his situation. Things were bad—undeniably so—but at least he had Max by his side. It could be a lot worse, he reminded himself, taking solace in the small moments of companionship.

The next morning dawned bright and chilly. Albert awoke and decided he had to visit the local shop to gather some provisions for himself and Max. He pulled the headscarf over his face again, securing it tightly. After clipping the lead onto Max, they set off to the village store.

As they entered the small grocer's shop, the bell above the door jingled softly. The wooden floor was meticulously clean, and a broom leaned against the door, ready for use. Shelves lined with neatly arranged goods filled the space, offering various fresh produce alongside essential hardware items. Gordon, the store owner, was a friendly man in his forties, bald and wearing a well-worn apron. He had a welcoming demeanour and always seemed eager to engage with customers.

However, today, the usual chatter from Gordon and two local women—Mrs. Crawshaw and Mrs. Shuttleworth—came to an abrupt halt as they turned to regard Albert with wide eyes. The atmosphere shifted, and the air felt tense. Albert felt like an outsider looking in. He took a moment to gather himself, pushing down the unease that crept into his chest. "Am I next? " He asked, breaking the silence. "Yes, son," Gordon replied, maintaining his calm as he gestured for the two women to leave. "They were just leaving." With that, he opened the door for Mrs. Crawshaw and Mrs. Shuttleworth, who stepped outside while casting curious glances over their shoulders. Albert could sense the unease in the air; he knew how he must look with the scarf covering most of his face. He stood at the counter, acutely aware of their stares, as Gordon began gathering the items from his shopping list. "Would you mind returning the milk bottle? " Gordon asked casually, handing over the goods. "The dairy keeps complaining that they keep going missing. "Of course," Albert replied, thankful for Gordon's kindness. He thanked him and made his way back outside, the bell jingling once more as he exited. As he walked further down the road, he spotted Mrs. Crawshaw and Mrs. Shuttleworth, still deep in conversation. Their eyes flicked towards him, and Albert could see their body language shift in response to his presence. It stung, but he brushed it off. People were simply unsure how to react, he told himself, adjusting the scarf that covered his face as he moved past them.

Once home, Albert set about preparing a meal for himself and Max. He decided on a simple dish of fried steak and eggs. cooking with an odd sense of normality. As the rich aroma filled the kitchen, Max watched eagerly, his eyes wide with anticipation. Albert chuckled, feeling a sense of satisfaction as he plated the food, placing a small chopped portion on the floor for Max. They settled down to eat together, a quiet companionship enveloping them.

As the weeks turned into a comfortable routine, the villagers began to adjust to the sight of Albert and Max moving about the streets. Some were friendly and welcoming, offering polite nods or a wave when he passed, while others remained suspicious, their eyes lingering a little too long on the headscarf that covered his face. The initial stares, though, slowly faded, and most of the village seemed to settle into an unspoken understanding: Albert was here to stay, and no one asked questions about the past.

Gordon, ever friendly, had told Albert that he would share what he could about the village's history and Albert's could discuss his own past whenever he felt ready. This patience, along with the grocer's daily greetings and small talk, provided Albert with a sense of connection. Not everyone was as warm, though. Mrs. Crawshaw and Mrs. Shuttleworth, who were often seen gossiping outside the store, remained wary of him. He would occasionally catch them whispering and casting glances his way, as though trying to piece together the mystery of the man behind the scarf.

One day, a local farmer named Mr. Briggs approached Albert while he was fixing a broken fence in his yard. "Need a hand with that?" he asked, and Albert was taken aback by the offer. The man's face was weathered from years of outdoor work, but his eyes held no suspicion—just a genuine willingness to help. They worked in silence for a while, sharing only a few words, but it was a small moment of camaraderie that Albert cherished. Still, not all encounters were so easy. A group of men outside the village pub gave him cold stares one evening as he passed by, their conversations quieting as he drew near. Albert felt their judgment, but he kept his head down, determined to go about his business without drawing attention.

Inside his house, Albert tried to make it more of a home. The air of neglect still clung to the place, and his first few attempts at cleaning were overwhelming. He started with the basics, sweeping the dusty floors and scrubbing the faded walls. The scent of old wood and dampness persisted, no matter how much he aired the rooms, but little by little, he made progress. There was a satisfaction in the physical work, even though it was tiring. Albert bought a few supplies from Gordon's shop—soap, brushes, and some paint—but doing it all on his own proved difficult. His hands, still weak from injury, often shook as he worked, and some days, he found it difficult to muster the strength to keep going.

One afternoon, Mrs. Crawshaw passed by and stopped to watch him struggling to hang a curtain. "Looks like you could use another pair of hands," she said, though her tone was more one of curiosity than genuine concern. Albert thanked her politely but declined. She lingered a little too long before walking away, her eyes flicking over the house with a critical gaze.

Still, there were brighter moments. One day, a small group of children, playing near a stream, waved to him as he walked by with Max. Their carefree laughter reminded Albert of a time before the war, and for the first time in what felt like years, he smiled—a genuine, unforced smile. Max barked playfully at the children, wagging his tail, and for a brief moment, the burden of Albert's past felt lighter.

Decorating the house took time, and the process was slow, but it gave Albert a purpose. He painted the walls a pale blue, covering up the faded cream that had dulled over the years, and slowly filled the shelves with small items he'd bought from the local shop. The furniture remained sparse, but the house started to feel more like his own. In the evenings, he would sit in the small garden, sipping tea as the sun set behind the chimneys, casting long shadows over the village.

After a few weeks, Albert decided to summon the courage to venture further afield. Life in the village had settled into a quiet routine, but he felt the need to see more—something beyond the familiar cobbled streets and watchful gazes of the locals. With his headscarf securely wrapped around his face and Max trotting at his side, he made his way to the station. The journey was brief, just a ten-minute ride to the nearest town, yet it felt like a significant step.

As the train pulled into the town station, Albert couldn't help but notice the contrast between the soot-stained buildings he'd passed on the journey and the grand station entrance, framed by towering Corinthian columns. The elegance seemed at odds with the heavy, industrial air that filled the town, but it was what he saw in the square outside that truly set him on edge.

There, in the middle of the square, stood a tank—hulking, mechanical, and utterly out of place in the otherwise civilian setting. Its steel body gleamed dully in the overcast light, and Albert could almost hear the clank of its treads on the battlefields of France. The tank was part of a war bond campaign, drawing a large crowd of curious townsfolk. Children clambered over its massive frame, their parents calling them down with smiles, completely unaware of the devastation such a machine could unleash. Albert stood for a moment, watching the scene. The tank reminded him too much of the brief war that had changed his life. He knew all too well what it could do, how it could tear through men and change lives in an instant. The people in the square, though eager and excited, had no idea of the true horror that machine represented. How could they? To them, it was a symbol of hope, of victory, a way to end the war sooner. The money they paid for war bonds was, in their minds, an investment in peace, in bringing their loved ones home. Albert could hardly blame them for their ignorance; they wanted the war to end just as much as he did. But still, seeing that tank there, polished and admired, stirred something dark within him. He looked away, unable to bear it any longer, and spotted a small café on the corner of the square. Its outdoor tables offered a reprieve from the noise of the crowd, so Albert made his way over and took a seat. The café reminded him of the ones he'd seen in Armentières, though he had never stayed long enough to enjoy them. As he sat down, he caught sight of the waitresses inside, whispering to each other and stealing glances at him through the window.

After a few moments, a young girl came out to take his order, her nervous smile betraying her curiosity. She gave Max a gentle pat before asking, "What can I get for you, sir?" Albert ordered tea. The waitress returned inside with Albert's order, her steps quick and nervous. Behind the counter, Mrs. Whitmore, one of the older waitresses, watched her closely. Mrs. Whitmore had been working at the tearoom for years, her sharp eyes and no-nonsense attitude earning her a reputation in the town. She was known for her strong views on the war, and her belief that every able-bodied man should be fighting in it. Her thin lips were set in a tight line as she glanced at Albert through the window, seeing only his back and the way he sat quietly at the table outside.

In her apron pocket, Mrs. Whitmore kept a collection of white feathers—small symbols of disgrace she was quick to bestow upon any man she deemed unfit for shirking his duty. The white feather had become a powerful emblem during the war, handed out to those not in uniform, marking them as cowards in the eyes of the public. To Mrs. Whitmore, it was a reminder of what was expected of men during these times: to fight, to sacrifice, to serve. She had no patience for those who stayed behind, and the sight of a young man out of uniform stirred her ire. Without a word, she pulled out one of the feathers, holding it up for the younger waitress to see. She gave a small nod towards Albert, her meaning clear. The young girl glanced nervously at the feather, then back at Mrs. Whitmore. "I don't think it's right," she whispered, glancing to the window. "He's... There's something wrong with his face. He's covering it. I don't think he's the kind you should give that to." Mrs. Whitmore raised an eyebrow, her expression hardening ever so slightly. She wasn't angry—her emotions ran deeper than that—but there was a steely resolve in her eyes. She had handed out more than a few feathers in her time, never second-guessing herself, never wondering whether it was deserved. To her, a man without a uniform was a man hiding from his duty, and that was that. She tapped the feather lightly against the tray, a subtle but unmistakable command. "There's no harm in reminding them," she said quietly, her voice controlled. "If he's able to sit in a café, he's able to fight." The young waitress shifted uneasily, her hands clasped in front of her. "But what if he's injured? It doesn't seem fair, Mrs. Whitmore." Mrs. Whitmore's gaze softened, but only slightly. She was not without compassion, but she also believed strongly in her role. "We can't always know for sure," she said, her tone still calm. "But sometimes, they need a reminder." The younger girl hesitated again, but Mrs. Whitmore was already moving. Taking the tray from her hands, she walked steadily towards the door, her movements measured and deliberate. She stepped outside, the light from the café spilling onto the cobbled square, and approached Albert's table. Albert sat still, Max lying quietly at his feet. He didn't notice Mrs. Whitmore at first, but when she placed the tea down on the table, he glanced up. She was studying him, her eyes flicking over his scarf, his posture. Her gaze wasn't aggressive, but searching, as if trying to determine whether he was one of those men who deserved the feather she so often carried.

Albert met her eyes without flinching, his expression calm but resolute. Though much of his face was hidden, his eyes spoke of a quiet strength, a man who had seen more than his share of hardship. Mrs. Whitmore lingered for a moment longer, still trying to assess him, but something in the way he held himself gave her pause. Without a word, she turned and walked back inside. There was no dramatic gesture, no lingering stare—just a quiet acknowledgment that perhaps this time, the feather wasn't needed. Inside the tearoom, she placed the tray down on the counter with a soft sigh, and after a moment, slipped the white feather back into her apron. She tucked it away with the others, ready for the next man she deemed deserving of the small but cutting symbol. The young waitress, who had been watching from the doorway, let out a quiet breath of relief. Mrs. Whitmore said nothing as she passed by, her expression unreadable. Albert, meanwhile, sat with his tea, oblivious to what had almost been handed to him. He raised the cup to his lips, the tea warm but tasting faintly of bitterness and judgement.

After the War, in a display of gratitude, the Government had presented several towns and cities in Britain with their own tank to put on display. A gift for the sale of War Bonds. It was in the square for a few weeks in 1919. However, it quickly became an unwanted relic. People no longer wanted reminders of the war and, only months after its arrival, the tank was quietly moved by the Council one night to a field on the outskirts of town where it was allowed to rust away.

Chapter Seven

ECHOES OF THE PAST

As the weeks and months passed, Albert and Max gradually settled into life in the small village. While the initial stares from the townsfolk had lessened, Albert could still occasionally feel the uncomfortable presence of gazes lingering on him. Most people had learnt to accept the stranger with the face covering, but the whispers still lingered behind closed doors. He often caught snippets of conversations, voices dropping to hushed tones as he walked by. Despite their attempts at normality, the war remained an unspoken topic whenever he was around. The villagers, it seemed, were keenly aware of the scars it left behind, even if they didn't directly acknowledge his own.

One morning, as the sun filtered through the clouds, the postman delivered a letter that would change everything for Albert. He opened the envelope, his pulse quickening as he slowly read the official-looking words. It was devastating news: the war pension he had been relying on—small as it was—was being stopped. The letter explained that, as Captain Ryecroft's valet, he had never been properly enlisted into the army, meaning he was still considered a civilian and therefore ineligible for the pension. Although the letter conveyed that they wouldn't seek repayment of past payments, it also stated that the funds would cease in just two weeks.

Horror washed over Albert as he realised the implications. What job could a disfigured, barely literate ex-soldier like him possibly secure? The thought of working in the mills or anywhere else where he would have to remove his face covering filled him with dread. He could already imagine the stares and whispers, the judgment in their eyes, and it caused him to sit down abruptly, a cold sweat breaking out across his forehead. Panic gripped him as he considered his future.

"Come on, Max," he finally said, forcing himself to move. "Let's go for our morning walk."

Max seemed to sense Albert's unease, trotting beside him with his tail wagging. They made their way through the familiar fields behind their terrace, but Albert's mind was elsewhere, consumed by the news. They decided to stop by the village store to pick up some groceries, hoping that the mundane task would distract him, even just for a moment. Upon entering the shop, Albert was greeted by the familiar scents of spices and freshly baked bread. Gordon, the shopkeeper, was busy chatting with Mrs. Crawshaw and Mrs. Shuttleworth. As soon as Albert stepped inside, their laughter faded, replaced by silence and hesitant glances. He felt the heat rise to his cheeks but forced himself to focus on his shopping list.

"Good morning, Albert! What can I get for you today?" Gordon asked, his tone cheerful but observant. "I need some groceries," Albert replied, trying to maintain a casual demeanour. As Albert approached the counter, he avoided looking at the two women, acutely aware of their stares. After what seemed like an eternity, they left.

"Albert," he began, his voice low and gentle, "you know if there's anything I can help you with... you can always talk to me."

For a moment, Albert hesitated, the words caught in his throat. His worries felt overwhelming, and he preferred not to burden anyone with his problems. But looking into Gordon's eyes, he recognised a sincerity that encouraged him to share.

"Well," he said slowly, sitting down on a nearby stool, "it's about my income." He glanced around the store, ensuring no one else was listening, then continued. "They've stopped it. I was never properly enlisted, so I'm not entitled to anything."

Gordon's expression shifted to one of deep concern. "That's terrible," he said softly. "What does that mean for you?"

"I don't know," Albert admitted, feeling the panic rise again. "What job could I possibly get? I can't work in the mills or anywhere else where I'd have to remove this." He gestured towards his headscarf, a shield against the world's judgment. "I can't bear the thought of the stares."

Gordon nodded thoughtfully, sensing the enormity of Albert's fear. "I understand how hard that must be for you. But you're not alone in this. If there's anything I can do to help, just let me know."

Albert looked down, wrestling with his emotions. "I just need time to think," he replied, feeling a mix of gratitude and shame. "But thank you, Gordon."

After Albert finished his shopping, he left the store. As he walked home, Max trotted happily alongside him, seemingly aware of the turmoil swirling in his owner's mind.

Meanwhile, once Albert was out of sight, Gordon turned his attention back to the store. A thoughtful expression crossed his face, and an idea began to form in his mind. He realised that perhaps he could help Albert in a way that would not only support him but also benefit the village.

That evening, as Albert prepared a simple meal for himself and Max, he found himself reflecting on the conversation with Gordon. It dawned on him that while he still faced challenges, the villagers were beginning to accept him. They may not understand the full extent of his experiences, but their kindness had started to chip away at the isolation he felt.

Chapter Eight
The Empire Picture House

The Empire Picture House opened its doors in 1909, standing as one of the first cinemas in the area and a beloved fixture in the small village. Each night, crowds would gather, a line of familiar faces eagerly awaiting the flickering magic of the silver screen. The same patrons returned night after night, a shared community drawn together by the stories unfolding in the dim light of the theatre.

By 1917, the film capturing the hearts of the audience was 'Kidnapped', a silent adventure based on the classic novel by Robert Louis Stevenson, starring Raymond McKee in the title role. The enchanting world of pirates and treasure, coupled with the dramatic score accompanying the images, provided an escape from the harsh realities of life, especially during the ongoing war.

However, trouble brewed behind the scenes. Willie, the projectionist, had gone missing, leaving Charles Bowes, the cinema's owner, in quite a predicament. Rumours swirled among the villagers, with many believing Willie had fled to avoid conscription. Some even speculated he was hiding in his grandmother's basement, sheltered until the war was over. Regardless of the truth, the absence of his projectionist meant that Charles was faced with a daunting challenge: he would have to manage the projector himself while also serving refreshments and acting as the usher, all while his wife, Ada, handled ticket sales.

Charles was in his late forties, too old for military service and too out of shape, but he carried himself with a sense of pride. He liked to think of himself as a working-class man, but the substantial inheritance left to him by his father had enabled him to buy a plot of land and build the Empire cinema just a few years prior. He envisioned the cinema not merely as a business venture but as a vital public service, offering the people of the village a respite from their daily grind in the mills and factories, an hour to lose themselves in fantastical worlds far removed from their realities.

Despite his philanthropic ideals, the cinema was thriving. The sound of laughter and conversation filled the air each night, creating a vibrant atmosphere as the villagers enjoyed the films. Charles relished the joy his establishment brought to the community, but the added responsibility of operating the projector loomed heavily over him.

One evening, as he sat in his small office behind the cinema, organising ticket sales and receipts, Gordon the shopkeeper entered, his expression serious yet hopeful.

"Charles, I need to talk to you," he said, closing the door behind him.

"What's on your mind, Gordon?" Charles asked, leaning back in his chair.

"I have an idea that could help both you and someone in need," Gordon replied.

Charles raised an eyebrow, intrigued. "Go on."

"I know a man who's looking for work—Albert Sykes, a war hero. He's had a rough time adjusting to life after the war, and I think he could be a good fit here."

Charles's eyes brightened. "You mean the man with the headscarf? I've seen him around. How does he feel about working in a cinema?"

"He's hesitant," Gordon admitted, "but he's in need of a job, and I think this could provide him a fresh start. The patrons won't judge him here; they'll be too busy enjoying the films."

A thoughtful silence fell between them as Charles considered the proposal. Employing a disabled war hero who sought to avoid judgemental stares resonated with his own sense of benevolence. It was a chance to do the right thing, to provide Albert with a sense of belonging while also solving his current staffing issue. "I'll give him an interview," Charles decided, nodding. "Let's see how he does."

"Great," Gordon said, relief washing over his features. "I'll let him know."

The next day, with Max trotting beside him, Albert made his way to the Empire Picture House, his stomach churning with nerves. He could hardly believe he had agreed to the interview, yet the prospect of a job was both exhilarating and terrifying. As he entered the cinema, the scents of tobacco smoke and furniture wax wafted through the air, momentarily distracting him from his anxiety. He approached the office, the headscarf still wrapped around his face, shielding him from the world outside. Inside, Charles looked up from behind his desk, his expression warm yet focused. "Have a seat. Could I have your name, please?" he asked.

"Albert Sykes," Albert replied, his voice steady despite his unease.

"Education?" Charles continued, flipping through a notebook.

"Well... I..." Albert stumbled over his words, unsure of how to respond. His education had been minimal at best, limited to what he had managed to learn in the village school before joining Lord Ryecroft's household.

"Never mind," Charles interjected, waving a hand dismissively. "It's overrated. Have you operated a projector before?"

Albert hesitated, the memories of his time as a valet flooding back. "I've..." he began, but the words caught in his throat.

"Never mind," Charles said again with a smile. "It's easy to learn. I can show you. When can you start?"

Albert felt the heavy pull of expectation as he began. "I..."

"Saturday? Excellent!" Charles exclaimed, his eyes sparkling with enthusiasm. "We'll have you trained up in no time."

Just like that, Albert found himself with a job. As he left the Empire Picture House, a sense of elation filled him. Max sensed the change in his demeanour and wagged his tail excitedly, as if he understood that this was a new beginning.

Returning home, Albert couldn't shake the feeling of hope blooming within him. The words of the doctor from his time in the hospital echoed in his mind: perhaps a bit of luck was coming his way. With each step, he felt a renewed sense of purpose, an opportunity to reclaim a part of himself that had been lost during the war.

As Saturday approached, Albert prepared for his first day at the cinema. The nerves lingered, but they were mingled with anticipation. He would be a part of something larger than himself, a contributor to the joy and laughter that filled the village each night at the Empire Picture House. With Max by his side, Albert stepped into a new chapter of his life, ready to embrace whatever challenges lay ahead.

Chapter Nine

THE MAN BEHIND THE LENS

IN THE EARLY YEARS of the Great War, the military and the government sought to control the narrative of the conflict at home, keeping the realities of war far removed from the public's view. Soldiers who managed to obtain cameras were forbidden from using them, while the press was almost entirely barred from the front lines. Any photographs that made their way back to England were heavily scrutinised and frequently censored. Filming was outright prohibited; the heavy equipment was ill-suited for the muddy terrain, and the army refused to assume responsibility for any injuries that might occur due to reckless directors poking their heads above the trenches.

Yet, in the next village along the valley from where Albert lived, an enterprising photographer named James Horsforth had found a way to continue his passion for filmmaking. Armed with the latest film equipment, he had been creating short silent films that were shown in local cinemas. These films typically featured a charming young lady on a swing, a caped villain lurking in the bushes, and a heroic figure who would chase the villain away to the delight of the young lady. The local audience adored these productions, largely because James often cast local people in his films, ensuring a packed house filled with familiar faces eager to see themselves on the silver screen.

However, with the onset of the war, James's ambitions took an unexpected turn. Initially, he had hoped to travel to France to document the conflict, but the military quickly quashed that idea. Determined to contribute to the war effort in his own way, James spent months devising a strategy to work around the military's restrictions. Eventually, he hit upon a brilliant idea that would allow him to continue making films and provide a lucrative opportunity.

Although the valley's landscape was predominantly hilly, there were patches of flat terrain that could convincingly resemble the French countryside. With little hesitation, James approached the Army, claiming he could produce films that would depict action at the front. To his surprise, the Army agreed, and soon young soldiers in training were digging trenches and creating craters from simulated explosions using shovels and picks to create his battleground film set. James positioned his cameras to capture every moment, transforming the mundane landscape into a stage for 'battles.'

James and Charles Bowes, the owner of the Empire Picture House, were good friends, bonded by their shared passion for cinema. When James learnt that Charles had a war hero working for him, he was eager to meet Albert, hoping to gain first-hand insight into life at the front lines. Although Albert's experiences in the war were limited, Charles persuaded him to meet James, believing that Albert's perspective would add authenticity to the next film project.

The following weekend, Albert found himself enlisted as an 'expert' on the film set. A new movie was to be filmed on Sunday, and both James and Charles were excited about the prospect of Albert's involvement. Despite his nerves, Albert agreed, motivated by the chance to contribute to a narrative that could resonate with the audience.

As Sunday approached, a mix of anticipation and anxiety washed over Albert. He had never been part of a film production before, and the idea of stepping into the role of an expert made him apprehensive. On the day of the shoot, he donned his headscarf—his protective covering—and made his way to the filming location and into the tent that had been erected for the film crew. Max trotting faithfully beside him. The whole area was blocked off to the curious villagers, as this was supposed to remain a secret.

As the mist began to rise on the fields, the young soldiers were hard at work digging trenches. Their faces were set with determination, their bodies moving rhythmically, spades hitting the earth in unison. They had been at it for hours, but they showed no sign of complaint. The sight of the freshly dug trenches under the fog gave the scene an eerie realism, the kind that would have any passerby thinking they had stumbled upon the front lines in France.

Sergeant Wellburn, a grizzled veteran with a weathered face, called the men to attention with a sharp bark of command. The soldiers snapped to, their spades clattering to the ground as they stood in line, their expressions a mix of nervousness and excitement. This was something different, a break from their usual drills.

James Horsforth, dressed in his typical dusty overcoat and flat cap, stepped forward. He had a sharp eye for detail, and his work with the camera was meticulous. The soldiers were still slightly awed by him, even though most of them had been in one of his films at some point. He had become something of a local celebrity, but today he had a different energy about him, knowing that this scene needed to be more authentic than anything he'd shot before.

"Today, men, we're going to be filming a gas attack scene," James announced, his voice carrying across the field. "And we have an expert and a war hero with us to give some advice."

A murmur went through the ranks of the young soldiers. They straightened up, eager to see who this expert might be. James himself wasn't entirely sure of Albert's background. He had only heard snippets from Charles, but that was enough to build a little mystique around the man.

Albert stepped out of the tent, his figure almost ghost-like in the grey light of the morning. His entire head was covered by a gas mask, making him look like one of the many faceless soldiers they had all imagined fighting on the front lines. His gait was slow but steady, his limp barely noticeable. Even without his face showing, his presence commanded attention.

"Captain Sykes from the err... Kings... Own... er... Rifle... Horses...?" James stammered, half asking, half announcing. Albert simply nodded confirming the statement without words, though internally, he winced at the fabricated title.

Sergeant Wellburn, whose face had gone from surprise to mild confusion, nodded as well. He seemed to sense that the details didn't matter as much as the spirit of the exercise. Taking his cue, he stepped forward, turning to address his men.

"Captain Sykes is a war hero," he declared, his gravelly voice echoing with conviction. "His mother has a whole cabinet of medals, and despite limping a little, he attracts young girls wherever he goes." The soldiers exchanged glances, impressed by the image that had been painted of this man standing before them. They didn't know what to make of him, but Sergeant Wellburn's words were enough to silence any scepticism.

"I've been told he'll be wearing his gas mask all afternoon," the sergeant continued, eyeing his soldiers one by one. "If he can do it, you lot can too. No complaints. Understand?"

A chorus of "Yes, Sergeant!" followed, and with that, they all got into position.

Smoke bombs were ignited, releasing thick clouds of white smoke that billowed over the field. The acrid smell of the smoke filled the air, adding to the tension. The cameras began to roll, capturing every detail of the staged battle. The soldiers, gas masks on, moved through the trench systems, their movements rehearsed but tense. For a few brief moments, they were no longer recruits in a film—they were soldiers on the front lines, preparing for the horror of a gas attack.

Albert stood at the edge of the scene, watching through the lenses of his mask. His heart ached with the memories he would rather not recall. The young men in front of him, with their fresh faces and their eagerness to prove themselves, reminded him of the boys he had seen back in France—boys who had gone into battle full of hope and many who never returned. The sadness was almost overwhelming, but he remained silent, rooted to his spot as the scene played out.

The filming wrapped up just as the sun began to dip lower in the sky, casting a golden hue over the smoke-filled field. The soldiers, still in their masks, climbed into the back of the army truck that would take them back to base. They were laughing and joking now, their earlier nerves replaced by the exhilaration of having completed the scene. They were proud of their performance, though none of them truly understood the gravity of the battle they had just simulated.

Albert, with Max trotting faithfully at his side, followed Charles and James to the Shakespeare Inn. The walk was silent at first, the only sounds coming from the crunch of gravel beneath their boots and the distant calls of birds. The war was never far from anyone's mind, but for now, the camaraderie of shared drinks was a welcome distraction.

Once inside the dimly lit pub, they settled into a quiet corner. Charles and James ordered drinks, and the conversation slowly shifted to lighter topics. But something inside Albert stirred as he sat there, the pub filled with warmth and life. The familiar faces of Charles and James, men who didn't look at him with pity but with quiet respect, made him feel something he hadn't felt in a long time: the faint stirrings of normality.

And then, unexpectedly, Albert reached up and removed the scarf that had covered his face for so long. The gesture was slow, almost tentative, as if he wasn't entirely sure it was the right thing to do. The pub fell momentarily silent as Charles and James glanced at him, caught off guard but not repelled by what they saw. Their eyes held no judgement, only quiet understanding.

They didn't speak. Instead, they simply nodded, acknowledging the bravery it had taken for Albert to reveal himself and to trust them with this part of himself that he had kept hidden for so long.

Albert felt a tap on his shoulder, and he looked up to see Frank, the barman, standing beside him. Frank placed a double whisky in front of him and gave him a firm pat on the back.

"That took some bottle, Albert," he said, his voice full of sincerity.

Albert smiled, a small, grateful smile that barely reached his lips but was full of meaning. He raised his glass, and the others followed suit. Together, they drank a silent toast to Albert and Max, and at that moment, Albert felt just a little less alone.

Chapter Ten

Arthur and Violet

By early 1918, Albert had begun to walk around the village with a bit more confidence. Though he still pulled his cap low over his face and kept his collar turned up, the removal of his face covering had done wonders for his spirit. No longer hiding completely, he was starting to engage more with the world around him, savouring the small joys of daily life that had once seemed so distant. The soft rustle of leaves in the trees, the distant sound of children playing, and the warm laughter of villagers chatting at the market brought a sense of normality that he had long yearned for. Max trotted loyally at his side, his slender frame a familiar and comforting presence, always eager to lend companionship. The dog seemed to sense that Albert's slow return to normality was something worth guarding, his watchful eyes scanning their surroundings as they walked.

By November 1918, the war was finally over. By the end of the year, troops had begun to trickle home, their return greeted with joy and jubilation. The air in the village was filled with a bittersweet mixture of relief and grief, as those who had survived reunited with their families while the families of the fallen mourned their losses. It was impossible to walk down the street without seeing some reminder of the sacrifices made. A widow standing at her gate, her eyes filled with unshed tears; a child playing with a wooden toy soldier, untouched by the tides of history; a group of men gathered at the local pub, their conversations filled with stories of bravery and camaraderie—every corner of the village held stories, both joyful and sorrowful. Each face Albert encountered held its tale, a tapestry of experience woven from the threads of war.

In other parts of the country, conscientious objectors—those who had refused to fight—were often treated with scorn. In the village, however, the atmosphere was different. Here, in the surrounding valleys, they were met with more understanding. The locals had long prided themselves on their empathy towards those who refused to take up arms. The COs, as they had come to be known, were listened to with respect. Some had been sent to France to perform menial tasks, while others had been imprisoned and subjected to brutal treatment: their ideals often met with harsh consequences. The village had become a refuge of sorts, a place where discussions about peace and the futility of war could flourish amid the echoes of conflict.

One such man was Arthur Forest. After being released from Wakefield prison in 1919, Arthur returned home, where Charles Bowes, ever the generous soul, gave him a temporary job at the Empire Cinema. Arthur quickly became a close friend of Albert and Max, the three of them bonding over their shared experiences of war and its aftermath, even though their paths through it had been so different. Arthur's easy-going demeanour and sharp wit were a balm for Albert's troubled soul, and together, they formed a brotherhood that transcended their individual hardships.

Arthur was a committed Marxist and was one of the many COs in the village. He argued the Great War was driven by "sordid capitalism" and should be resisted by the working classes. When his appeal against conscription failed in 1916, he took matters into his own hands. That summer, Arthur took his bicycle, caught the train to Scotland, and cycled through the vast and remote Highlands, trying to avoid the authorities. He cycled on minor roads and, for several weeks, he slept under the stars and survived by performing odd jobs—once even helping at a fishing dock in Aberdeen. At one point, Arthur stumbled upon a small group of local children, who found his "secret agent" escapades fascinating. They insisted on hiding him in a barn and bringing him food like a true spy—a light-hearted moment in his otherwise difficult journey.

By September, Arthur's funds had dwindled, and with winter fast approaching, he returned home. Upon arrival, he turned himself in and was swiftly handed over to the army. Despite his solitary defiance, sympathetic locals cheered on him by singing "The Red Flag" as Arthur was bundled into an Army van and driven away to stand trial. Refusing to comply with any military orders, he was imprisoned, enduring solitary confinement at Wormwood Scrubs for a period. The isolation took its toll, leading to a nervous breakdown. Nevertheless, he persisted in his beliefs.

Arthur's family were fully supportive of his stance. His older sister, born two years before him, had been blind since birth, but her lack of sight never dampened her spirit. Violet was a fierce supporter of her brother's stand against the war and shared his deep-rooted political beliefs. Violet, despite her own challenges, was a tireless advocate for peace and social justice, embodying the values their family held dear. The Forest family was deeply united in their convictions. Their father, Reverend Thomas Forest, was an outspoken Anglican clergyman known for his anti-war sermons. From the pulpit of St. James' Church, he often condemned the war as a senseless conflict driven by the elite. His congregation, largely made up of working-class families, were sympathetic to his views, and Reverend Forest's words often inspired others to question the war's legitimacy.

Despite her blindness, Violet was deeply involved in her father's work, regularly assisting with church meetings and participating in local charity efforts. When Arthur was imprisoned, Violet became his lifeline. Accompanied by their parents, she visited him as often as possible, sitting by his side and sharing news of the family's ongoing work in the peace movement. With remarkable memory, Violet would recite letters from sympathisers that had been sent to her, offering Arthur a sense of connection to the outside world. Her unwavering emotional support in those dark moments was a source of strength for Arthur, helping him endure the isolation of prison. The bond between the siblings was unbreakable—rooted in shared beliefs and reinforced by Violet's persistent encouragement. Her visits became a beacon of hope, and their mutual support turned out to be one of the strongest pillars in Arthur's most challenging times.

One afternoon, as Arthur, Albert, and Violet sat in the cinema's small projection room, a film playing in the background, Arthur shared his thoughts with Albert. "I believe I've got more in common with projectionists in Germany than I do with the English upper classes," he said, adjusting the lenses on the projector with careful precision. His words were full of conviction, and Albert nodded in agreement, understanding the sentiment. Albert had spent most of his life attending to the every need of one upper-class family. Pressing clothes, preparing meals, cleaning, washing, and looking after their horses. Even though Lord Ryecroft could be called a good employer, everything revolved around him and his family.

People like Albert were just the little people whose purpose was just to attend to their every need.

"We can do something to improve the lives of the mill workers and textile workers around here," offered Violet. Albert nodded in agreement. He didn't realise that the nod he gave to a seemingly open suggestion would change his life in an unexpected way.

"I'm thinking of standing for the Labour Party in the next election, Albert," Arthur announced, "and I'd like you and Max to be my campaign managers." Albert was taken aback but flattered. Campaigning wasn't something he had ever considered, but the thought of doing something meaningful, something that would shape the future of the village, appealed to him. The idea of being involved in the community and using his experiences to foster understanding and compassion ignited a spark within him.

Before he could answer, a clattering sound filled the room, followed by whistles and boos from the cinema auditorium. In the depths of their conversation, they had forgotten to prepare and change the next film reel for the movie showing. Quickly, Albert stood up, took the film from the canister on the table, and threaded it through the projector before setting it running. An enthusiastic cheer came up from the auditorium as *Broken Blossoms* with Lillian Gish began to play on the screen again. "That was close!" said Albert.

He thought back to the war propaganda film he had been cajoled into being involved with a couple of years prior but considered it better not to tell Arthur about it as he knew it wouldn't sit well with him. Of course, Arthur knew anyway, but though it best not to mention it either.

Arthur left the projection room, giving Albert time alone with Violet. "So," Violet said, with a knowing smile, "will you be his campaign manager?" "Of course," Albert replied, realising he hadn't answered the question in all the flurry.

The following day, in the quiet stillness of St. James' Church, Arthur stood at the pulpit, practising his oratory skills. His voice echoed in the empty nave as he rehearsed for his upcoming speeches. Sitting in the pews, Violet, Albert, and Max offered encouragement, urging him to focus on being passionate and compassionate rather than adopting a 'fire and brimstone' style of preaching. They knew Arthur had a powerful message, and they believed delivering it with genuine conviction would resonate more with people.

After the practice session, Arthur gathered his notes and prepared to head off for his evening shift at the cinema. He waved off the suggestions to rehearse further, feeling more confident in his abilities. Together, Violet, Albert, and Max decided to enjoy a leisurely walk along the canal, letting the cool air and peaceful surroundings ease the strain of their hard work. It was a rare moment of calm in the midst of an otherwise hectic campaign, one that reminded them why they were so committed to the cause.

Two weeks later, Arthur was chosen to fight for the seat in the 1922 election, though more importantly for Albert, a romance had started to blossom between himself and Violet. The weeks that followed were filled with more walks on the canal and other pastimes, though they had both decided that the dancehall was not for them. The local football team was doing very well, so several Saturday afternoons were spent on the terraces shouting and chanting, with Albert describing to Violet the action on the pitch.

As the election drew closer, Arthur, Albert, and Violet threw themselves wholeheartedly into campaigning. Every morning, they set out with bundles of leaflets and a clear purpose, knocking on doors, speaking to residents, and listening to their concerns. In every neighbourhood, from the mill workers' cottages to the quiet, cobbled streets where shopkeepers lived, they spread the message of change. Arthur was determined to represent the working class and to offer an alternative to the old guard of politics. Arthur's speeches became a fixture in the town. He would set up a small stage in the market square, rallying those who gathered with passionate calls for fair wages and better working conditions. His voice carried across the park on Sunday afternoons, where families on their day of rest would stop to listen as he explained how the current government had failed them. The Mechanics Institute debates were tense but energising; Arthur held his own against more experienced candidates, calling out the complacency of the sitting Liberal MP and pointing to the harsh realities the working people faced.

Albert and Violet worked tirelessly behind the scenes, organising meetings, distributing posters, and ensuring Arthur was seen and heard everywhere they thought a crowd might gather. Violet, despite her blindness, became the heart of the campaign. She had a way of speaking to people that made them feel truly heard, and her dedication to the cause inspired others to join their movement.

As Election Day neared, the trio felt a surge of optimism. They had worked harder than ever, and the support they received gave them hope that change was within reach. However, when the votes were counted, Arthur narrowly lost the seat to the sitting Liberal candidate. The Conservatives won the overall election, with Bonar Law becoming Prime Minister, albeit with a reduced majority. The loss was a bitter pill to swallow, especially after all the hard work they had put in. For a moment, it felt as though all their efforts had been for nothing. But Arthur, ever resilient, refused to be deterred. He quickly shifted his focus to the local council election, knowing that change could still happen on a smaller scale. The defeat only strengthened his resolve to fight for the rights of the town's working class.

That same year, the local football team achieved something extraordinary—they defeated Preston North End at Wembley to win the FA Cup. The whole town erupted in celebration. Now, the team paraded the trophy from the top of an open-top omnibus through the streets, cheered on by hundreds of people gathered in the town square. Among them were Albert and Violet, watching with pride as the cup gleamed in the sunlight. Max, also an ardent fan, decided on this occasion to spend the afternoon asleep on the settee at home

For Albert and Violet, these moments felt like the culmination of all their hard work. The campaign had brought them closer together, and now, as they stood in the crowd with Albert naming the players who took it in turns to hold the FA Cup aloft, they couldn't help but feel that life was falling into place. Their future, once filled with uncertainty, now seemed full of promise and possibilities. Despite the challenges ahead, they knew they were on the right path, and together, they would keep moving forward.

Chapter Eleven
New Beginnings

Towards the end of 1923, Albert found the courage to propose to Violet. It was a simple yet heartfelt moment, one that encapsulated their shared journey.

Their wedding in 1925 was a small affair, held in St. James' church, with Violet and Arthur's father, Reverend Thomas Forest, carrying out the service. Arthur had not only become a local councillor but also been elected mayor that year. Julia Ryecroft, now married and living in her own grand estate, travelled to attend the ceremony, bringing her husband and a whippet named Penny. The sight of the two sleek dogs, Max and Penny, playing together outside the church brought a smile to everyone's faces, a moment of joy amidst the solemnity of the occasion.

As Albert stood at the altar, surrounded by loved ones, he couldn't help but reflect on how far he had come. The years of hiding and feeling ashamed of his scars were behind him, replaced by a sense of belonging and acceptance. With Violet by his side, her unwavering support a source of strength, and Max always there to remind him of the simple joys in life, Albert had found something he had long thought lost: peace. The vows they exchanged felt like a culmination of their shared experiences, a promise to support each other through thick and thin. As they stepped out of the church, greeted by the cheers of family and friends, Albert felt an overwhelming sense of gratitude wash over him.

As the villagers raised their glasses to toast the newlyweds, laughter and music filled the air, the future seeming full of hope and promise. Albert felt a sense of belonging he had longed for – a connection to his community and to Violet that transcended the pain of his past.

MAX:
ESCAPE *FROM* BERLIN

Contents

1. Shadows over Berlin — 86
2. The Descent — 92
3. A Flicker in the Darkness — 99
4. The Phoney War — 106
5. The Escape — 113
6. A Fragile Dawn — 119
7. The Unseen Enemy — 126
8. Road to the Maginot Line — 131
9. The Perilous Crossing — 136
10. An Ominous Reckoning — 143
11. Betrayal at Longuyon — 149
12. Ghosts in the Mist — 161
13. The Call for Help — 166
14. Fires in the Square — 171
15. A Path Less Taken — 177
16. Crossing the Divide — 185
17. A Haunting Horizon — 190
18. Epilogue: After the Storm — 199

Chapter One

Shadows over Berlin

BERLIN, 1939. THE CITY buzzed with an undercurrent of unease, as if the very air carried the weight of the coming storm. The streets were busy, yet a quiet anxiety lingered in every interaction, every glance. The grandiose buildings along Wilhelmstrasse loomed over pedestrians, their stone facades imposing in their silence. Among them stood the British Embassy, a relic of another time, when diplomacy had seemed a viable option to maintain peace in Europe. The embassy was a hive of activity, where decisions made in its grand offices might alter the course of history.

Inside, Charles Sterling, a seasoned diplomat with the weariness of his years etched into his features, sat behind a heavy oak desk. His office was tidy, the neatness a reflection of his methodical mind. A stack of papers lay before him, reports that needed to be sent back to London, each one detailing the worsening situation in Germany. Charles was a man of quiet authority, not given to dramatic or unnecessary emotion. His sandy hair showed streaks of grey, and fine lines criss-crossed his forehead from years of navigating the treacherous waters of international politics. He wore a three-piece suit, meticulously pressed, the pocket watch chain glinting under the light from the window. But it was his eyes—pale blue, almost steely—that revealed the depth of his experience and the toll the last few years had taken on him.

Covering his desk were papers strewn about. Each word inscribed on those pages emphasised the harsh truth he had been hesitant to acknowledge: diplomacy was proving unsuccessful. The Nazi regime's relentless aggression, the annexation of territories, the oppressive grip on its own people—everything pointed to the inevitable. War with Britain was not just a possibility; it was a looming certainty.

As Charles reviewed the latest intelligence reports, the door to his office opened without a knock. It was customary for his superior, Sir Neville Henderson, the British Ambassador to Germany, to dispense with formalities when it suited him. Henderson was a tall man, thin to the point of appearing gaunt, with sharp features that might have seemed aristocratic were it not for the deep-set worry that often shadowed his eyes. "Charles," Henderson began, his voice clipped as always, though it carried an undercurrent of something else today—perhaps resignation, or was it fear? "We've just received word from London. The situation is escalating faster than expected." Charles looked up, meeting Henderson's gaze. "What does London propose?" he asked, though he already suspected the answer. Henderson hesitated – something unusual for a man known for his decisiveness, misguided as it might often be. "Chamberlain still believes we can reason with them, though the window for negotiation is narrowing. We've been instructed to maintain our current stance, but... preparations for the closing of the Embassy and being recalled have begun." Charles sat back in his chair, considering the implications. "And the Germans? What of their intentions? Surely, even Ribbentrop must see the folly of pushing this any further." Henderson's lips tightened into a thin line. "Ribbentrop? He's nothing more than Hitler's mouthpiece. The man believes in the inevitability of war as fervently as any true believer in their faith. He won't back down, not now." Charles nodded, Henderson's words sank in, leaving a quiet unease between them. The ambassador glanced out of the window, towards the city that sprawled beyond the embassy walls.

A sharp rap on the door interrupted the conversation. Henderson's secretary, a young man with an anxious demeanour, appeared in the doorway. "Sir Neville, there's a call for you from London. They say it's urgent." Henderson nodded curtly. "I'll take it in my office." He turned back to Charles. "We may have to act sooner than expected." With that, Henderson swept out of the room, leaving Charles alone with his thoughts. The clock ticked on, its rhythm quietly measuring the moments passing by. Charles rose from his desk, moving to the window that overlooked Wilhelmstrasse. Below, people went about their day, but there was an undercurrent of unease in their hurried steps and in the furtive glances exchanged between strangers.

The city was holding its breath, waiting for the inevitable. Berlin had always been a city of contrasts, where the past and the future collided with a force that was both creative and destructive. But now, the vibrancy of its streets, the brilliance of its architecture, seemed to be overshadowed by the dark clouds of war gathering on the horizon. Charles' thoughts drifted to his family. Margaret, his wife, and their two children, Lucy and Peter, had been in Berlin with him for several years now. Margaret had adjusted to the diplomatic life with grace, though she had always worried about the strain it placed on their family. Lucy and Peter weren't old enough to grasp the seriousness of the situation or fully comprehend the implications of the unrest brewing around them. His thoughts were interrupted by the distant sound of marching boots, a sound that had become all too common lately. Charles knew what it meant—another parade, another display of power meant to instil fear and obedience. He turned away from the window, unable to bear the sight of the swastika banners fluttering in the wind.

The Embassy had always been a sanctuary of sorts, a small piece of Britain in the heart of Berlin, but now it felt more like a prison. The world outside was closing in, and Charles knew that soon, even the embassy's walls would not be enough to keep the dangers at bay. He returned to his desk, staring at the papers before him. The words blurred as his mind wandered. How had it come to this? The world had been at peace, or so it seemed, only a few years ago. Now, everything was unravelling, and the ties that had bound nations together in diplomacy and mutual respect were fraying beyond repair. That evening, he paced in his office long after most of the staff had gone home. He struggled to concentrate, with an uneasy feeling in the air and a sense that the world teetered on the edge of disaster clouding his mind. The sudden chime of the clock striking seven jolted him from his thoughts.

The realisation that he had been in the office for hours, making no progress, gnawed at him. Frustrated, Charles stepped outside to walk home, hoping that the cool night air might clear his mind. Leaving the embassy, he walked along Wilhelmstrasse, the usually bustling street now eerily quiet. The grand buildings that lined the street were shrouded in darkness, their imposing facades taking on a more sinister aspect under the pale moonlight. As he walked, his thoughts returned to Henderson's earlier words. The ambassador's pessimism had been unusual, and it left him feeling unsettled. He had always believed in the power of diplomacy, but now he couldn't shake the sense that it might be too late.

His feet led him towards the Hotel Adlon, its opulent exterior sharply opposing the growing bleakness of the city around it. The hotel had been a symbol of Berlin's golden age, a gathering place for the city's elite and international dignitaries. But tonight, even the Adlon seemed to have lost some of its lustre, the grand entrance and marble pillars appearing more foreboding than welcoming. As he passed the hotel, he noticed a group of men loitering near the entrance. They wore the brown shirts that had become synonymous with the Nazi regime, their faces hard and unfriendly. Charles instinctively pulled his coat tighter around himself, hoping to avoid their attention. But it was too late. One man called out to him, his voice laced with suspicion. "Hey, you there! What are you doing out at this hour?" Charles slowed his pace, considering his options. He could try to talk his way out of the situation, or he could keep walking and hope they wouldn't follow. Before he could decide, the men approached him, their movements swift and menacing. "You don't look like one of us," another man sneered, his eyes narrowing as he studied Charles. "What's your business here?" Charles's pulse quickened as the menacing brownshirts closed in on him. "You're a foreigner, aren't you?" one of them sneered, his eyes narrowing with suspicion. "What's your name?"

Charles, fully aware that revealing his identity could put him in even greater danger, played along. "Hans Müller," he said, choosing the most common German name that came to mind. "I work at the Ministry of Agriculture." The man who had spoken first frowned, clearly unconvinced. "Müller, huh? Show us your papers." Charles cursed silently, realising he had no identification with him. "I left them at home," he said, trying to sound casual. "I didn't think I'd need them for a short walk." But the men weren't satisfied. One of them stepped forward and struck Charles across the face. The force of the blow sent him staggering back, and before he could recover, the others joined in. Punches and kicks rained down on him, leaving him dazed and gasping for breath. "Get him up," one of them barked, and two of the men roughly hauled Charles to his feet. They began dragging him down the street, ignoring his feeble attempts to resist. his heart raced with fear, his mind scrambling for a way out of this dire situation. But the pain that throbbed through his body with every step clouded his thoughts.

After what felt like an eternity, they reached a police station, a dark, foreboding building with iron bars on the windows. The brownshirts roughly shoved him through the entrance, their boots echoing off the stone floors as they marched him towards the front desk. The desk sergeant looked up, his face a mask of boredom, until he saw the bloodied and battered man. His eyes flicked to the brownshirts, and a look of understanding passed between them. "Caught this one sneaking around," one brownshirt said, his tone dripping with contempt. "Claims he's a German, but we think he's lying."

The sergeant nodded curtly and gestured to the two officers. "Take him to the cells. We'll deal with him later." The officers grabbed Charles by the arms and dragged him down a dimly lit corridor, his feet barely touching the ground. They reached a heavy iron door, which one officer unlocked with a loud, grating sound. They shoved him inside, and he stumbled, falling hard onto the cold, damp floor. The door slammed shut behind him with a finality that sent a shiver down his spine.

Charles lay there for a moment, his body aching from the beating he had endured.

Chapter Two

THE DESCENT

THE CELL WAS COLD and damp, a far cry from the comfort of the embassy or his home in Charlottenburg. Charles Sterling sat on the hard, wooden bench that lined one wall, his thoughts racing as he tried to make sense of the last few hours. As he sat in the dim light of the cell, he realised how vulnerable he truly was. Without documentation, without anyone to vouch for him, he was just another prisoner in a city on the brink of war.

The hours dragged on, marked only by the distant sounds of doors opening and closing and the occasional shout or curse from other prisoners. He tried to keep his mind occupied, replaying the events of the day and considering his options. But there was little comfort to be found in strategy; his fate was now in the hands of his captors, and he had no way of knowing what they planned to do with him. Time lost all meaning as he sat in the darkness, the walls of the cell pressing in on him. He did not know how long he had been there—hours, perhaps days. The isolation was maddening, and the silence only deepened his sense of helplessness. Occasionally, he could hear the muffled voices of the guards as they passed by his cell, but they never spoke to him directly, and his own attempts to communicate were met with cold indifference. It was during one of these stretches of silence that he overheard a conversation between two guards just outside his cell door. Their voices were low, but in the quiet of the cell block, every word carried. "Did you hear?" one guard said, his tone conspiratorial. "The British ambassador was in a right state when he delivered the ultimatum to Ribbentrop. Practically shaking, he was." The other guard chuckled. "And what good did it do him? Ribbentrop didn't even bother to meet with him. Sent his bloody translator instead." "Typical," the first guard muttered. "They think they can push us around, but they'll see. We've been ready for this for years."

A surge of dread washed over Charles as he fully grasped the meaning behind their words. An ultimatum. That could only mean one thing—war. And if Ribbentrop had refused to meet with Henderson, then the situation was even more dire than he had feared. The guards' voices faded as they moved down the corridor, leaving Charles alone once again. But the information they had unwittingly shared reverberated in his mind. War had been declared. Britain and Germany were now officially at odds, and here he was, trapped in a cell in the heart of enemy territory. What would happen to Margaret and the children? Were they still safe in Berlin, or had they been caught up in the chaos that must surely be sweeping the city? Charles knew he had to get out, but at the same time, he couldn't afford to give his true identity away. The walls of his cell seemed unbreakable, the guards implacable in their duty. He stood up, pacing the small space in an attempt to burn off the restless energy that coursed through him. His mind raced, searching for a solution, but every avenue he considered seemed to lead to a dead end. The Embassy could have been evacuated by now; the staff ordered out of Berlin along with the rest of the British nationals. And even if they had managed to contact the German authorities about his disappearance, it was unlikely that the Nazi regime would be willing to cooperate now that war had been declared.

As the hours wore on, Charles felt his resolve harden. He could not afford to wait passively for a rescue that might never come. If he wanted to survive, if he wanted to find his family, he would have to take matters into his own hands. His chance came on the fourth or fifth day of his imprisonment. The cell door clanged open, and a burly officer gestured for him to follow. Charles' muscles protested as he stood, the long hours of confinement having taken their toll. He was led down a narrow corridor, past several other cells, until they reached a small, dimly lit room. "Sit," the officer barked, pointing to a wooden chair in the centre of the room. Charles complied, noting the empty desk that faced him. He assumed he was about to be interrogated, but as the minutes ticked by, it became clear that the officer was waiting for someone else to arrive. The silence stretched on, broken only by the occasional scrape of the officer's boots on the stone floor as he shifted his weight.

Eventually the door opened again, and a man in a dark uniform entered. He was tall and thin, with a face that might have been handsome were it not for the cruel twist to his mouth and the coldness in his eyes. He took a seat behind the desk, his gaze never leaving Charles' face. "You're in a difficult position, Herr Müller," the man began, his voice smooth and detached. "No identification, no papers, and a suspicious story. It doesn't look good for you." Charles swallowed, forcing himself to maintain a calm facade. "I've already told your men my papers were at home. I was out for a walk when I was accosted by those men." The man raised an eyebrow, as if amused by Charles' attempt to defend himself. "A convenient excuse, don't you think?" Charles' heart skipped a beat, but he kept his expression neutral. "I'm just a bureaucrat. My job is to manage agricultural reports, nothing more." The man leaned back in his chair, studying Charles intently. "A bureaucrat with no papers, no identification, and no clear story. It's not a convincing tale, Herr Müller. Not at all." Charles knew he was treading on thin ice. He had to be careful, or this interrogation could quickly turn into something much more dangerous. "I understand your scepticism, but I assure you, I'm not a threat to anyone. My work is strictly administrative." The man's lips curled into a faint smile, though there was no warmth in it. "We'll see about that." He gestured to the officer, who produced a small notebook from his pocket and began to take notes. Let's start with the basics," the man continued. "Where were you born, Herr Müller?" Charles hesitated for a fraction of a second before responding. "Bremen." "And your date of birth?" "January 12th, 1903." The man nodded, jotting down the information. "And your current address?" "Frederickstrasse 22."

The interrogation continued, with the man asking increasingly detailed questions about Charles' supposed life in Berlin. Charles answered each one as best he could, drawing on his knowledge of the city and its culture to craft a plausible story. But he knew that any slip up could give him away, and the tension in the room was palpable. Finally, the man seemed to grow bored with the questioning. He closed his notebook and leaned forward, his eyes narrowing. "You're not telling me everything, Herr Müller. I can sense it. You're hiding something." Sterling's mind raced, searching for a way out of this trap. He decided to take a gamble, hoping to turn the man's suspicions to his advantage. "I'm not hiding anything, but I understand why you might think so. The truth is, I've been having some trouble with my speech recently. It's made me hesitant to talk, especially under these circumstances." The man raised an eyebrow, clearly intrigued. "Trouble with your speech? What kind of trouble?" Charles cleared his throat, making a show of stumbling over his words. "A... a stammer. It... it's worse when I'm nervous." The man watched him closely, as if trying to determine whether Charles was telling the truth. After a moment, he nodded. "Very well, Herr Müller. I'll take that into account. But remember, if I find out you've been lying to me, there will be consequences." Charles nodded, relieved that his ruse seemed to have worked. "I understand." The man stood up, signalling that the interrogation was over. "You'll be released, but don't think for a moment that you're free. We'll be watching you, Herr Müller. One wrong move, and you'll find yourself back here—or worse." Charles nodded again. He knew he had only bought himself a temporary reprieve. The real challenge would be surviving outside the confines of the police station. The officer led him out of the interrogation room and back through the winding corridors to the entrance of the building. Without another word, the officer pushed open the door and gestured for him to leave. Charles stepped out into the cool night air, feeling a mixture of relief and trepidation. He had escaped the immediate danger, but he was far from safe.

The streets of Berlin were eerily quiet, the usual bustle of the city replaced by an oppressive silence. The sky was overcast, the clouds heavy with the threat of rain. He had to move quickly to get as far away from the police station as possible before anyone could change their mind about releasing him.

He walked briskly, keeping to the shadows as he made his way through the city. The landmarks that had once been so familiar now seemed alien and threatening, their grandeur overshadowed by the darkness of the night and the fear that gripped him.

As he approached Charlottenburg, where his home was, his thoughts shifted to his family. He guessed they were likely already on their way out of the city, evacuated along with the other British nationals. But he couldn't be certain, and the possibility that they were still in Berlin gnawed at him. When he finally reached his street, the sight of his house brought a pang of longing. As he approached, he noticed the curtains were drawn and the windows were dark. He also noticed his car, usually parked in front of the house, was gone. The house itself looked abandoned, its once-welcoming facade now cold and uninviting. He tried the front door, but it was locked. He moved to the side of the house, where a small window next to the door had been left slightly open. With some effort, he managed to push it wider and climb inside. The interior of the house was eerily quiet, the rooms empty and devoid of the warmth that had once filled them. His footsteps echoed on the wooden floors as he moved from room to room, searching for any sign of his family. But the house had been stripped of all personal belongings. Most of the furniture was gone, the shelves bare. It was as if his family had never lived there at all. Charles felt a wave of despair wash over him. He had hoped to find some trace of them, some clue as to where they had gone. But there was nothing, only the cold emptiness of the house that had once been their home. He made his way to the bedroom, where the bed still stood in the centre of the room. Exhausted and overwhelmed, he lay down on the bare mattress, his mind racing as he tried to formulate a plan.

He was alone in a city that had become increasingly hostile, with no money, no resources, and no way of knowing where his family was. But as he stared up at the ceiling, he knew one thing for certain: he would find them, no matter what it took.

Chapter Three

A FLICKER IN THE DARKNESS

THE MORNING SUN PIERCED through the thick curtains of Charles Sterling's bedroom, casting faint lines of light across the otherwise dark room. His eyes fluttered open, and for a moment, he was disoriented, unsure if he was awake or still trapped in a nightmare. The events of the past few days were a blur, but the stark reality quickly set in. He was a British national stranded in Berlin, a city now teetering on the edge of madness as the war unfolded around him.

With a groan, he pushed himself up from the bed. His muscles ached from sleeping in awkward positions, and his mind was fogged by the ever-present anxiety that shadowed him. The house was unnervingly quiet, devoid of the usual sounds of life that had once filled it. The absence of Margaret's soft humming as she moved about, the children's laughter, and even the clattering of breakfast being prepared—it all left a gaping void that only deepened the sense of isolation. They were far away now; he hoped. He had no way of knowing for certain if they had made it out, but he clung to the belief that Margaret, Lucy, and Peter were safe.

As he stood, Charles noticed movement outside the window, a subtle shift in the corner of his eye. He approached the window cautiously, drawing back the heavy curtain just enough to peer out. The garden next door, belonging to the Schmitts, his elderly neighbours, came into view. There in the garden, was Max his loyal dog. Max was bounding about, his tail wagging as he explored the familiar territory. The sight of him, so blissfully unaware of the chaos that had descended upon the world, brought a fleeting smile to Charles's lips.

But that smile quickly faded. Why was Max in the Schmitts' garden? Charles's mind raced. Margaret must have asked them to take care of Max before she left. The Schmitts had always been good neighbours, kind and reliable. But now, in the heart of Nazi Germany, could he still trust them? Where did their loyalties truly lie in this new, terrifying world?

The Schmitts were an elderly couple who had lived next door for as long as Charles could remember. They were quiet, unassuming people who kept to themselves but were always willing to lend a hand when needed. Their son, Hans, had been drafted into the army and was now stationed on the German-Polish border, according to the last letter they had received from him. Their granddaughter, Lottie, was twelve years old and stayed at their house a lot because of the war. Lottie loved Max; she often played with him in the garden, her laughter echoing through the hedges.

As Charles watched, the back door of the Schmitts' house opened, and Lottie skipped out into the garden. Her blonde hair was tied back in a loose ponytail, and she wore a simple dress, slightly worn but clean. She called out to Max, her voice bright and cheerful, and the dog bounded over to her, tail wagging furiously. Lottie knelt down to pet him, her laughter filling the air as Max licked her face with unrestrained affection.

Charles felt a pang of sadness as he watched them. Lottie's innocence and carefree joy felt distant from the challenging situation he was in. For a moment, he was tempted to believe that things could still be normal and that the world hadn't been turned upside down. But that was a dangerous illusion, and he couldn't afford to indulge in it. The world had changed irrevocably, and every action, every word, was now a matter of survival.

As if sensing his gaze, Lottie suddenly looked up and directly at the window where Charles stood. Their eyes met, and Charles's heart skipped a beat. He had been careless, too caught up in his thoughts to remember the need for caution. For a brief moment, they stared at each other, neither moving. Then, in a panic, Charles stepped back from the window, cursing himself for being so reckless.

He stood still, his chest thudding as he waited for the inevitable. What would Lottie do? Would she tell her grandparents? Would they inform the authorities? The fear of discovery – of being dragged from his home and thrown into a Nazi prison gripped him like a vice.

And then there was a knock at the door.

The sound echoed through the empty house, sharp and foreboding. Charles's blood ran cold. It was a sound he had been dreading, a sound that could only mean one thing: he had been found. Then there was another knock, more insistently this time, demanding his response.

Charles took a deep breath, trying to steady his nerves. There was no choice but to answer. Hiding would only raise suspicion and make things worse. He made his way downstairs, each step feeling heavier than the last, his mind racing with possibilities. When he reached the front door, he hesitated for a moment, steeling himself for what might come next. Then, with a deep breath, he opened the door. On the doorstep stood Mr. and Mrs. Schmitt. The elderly couple looked both worried and determined, their faces etched with the lines of age and the strain of the last few days. Mr. Schmitt was of a medium build and lean, his posture stiff, while Mrs. Schmitt was shorter, with a kind but anxious expression. "Can we come in? "Mr. Schmitt said in German, his voice low and urgent. He glanced around the street, as if checking to see if anyone was watching. " Charles didn't hesitate. He stepped aside, allowing the Schmitts to enter the house, and quickly closed the door behind them, securing the latch with trembling hands. The sudden invasion of their presence in his home brought a new wave of anxiety. What had they seen? What did they know? Mrs. Schmitt looked at him with a mix of concern and fear. "What happened?" she asked softly, also in German. "Why are you still here? We thought you had left with the others."

Charles motioned for them to follow him into the living room. The room was mostly empty, the furniture sparse after Margaret had taken what she could with her. The Schmitts sat down on the remaining chairs, their eyes never leaving Charles. He sat across from them, keenly aware of their gaze. There was no point in lying; he needed their help, and that required trust, however precarious. "I've been in a cell in the Police station," Charles began, his voice steady despite the fear gnawing at his insides. "They interrogated me for days, but I managed to convince them that I was just a low-level German clerk, nothing more. They didn't really know what to do with me, so they let me go." Mrs. Schmitt gasped, her hand flying to her mouth. "I told them what they wanted to hear, and I think they believed me. But I don't know how long that will last. They could come back at any time." Mr. Schmitt nodded gravely. "Your family are safe" he said. "They were evacuated, Margaret, Lucy, and Peter—they were put on a train to Switzerland a few weeks ago." Mrs. Schmitt reached out and placed a comforting hand on Charles's arm. "Your wife came to us before she left," she said gently. "She asked if we would take care of Max. She was so worried about you."

Charles felt a rush of gratitude towards Margaret. Even in the chaos of their departure, she had thought to ensure that Max was cared for. The realisation that she had trusted the Schmitts gave him a small measure of comfort. But it also made the stakes even more real. If the Schmitts turned against him, if they decided he was too much of a risk… "We'll keep your secret," Mr. Schmitt said firmly, cutting through Charles's spiralling thoughts. "As long as we can. But you must be careful, Herr Sterling. These are dangerous times. The wrong word, the wrong action—it could mean the end for all of us." "I understand," Charles replied, his voice resolute. "I'll stay out of sight. I won't put any of us in danger."

Mrs. Schmitt squeezed his arm before withdrawing her hand. "We'll bring you food," she said. "And anything else you might need. But you must stay hidden. Don't let anyone see you, not even Lottie."

Charles nodded, deeply moved by their willingness to help him. "Thank you," he said, the words feeling inadequate. "I don't know how I can ever repay you for this."

The three of them sat in silence for a moment. Charles knew that by agreeing to help him, the Schmitts were risking their lives. In Nazi Germany, aiding an enemy national was a crime punishable by death. The gravity of what they were doing was not lost on him. "Do you have a plan?" Mr. Schmitt asked finally, breaking the silence. Charles shook his head. "Not yet," he admitted. "Right now, I'm just trying to survive. I need to find a way out of the country, but I don't know how. The borders are heavily guarded, and I have no papers. If I'm caught…" Mrs.

Schmitt nodded sympathetically. "It won't be easy," she said. "But we'll help you however we can. You can't stay here forever, though. Someone will eventually notice."

Charles knew she was right. The walls were closing in, and his options were limited. He needed a plan, and he needed it soon. The Schmitts stood to leave, and Charles escorted them to the back door, the route they had come in to avoid prying eyes. As they stepped outside, Mr. Schmitt turned back to Charles. "Stay strong, Herr Sterling," he said quietly. "We'll get through this. But you must stay vigilant. The war has changed everything, and we can trust no one." Charles nodded, watching as they disappeared into the garden, their figures fading into the shadows. He closed the door behind them, locking it securely. Alone again, the silence of the house descended upon him like a heavy shroud.

He returned to the living room, sitting down in one of the remaining chairs, but he felt a renewed sense of determination. The Schmitts were right—he had to be careful, vigilant. But he wasn't entirely alone. With their help, there was a chance, however slim, that he could find a way out of this nightmare and reunite with his family.

The day stretched on, each minute feeling like an hour. Charles kept to the shadows, avoiding the windows and keeping the lights off. Every sound from outside made him tense, his heart pounding in his chest. He knew he couldn't stay like this indefinitely. The walls felt like they were closing in, and the air in the house was stifling. He longed for fresh air, for the freedom to walk outside without fear. But those days were gone, at least for now.

As night fell, the darkness outside seemed to seep into the house, filling every corner with shadows. Charles sat in the gloom, his thoughts a tangled mess of fear, hope, and determination. The Schmitts' words echoed in his mind: Trust no one. It was advice he knew he had to follow if he wanted to survive. The war had turned the world into a place where even the smallest act of trust could lead to betrayal.

But despite the fear, despite the uncertainty, Charles felt a flicker of hope. The Schmitts had promised to help him. It wasn't much, but it was enough to keep him going and to keep him fighting. He had to believe that there was a way out and that he would see his family again.

Chapter Four
The Phoney War

The days blurred into weeks, and Charles Sterling's world shrank to the confines of his once lively home. The rooms that had echoed with the sounds of his children's laughter and Margaret's soothing voice were now silent, save for the occasional bark of Max or the creak of the old house settling. Time had lost its meaning in the stillness of war. The Phoney War, as the newspapers had dubbed it, was in full swing—a strange, uneasy period where Germany had invaded Poland, and yet the frontlines across Europe remained eerily quiet. It was a stalemate, a deceptive calm before the inevitable storm.

Charles spent his days in near-total isolation, moving from room to room with the care and precision of a ghost. Every step was measured, every action deliberate. The slightest noise could betray his presence, and he lived in constant fear that one day someone would notice the subtle signs of life in the supposedly abandoned house. The Schmitts were his only contact with the outside world, but even their visits had become infrequent, a testament to the growing fear that permeated the city.

It was during one of these monotonous days, as he sat in the dim light of the drawing room, that Charles heard the distant hum of an aircraft.

He tensed immediately, his ears straining to catch the sound. Planes were not an uncommon sight over Berlin, but this one seemed different—closer, more deliberate. The hum grew louder, and then, suddenly, there was a strange fluttering noise, like the sound of birds taking flight. Charles hurried to the window, peering cautiously through a small gap in the curtains.

Outside, the sky was filled with tiny white specks, like snowflakes, drifting lazily to the ground. But this was no winter storm. As the objects descended, he realised what they were: leaflets, thousands of them, carried by the wind and scattered across the city. One of them landed in his back garden, mere feet from the door. He knew the risk of leaving the safety of the house, even for a moment, but curiosity gnawed at him. What message had been deemed important enough to be dropped over Berlin? Against all his better instincts, he moved quickly to the back door, cracking it open just enough to reach out and grab the leaflet that had settled near the threshold. He snatched it up and retreated inside, locking the door behind him.

The paper was coarse and flimsy, the ink slightly smudged from its descent. Charles unfolded it with trembling hands, his eyes scanning the bold print. The leaflet was in German, but it was clear who had sent it: the RAF. The message was stark and unflinching, a warning to the German people about the evils of Nazism. The leaflet proclaimed that the Allies had the capability to bomb Berlin at will, and that no one in the city was safe from their reach. It was both a threat and a promise that the war, despite the current stalemate, was far from over. It also gave notice of a massive Expeditionary Force currently amassing on the French/Belgian border ready to repel any military movements in that direction.

Charles read the leaflet twice, his mind racing. The words were designed to sow fear and doubt among the German populace, but to him, they were a lifeline, a sign that the outside world had not forgotten him. The RAF's message was clear: the Allies were watching, waiting for the right moment to strike. It was a small comfort, but a comfort nonetheless, in his increasingly bleak existence.

Christmas of 1939 came and went, a cold and lonely affair that only deepened the sense of isolation. The Schmitts, once a comforting presence, now only dropped off food at his doorstep to the side entrance briefly, as if fearing that even the slightest prolonged interaction might draw unwanted attention. Their fear was palpable, and it infected Charles as well. The food they brought was scarce – just enough to keep him and Max alive, but never more. Too much food, Mrs. Schmitt had whispered once, might raise suspicion among the neighbours, who were already growing curious about the old couple's sudden increase in provisions.

Max, at least, was a source of solace. The dog had sensed the unease in the air and, in his own way, seemed to understand the gravity of the situation. He rarely barked now, and when he did, it was only a soft, low growl—a warning, not a call for attention. Max spent most of his time close to Charles, his presence offering quiet reassurance in the otherwise empty house. On New Year's Eve, as Charles sat in the darkened living room, he scratched Max's ears and spoke to him in a low voice, telling him stories of better days and of holidays filled with joy and laughter. Max listened intently, his dark eyes fixed on Charles, as if he too longed for those days to return.

But the days of joy felt distant, buried beneath the overwhelming strain of war as January melted into February in a haze of cold and fear. Charles kept himself busy with small tasks - anything to keep his mind from dwelling too long on the hopelessness of his situation. He read and reread the few books that had been left behind, studied the map of Europe that hung on the wall, and meticulously cleaned the house, erasing any trace of his presence after every meal. The routine was maddening but necessary.

Then, one cold morning in March, the fragile routine was shattered. A loud crash from downstairs jolted Charles awake. He was out of bed instantly. For a moment, fear paralysed him, unsure of what to do. Then instinct kicked in—months of living on the edge had taught him to be cautious and to always have an escape plan. He grabbed the thin bedsheet and motioned for Max to follow him.

Together, they moved silently through the darkened house, heading for the attic. Charles had prepared this hiding place months ago, – a small space under the eaves where he and Max could remain hidden if the worst happened. As they climbed the narrow stairs, Charles's mind raced. Who were the intruders? Had the Gestapo finally come for him? Or was it something worse—had the neighbours reported the Schmitts, leading the authorities to his door?

When they reached the attic, Charles pulled Max close and whispered in his ear. "Quiet now, Max," he said, his voice barely a breath. "No sound, not a peep." Max, as if understanding the gravity of the situation, pressed close to Charles and remained still, his breathing slow and steady.

Charles arranged the bedsheet over them, a makeshift covering that might help them blend into the shadows. They remained as silent as statues, their hearts beating in unison as they listened intently to the sounds from below.

Footsteps. Several pairs of them, moving purposefully through the house. Charles strained to hear the voices that accompanied them, trying to make out words, but the sound was muffled. He could catch only snippets—"search," "good place," "ministry men." His blood ran cold. Whoever they were, they were here for a reason, and that reason likely spelt the end for him.

The voices grew louder as the intruders moved through the house. Charles heard the distinct clatter of doors being opened, and furniture being shifted. They were searching for something, or someone. His pulse quickened as the footsteps drew closer to the attic stairs. A deep voice, gruff and authoritative, spoke up. "This place will do," the man said, his words carrying up the stairs. "Plenty of space. No one will think to look here."

Charles's breath caught in his throat. His mind raced with possibilities, each more terrifying than the last. Were they planning to move into the house? Was it being requisitioned for some official purpose? If so, his days of hiding were numbered. There would be no way to remain undetected if the house was occupied. He and Max would be discovered, and when they were, the consequences would be dire.

For what felt like an eternity, Charles and Max remained perfectly still, listening as the intruders continued their work. The sound of heavy objects being moved echoed through the house, followed by the creak of the floorboards as the men walked from room to room. Charles could feel Max's steady heartbeat against his leg, a grounding presence in the midst of his rising panic.

Then, suddenly, the voices retreated. The footsteps grew fainter, and after a few tense moments, the front door slammed shut. Silence descended once more, thick and oppressive, echoing with what had just transpired.

Charles didn't move for several minutes, waiting to be sure that the intruders were truly gone. His mind was spinning with the implications of what he had overheard. The phrase "good place" stuck in his head. Were they talking about the house? Had they chosen it for some specific purpose? And if so, what did that mean for him?

Finally, when he was certain that the house was empty again, Charles let out a slow, shaky breath. He loosened his grip on Max, who looked up at him with wide, worried eyes. "It's okay, Max," he whispered, though the words felt hollow. "We're safe... for now."

Carefully, Charles crept out of the attic, his muscles aching from the tension of the past hour. He moved through the house, examining each room for signs of what the intruders had done. To his dismay, it was clear that they had been thorough. The small amount of furniture had been rearranged, and in the living room, a large trunk had been left behind. It was a military issue, and when Charles cautiously opened it, he found it filled with paperwork, maps, and other documents—none of which he dared examine too closely.

His heart sank as the reality of his situation hit him. The military or some branch of the government had most likely commandeered the house. It was only a matter of time before they returned to begin their operations. When that happened, there would be no way for him to remain hidden. His sanctuary had been compromised.

That night, as Charles lay in bed with Max curled up beside him, he couldn't shake the feeling of impending doom. The house that had once been his refuge was now a trap, and he was the prey. The Schmitts had warned him to be careful, to trust no one, and now those words seemed more prophetic than ever.

He needed a new plan. The longer he stayed, the more dangerous it became. But where could he go? And how could he escape a city that was tightening its grip with every passing day?

As sleep finally claimed him, Charles knew that his time was running out. The Phoney War might be a stalemate for now, but for him, the real battle was just beginning.

Chapter Five
The Escape

Charles Sterling sat in the darkened corner of his house, his mind racing as he replayed the events of the previous day. The intruders had left, but the fear they had instilled lingered in every creak and shadow. His sanctuary was no longer safe, and the precariousness of his situation pressed on his mind. He knew he couldn't stay, but the question of where to go and how to get there seemed impossible to answer.

A soft knock on the back door jolted him from his thoughts. He moved cautiously through the house, peering through a crack in the curtain. It was the Schmitts, their faces pale and anxious. Charles unlocked the door and let them in, noting the fear in their eyes.

"We have to talk," Mr. Schmitt said in a low voice, his words trembling with urgency. "You must leave now, Charles. It's no longer safe here."

Charles nodded, his throat tight. He had known this moment would come, but the suddenness of it still caught him off guard. "But how?" he whispered, the question lingering in the tense silence. "I have no way to get out of the city, no papers, no plan."

Mrs. Schmitt glanced at her husband before speaking, her voice barely above a whisper. "The Beckers across the road—they have a car. I have a key to their house. I sometimes do some cleaning for them when they're away. We could... we could take their car."

Charles stared at her, the implications of her suggestion sinking in. "Steal their car?" he asked, his voice thick with disbelief. "What if they report it? A single phone call, and every roadblock in Germany will be looking for me." Mr. Schmitt nodded, his expression grim. "You're right, it's risky. But what choice do you have? The house has been compromised. They'll be back, and next time, they might find you. We can't think of anything else. The car might be your only chance." Charles looked between the two of them, the desperation in their eyes mirroring his own. He knew they were right—staying in the house was no longer an option. But the idea of stealing a car and of fleeing through the streets of Berlin sent a shiver of dread down his spine. It was a gamble, but as he weighed the options, it became clear that it was a gamble he would have to take.

Mrs. Schmitt outlined the plan. The Beckers often went to the cinema on Friday evenings, and tonight was no exception. They would leave around nine, and she would slip into their house to take the car keys. Charles could then make his escape under the cover of night. "It's not perfect," Mrs. Schmitt admitted, her hands trembling slightly as she spoke. "But it's the best we can do." Charles felt a surge of gratitude for the elderly couple. They were risking their lives for him, a man who had brought nothing but danger to their doorstep. "Thank you," he said quietly, his voice thick with emotion. "I don't know how I'll ever repay you." Mrs. Schmitt smiled weakly, patting his hand. "Just stay safe, Charles. That's all the repayment we need."

They spent the next few hours preparing for the escape. With nothing to pack, just the food the Schmitts had been able to provide, it didn't take long. He moved through the house one last time, taking in the familiar surroundings, knowing he might never return.

As eight o'clock approached, the sense of anticipation began to build. Charles watched from a gap in the curtains as the Beckers left their house, walking arm in arm down the street. He could almost imagine they were an ordinary couple on an ordinary night out, if not for the fact that their absence would soon become the key to his survival.

Mrs. Schmitt waited a few minutes after the Beckers left before slipping across the street. Charles and Mr. Schmitt watched from the shadows as she unlocked the front door of the Beckers' house and disappeared inside. The seconds stretched into agonising minutes before she emerged, holding the car keys tightly in her hand.

She hurried back to Charles's house, her face pale but determined. "I've got them," she said breathlessly, handing the keys to Charles. "It's all set. You should go now, while it's still quiet." But just as Charles was about to step out into the street, a sight in the distance made them all freeze. Charles's heart sank as he saw the Beckers returning, their expressions troubled. "Have they changed their mind? Have they forgotten something?," Mrs Schmitt whispered frantically, her eyes wide with fear. "They've come back."

Charles watched in horror as the Beckers approached their house, unaware that their car keys were no longer inside. He could see Mr. Beckers' brow furrowed in concern as they stopped at their front door before going inside. They hadn't noticed the Schmitts across the street yet, but it was only a matter of time. Panic set in among Charles and The Schmitts. They had counted on having a few hours' head start, but now that time had been reduced to mere minutes. Charles could feel the Schmitts' anxiety radiating off them, and he knew that every second they hesitated was a second closer to discovery.

"We can't wait any longer," Mr. Schmitt whispered urgently. "You have to go, now!" Charles nodded, taking a deep breath to steady his nerves. "Thank you," he said, his voice low and firm. "I'll never forget what you've done for me."

With that, he stepped out into the night, clutching the car keys tightly in his hand. The street was quiet, the only sound was the distant murmur of Berlin's nightlife. Charles moved quickly, slipping into the driver's seat of the Beckers' car, parked a few doors down from his own house. He held his breath as he inserted the key into the ignition, praying that the engine wouldn't roar to life too loudly. The car started with a low purr, and Charles exhaled in relief. He glanced back at the Schmitts, who were watching him from the shadows of their doorway, their faces a mix of fear and hope. He gave them a final nod, then turned his attention to the road ahead. As quietly as possible, he pulled away from the curb, his eyes flicking between the rearview mirror and the road ahead. A rush of adrenaline coursed through him, each pulse sharp and loud. He knew he had to get out of sight before Mr. Becker noticed his car missing. His foot pressed down on the accelerator, urging the car to move faster, but not too fast—he couldn't afford to draw attention.

From the front bedroom of their home, whilst pulling the curtains closed, Mr. Becker stood frozen. He had just seen Charles Sterling, the British man who had moved in across the street with his family a few years ago. The British man, who was supposed to have fled the city months ago when the war began, steal his car.

Mr Beckers' hand moved towards the telephone on the wall. He knew what he should do, what anyone should do when a car is stolen. Mrs Becker appeared at his side, her hand resting gently on his arm. "What is it?" she asked softly. Mr. Becker hesitated, his hand hovering over the phone. Then, with a sigh, put down the receiver. "Nothing," he said quietly. "It's nothing." Charles, unaware of the near miss, continued driving until the cityscape gave way to the open roads leading out of Berlin. He kept a careful eye on the road behind him, half-expecting to see flashing lights or hear the wail of sirens at any moment. But the night remained eerily silent, the only sound being the hum of the car's engine and the rhythmic thudding of his own heart.

Finally, after what felt like an eternity, Charles reached the outskirts of the city. He pulled over to the side of the road, his hands trembling on the steering wheel. He needed a moment to collect himself and to plan his next move. As he sat in the darkness, the strain in his body slowly began to ease. He took a deep breath, savouring the cool night air that drifted through the open window. For the first time in weeks, he felt a spark of optimism. He was out of Berlin, and though the road ahead was uncertain, he had at least made it this far.

Just as he was about to start the car again, he heard a soft whimper from the back seat. Charles froze as he slowly turned to look behind him. There, nestled among the blankets and the small case of belongings, was Max. His loyal dog had somehow slipped into the car without Charles noticing, and now lay curled up, his wide eyes fixed on his master. Charles stared at Max in disbelief, a mix of emotions swirling inside him. Relief, frustration, and an overwhelming sense of gratitude washed over him as he reached back to pat the dog's head. "Max," he whispered, his voice thick with emotion. "What are you doing here?" Max wagged his tail, his eyes filled with a trust and loyalty that brought tears to Charles's eyes. He hadn't even thought about Max when he'd made his escape—there had been no time, no opportunity to ensure his safety. And yet, here he was, as if he had known all along that Charles would need him. With a soft sigh, Charles turned back to the road, his resolve hardening. He wasn't alone any more.

Max was with him, and together, they would face whatever challenges lay ahead.

The road stretched out before them, dark and unknown, but Charles felt a renewed sense of determination. He might be a fugitive, but he was not without hope. The Schmitts had given him a chance, and now, with Max by his side, he would do everything in his power to survive and find his way to safety.

As the car moved forward into the night, Charles couldn't help but feel a small spark of hope. The war had taken so much from him, but it had not yet taken everything. He still had his life, his will to survive, and the loyal companionship of Max. And as long as he had that, he knew he could keep going, one mile at a time.

Chapter Six

A Fragile Dawn

As the first light of a new dawn began to filter through the dense canopy of trees, Charles Sterling gripped the steering wheel tightly, his knuckles white from the pressure. The faint rays of sunlight should have brought with them a sense of hope, a reminder that darkness does not last forever. But Charles, still miles from home and safety, found no comfort in the dawn. He was a fugitive in a foreign land, pursued not by a single adversary but by an entire nation that had declared war on his own.

The road ahead was narrow, lined with towering trees that cast long, eerie shadows across the path. For a brief moment, Charles let himself believe that they might make it out of this forest, that they might find a safe haven before nightfall. But that hope was shattered when the car emitted a loud splutter, jolting violently as the engine began to fail. Charles felt a jolt as the vehicle shuddered and then, with a final, despairing cough, came to a complete halt.

"No," Charles whispered, his voice barely audible. He tried turning the key again, willing the engine to roar back to life, but it was no use. The car had run out of petrol.

In their frantic rush to escape Berlin, they had neglected to check the fuel gauge. It was a mistake that now threatened to leave them stranded in the middle of nowhere, vulnerable and exposed.

With a heavy sigh, Charles leaned back in his seat, closing his eyes as the reality of their situation sank in. They were deep in enemy territory, far from any semblance of safety, and without a working vehicle, their chances of making it to the border were dwindling rapidly.

Max, sensing his master's distress, nudged Charles's arm with his nose. The dog's warm, comforting presence was the only thing that kept Charles from succumbing to despair. "It's all right, boy," Charles murmured, though the words felt hollow even as he spoke them. "We'll figure something out." He and Max stepped out of the car, the cold morning air hitting them like a slap in the face. Charles surveyed their surroundings, trying to determine their next move. They were on a desolate stretch of road, bordered by thick woods on either side. There was no sign of civilisation, no sound of approaching vehicles—just the quiet, oppressive silence of the forest.

Charles realised that they had no other option but to push the car off the road and into a thick clump of trees, where it would be less visible to passersby. Once the car was hidden as best as they could manage, Charles grabbed his small case from the back seat, slung it over his shoulder, and together with Max, set off on foot.

The forest seemed to close in around them as they walked, the trees standing like silent sentinels, their branches swaying gently in the breeze. Charles tried to keep his mind on the task at hand, but the seriousness of their predicament pressed down on him, making it hard to concentrate. Every rustle in the underbrush, every crack of a twig, set his nerves on edge. They were in enemy territory, and he knew one wrong move could be their last.

They hadn't been walking for long when Charles noticed a thin column of smoke rising in the distance. He stopped, squinting through the trees to get a better look. Smoke meant fire, and fire meant people. But who were they? Friends or foes?

"Stay close, Max," Charles whispered as they cautiously made their way towards the source of the smoke. As they drew nearer, the outline of a small hut became visible through the trees. It was a simple structure, made of rough-hewn logs, with a thatched roof and a small chimney from which the smoke curled lazily into the sky. A stack of firewood was piled neatly against one wall, and the scent of burning wood filled the air.

Charles stopped a few paces away from the hut, crouching down behind a thick bush to observe the scene. The hut was isolated, far from any town or village, and it seemed unlikely that anyone of significance inhabited it. Perhaps it belonged to a woodsman or a farmer, someone who lived off the land and kept to themselves. But Charles couldn't afford to take any chances. He needed to know if this person was a friend or foe before revealing himself.

Max sniffed the air; his ears perked up as he scanned the surroundings. Charles watched the hut for several minutes, but there was no sign of movement, no indication of who might be inside. He considered his options. He needed help—food, water, and, most importantly, petrol. But if the occupant of the hut was loyal to the regime, then approaching them could mean a certain capture. Charles knew he needed an alibi, a story that would explain his presence without arousing suspicion. After a moment's thought, he settled on a plausible lie: he was a travelling salesman, lost and in need of fuel. Just as he began to rehearse the story in his mind, a sharp click sounded behind him. The sound was unmistakable—a gun being cocked. Charles froze, his breath catching in his throat. Slowly, he raised his hands, signalling surrender. Max growled softly, a low rumble in his throat, but Charles knew that the dog's bark was worse than his bite. "Easy, Max," he whispered in his best German, trying to keep his voice calm. "*Ruhig, Junge.*"

"Who are you, and what are you doing here?" The voice was gruff, laced with suspicion. Charles didn't dare turn around, keeping his hands raised as he spoke. "I'm just a travelling salesman," he said, forcing his voice to remain steady. "My car ran out of petrol a little way back, and I was searching for help. I mean no harm." There was a tense silence, and Charles could feel the man's eyes boring into the back of his head, assessing him. Then, unexpectedly, the man barked out a short laugh. "A travelling salesman, eh?" the man said, his voice carrying a note of scepticism. "Out here, in the middle of nowhere? That's a new one." Charles swallowed hard, his mind racing for a way to convince the man of his story. "It's the truth," he insisted. "I was headed to the next town, but I must have taken a wrong turn somewhere. Then the car ran out of fuel, and... well, here I am." The man behind him remained silent for a moment, then he let out a grunt. "Turn around, slowly," he ordered.

Charles obeyed, turning to face his captor. The man was exactly what he had expected—a tall, broad-shouldered woodsman with a thick beard and piercing eyes that seemed to see right through Charles's flimsy story.

He held a hunting rifle in one hand; the barrel pointed directly at Charles's chest. "You don't look like much of a threat," the woodsman said, lowering the rifle slightly. He gave Charles and Max a once-over, his expression unreadable. "And you don't look like much of a salesman either." Charles forced a weak smile, trying to appear harmless. "I'm just seeking a little help," he said. "Some petrol, if you've got any to spare." The woodsman eyed him for a moment longer. Then, to Charles's surprise, he lowered the rifle completely and let out a chuckle. "Petrol, eh? Not much use for that out here. But come on in. I was just making breakfast." Charles blinked, caught off guard by the man's sudden change in demeanour. "Thank you," he said, still wary but grateful for the chance to rest and eat. He followed the woodsman to the hut, Max trailing closely behind. Inside, the hut was as rustic as Charles had imagined—a single room with a bed in one corner, a small stove in another, and a table with two chairs in the centre. The walls were lined with shelves holding jars of preserves, and a few basic tools were scattered about. It was a simple, utilitarian space, but it was warm and smelt of cooking food.

"Name's Klaus," the woodsman said, setting his rifle down by the door. "And you?" "Karl," he replied, taking a seat at the table. Max settled at his feet, still on edge but sensing that the immediate danger had passed. Klaus ladled out a thick stew from the pot on the stove, placing a bowl in front of Charles, along with a chunk of bread. "Eat up," he said. "You look like you could use it." Charles hesitated for a moment, then took a cautious bite. The stew was hearty and flavourful, and he realised just how hungry he was as he ate. The bread was rough but fresh, and it was the best meal he'd had in days. As they ate, Klaus watched him closely, a hint of curiosity in his eyes. "So, a travelling salesman," he said, a faint smile tugging at the corners of his mouth. "What exactly are you selling, Karl?" Charles had expected this question and had prepared his answer. "Household goods," he replied

smoothly. "Cooking utensils, cleaning supplies, that sort of thing. I travel from town to town, making a living on the road." Klaus raised an eyebrow, clearly unconvinced. "Not much call for that out here," he remarked. "Especially not with a war on." Charles's pulse quickened, but he forced himself to stay calm. "I wasn't planning on being out here," he explained. "I was headed to the next town, like I said. But I got lost, and then the car ran out of petrol. It's been a rough couple of days."
Klaus grunted in response, taking another bite of his stew. "You're either very unlucky or a terrible liar.....your German isn't too bad, though." he said after a moment. He opened his mouth to protest, but Klaus held up a hand to stop him. "Relax, Karl. I don't much care either way. We're all just trying to survive these days. I'm not a political animal, but I know evil when I see it." Charles nodded, though his mind was racing. He didn't know what to make of Klaus's words. Was he being honest, or was he simply playing along, waiting for the right moment to turn him in?

Before Charles could dwell on it further, a low rumbling sound began to build in the distance. At first, it was faint, barely noticeable over the crackling of the fire. But it quickly grew louder, the ground beneath them starting to vibrate. Klaus's expression darkened as he stood up and moved to the window. He peered out into the forest, his face tense. "Tanks," he muttered, his voice grim. "They're getting closer." Charles felt a surge of panic. If the tanks were this close, it meant the military was nearby, and he couldn't afford to be found. "I need to leave," he said, standing up abruptly. "If they find me here—"

Klaus turned to him, his expression serious. "If they find you here, they'll arrest you," he said. "And they'll arrest me, too, for helping you. We can't let that happen." "What do we do?" Charles asked, his voice tight with fear. Klaus didn't hesitate. "There's a hideout behind the hut," he said urgently. "It's a small bunker I use for emergencies. You and your dog can stay there until the tanks pass." Charles nodded. He gathered his things and followed Klaus outside. The tanks' rumble was now a constant background noise, growing louder and more oppressive. Klaus led Charles and Max to a small, discreet opening in the ground hidden behind a thicket of bushes. The entrance to the bunker was covered with branches and leaves, barely noticeable against the forest floor. "This is it," Klaus said, pushing aside the foliage to reveal the entrance. "Get inside and stay quiet. I'll keep an eye on things from here."

Charles squeezed down into the bunker, helping Max through the narrow opening. The interior was cramped and dark, with just enough room for them to crouch. The air was musty, but it was dry and secure. As Klaus replaced the branches over the entrance, the bunker was plunged into near darkness. Charles could hear the muffled sounds of Klaus moving around outside, the distant rumble of tanks growing louder. He held his breath, listening for any signs of trouble. Max curled up beside him, sensing the unease and staying close.

Minutes dragged by, each second stretching into what felt like hours. Charles's mind raced with worry. What if Klaus was caught? What if the tanks discovered their hiding place? The uncertainty was almost unbearable.

Chapter Seven

The Unseen Enemy

From his hiding place near the woodcutter's hut, Charles could feel the earth tremble with each rumble of the tanks rolling down the road. The deafening roar of engines and the clattering of metal tracks against the ground filled the air, echoing through the dense forest that surrounded them. Charles peered through a small gap in the woven wooden fencing covering the den.

What he saw was both awe-inspiring and terrifying—a seemingly endless convoy of German tanks, their hulking forms dominating the narrow road. Alongside them, soldiers moved not in the disciplined march of a traditional army but in a chaotic, almost frantic manner. They were jogging, some even running, their faces flushed with excitement or something more unnatural. Groups of soldiers laughed loudly, climbing on the tanks, cheering, and singing as if they were part of a twisted celebration rather than an invasion force. This was no ordinary army. Charles realised with a sinking feeling that the Phoney War was over. Germany was no longer biding its time; it was preparing to unleash a blitzkrieg across Europe, one that would leave devastation in its wake.

Charles watched the soldiers on the road, moving with unnerving speed and intensity. Just a few years ago, German chemists had created a mysterious drug, now a key weapon in the military's arsenal. It gave soldiers unnatural energy, erased their need for sleep, and filled them with a reckless sense of invincibility—like superpowers in pill form. He could just about see the telltale signs in the soldiers passing by: wide, glazed eyes, manic grins, and an unrelenting drive that kept them moving at a breakneck pace. This wasn't just an army—it was a force fuelled by something far more dangerous than anyone had anticipated. Charles knew what this meant. The German military, drugged and driven to extremes, was on the verge of unleashing a lightning-fast, brutal assault that would tear through Belgium, Holland, and France in a matter of days. The Allies were preparing for a conventional battle, but they had no idea of the drug-fuelled onslaught coming their way. He had to get this information to the British government as soon as possible. Thousands of lives hung in the balance. For now, all he could do was wait and watch the storm gather. As the tanks and troops continued to pass by, Charles couldn't help but wonder about the logistics behind this massive operation. The Germans had managed to keep this invasion force hidden until the last possible moment, and now they were mobilising with terrifying efficiency. The realisation of the sheer scale of the German war machine sent a chill down his spine. His attention was abruptly diverted when he noticed something unusual in the distance. A sleek black staff car was approaching, moving slowly along the road behind the convoy. As it drew closer, Charles could make out the figure of a high-ranking German officer sitting in the back seat, his uniform adorned with medals and insignia that marked him as a person of significant authority.

The car came to a stop near the woodcutter's hut, and to Charles's dismay, Klaus, the woodcutter who had sheltered him, emerged from his hiding place to greet the officer. Charles watched in horror as the two men exchanged words, their conversation punctuated by laughter. A wave of dread washed over him—had Klaus betrayed him? Was this the moment his cover would be blown, leading to his capture or death? He held his breath, unable to tear his eyes away from the scene unfolding before him. The officer stepped out of the car, and for a tense moment, Charles lost sight of him. He could only imagine what was happening as Klaus and the officer moved out of his line of vision. Was the officer searching for him? Had Klaus given him away? After what felt like an eternity, the officer reappeared, heading back to his car. He opened the boot and removed something, placing it by the side of the road. Charles couldn't see what it was, but the casual way in which the two men continued their interaction suggested that it was nothing out of the ordinary. The officer and Klaus shook hands, exchanged a few more words, and then the staff car drove off, leaving Klaus alone by the roadside. Charles watched in disbelief as Klaus sat down in an old chair, positioning himself to observe the passing soldiers. As they moved by, several of them stopped to shake Klaus's hand, sharing a joke or a laugh before continuing down the road. The entire scene felt surreal, as if Klaus were some kind of local celebrity or a respected figure among the troops.

Finally, after what seemed like hours, the convoy began to thin out, the last of the tanks and soldiers disappearing down the road. The deafening noise faded into the distance, replaced by the eerie silence of the forest. Charles remained motionless, still unsure of what to make of Klaus's actions. Could he trust the man who had so easily fraternised with the enemy? His thoughts were interrupted by a soft creak as the lid of the den was lifted. Charles tensed, ready to defend himself if necessary, but it was Klaus who appeared, his expression unreadable. "I have a present for you," Klaus said, his voice low and conspiratorial. He gestured for Charles and Max to follow him.

Cautiously, Charles emerged from the den, his eyes scanning the area for any sign of danger. Max stayed close by his side, his ears perked up and alert. Klaus led them to the roadside, where, to Charles's astonishment, two jerry cans full of petrol were sitting, glinting in the morning light. Klaus gave Charles a knowing look. "These were given to you, unwittingly, by the German General himself," he said with a wry smile.

Charles could hardly believe what he was hearing. The officer who had just passed through, laughing and joking with Klaus, had inadvertently provided them with the very thing they needed to continue their journey. It was a stroke of luck that seemed almost too good to be true. Before Charles could express his gratitude, Klaus continued speaking. "The soldiers you saw…they've been ordered to make their way to the edge of the Ardennes Forest. They're preparing for an invasion that will surprise everyone. They're going to bypass the Maginot Line and sweep through the Low Countries, trapping the British forces before they even know what's happening." Charles listened intently, the implications of Klaus's words sinking in. He suspected that the British Expeditionary Force were still stationed in northern France, expecting an attack to come from the east. If the Germans succeeded in their plan, thousands of Allied troops would be caught in a deadly trap with no way out.

Klaus's expression softened as he looked at Charles. "You need to get this information to your people," he said. "There's no time to lose. The Nazis are moving fast. " Charles nodded. He would need to travel quickly and carefully, avoiding any further encounters with the German forces. The journey to the French border would be perilous, but the stakes were too high to turn back now.

Chapter Eight
Road to the Maginot Line

Long shadows stretched across the dense forest as Charles Sterling prepared to set off on what could be the most perilous journey of his life. The sound of the German army's passing convoy still echoed faintly in his ears, even though the last of the tanks and soldiers had rumbled by an hour ago. The air was thick with the residue of dust and exhaust fumes, and the oppressive silence that followed such a force only heightened Charles's sense of urgency. Time was not on his side. He stood by the edge of the clearing, the car idling quietly behind him, its engine purring like a restless beast. Max, his faithful companion, sat in the passenger seat, ears perked and eyes alert, as if sensing the gravity of their mission. The old woodcutter, Klaus, had been right about one thing: they had a long and dangerous road ahead of them, and every moment counted. Klaus had given them enough petrol to make the journey, a gift that could only have been obtained through the sheer audacity of fooling a German general. Charles still marvelled at the woodcutter's nerve, shaking his head as he recalled the casual way Klaus had handed him the jerry cans, as if they were nothing more than a couple of bottles of schnapps. But Klaus had also given Charles something else, something far more valuable: a makeshift map, drawn on a scrap of paper.

Charles glanced at the passenger seat beside Max. "Another present," Klaus had said with a grin, handing him a rusted pan with a hole in the bottom. "You are a travelling saucepan salesman, right?" The absurdity of the disguise had made Charles laugh at the time, but now, as he prepared to leave, he wondered if it would be enough to get them through the many checkpoints that he assumed lay ahead. It was a thin ruse, but it was all he had. The car jolted slightly as Charles slid behind the wheel, the leather seat creaking under his weight. He adjusted the rearview mirror, looking back at the woodcutter's hut one last time. Klaus stood by the door, watching them with a mixture of concern and determination. Charles gave him a nod, a silent promise he would get home in one piece and set off.

As the car rolled onto the narrow dirt road leading away from the hut, Charles felt a heavy weight settle on his shoulders. He had been in dangerous situations before, but nothing like this. The stakes had never been so high. The German army was on the move, advancing with lightning speed, intent on cutting off the British Expeditionary Force in northern France. If they succeeded, it would be a disaster of unimaginable proportions. Charles knew he had to reach the French border before the Germans did, but the journey ahead was fraught with peril.

The small town of Kassel was now a fading memory behind him, a place where he had found temporary refuge but could no longer stay. Klaus had told him it was a ten-hour drive to the French border if they were lucky. But luck had a way of running out when you needed it most. Charles knew they would have to drive slowly at first, weaving southward to avoid catching up with the German division that had just passed. The thought of inadvertently running into the tail end of that force sent a shiver down his spine. He couldn't afford any delays—not now.

The car hummed along the road, the landscape blurring into a mix of forest and farmland as they moved further south. Charles kept one eye on the road and the other on the horizon, searching for any signs of trouble. He knew that the route Klaus had mapped out for him was risky, but it was also their best chance of avoiding the main highways where other road users were likely to be concentrated. Charles had memorised the map of Germany back in the British embassy, and between that and Klaus's rough sketch, he was confident they could navigate their way around Frankfurt and head southwest towards Strasbourg.

The afternoon passed slowly as the sun dipped lower, casting a warm orange glow across the countryside. Charles drove in silence, the only sound being the steady rumble of the engine and the occasional rustle of leaves as they passed by. Max lay curled up on the passenger seat, his head resting on his paws, but his eyes never left Charles. The dog seemed to sense the seriousness of the moment, his usual playful energy giving way to a calm alertness. As they drove, Charles's thoughts wandered back to the events that had brought him to this point.

The end of the First World War had seen the French construct the Maginot Line, a formidable barrier of concrete fortifications, obstacles, and weapon installations designed to deter any future invasions. The line stretched across the eastern side of France, an imposing wall that was meant to keep the Germans at bay. But even the best-laid plans could have fatal flaws, and the Maginot Line was no exception.

The French had believed that the dense Ardennes Forest would be an impenetrable natural barrier, too difficult for any army to traverse. They had focused their defences elsewhere, leaving the Ardennes vulnerable. And now, in a cruel twist of fate, that very weakness was being exploited by the Germans. They were not coming through the expected routes; they were sweeping through Belgium and northern France, bypassing the

Maginot Line entirely, and setting the stage for a catastrophic trap that could ensnare the British Expeditionary Force at Dunkirk.

Charles's grip tightened on the steering wheel as he thought of the thousands of Allied troops who would be caught in that trap if the Germans succeeded. He had to reach the French border in time to warn the British government, to give them a chance to prepare, to escape. But first, he had to get there. The car continued its journey southward, the road winding through the German countryside as the afternoon light began to fade. Charles was acutely aware of passing time, the minutes ticking away with each mile they covered. They were making good progress, but he knew that nightfall would bring new challenges. The cover of darkness could be both a blessing and a curse—hiding them from prying eyes but also making it harder to navigate unfamiliar roads.

As the sun dipped below the horizon, Charles flicked on the car's headlights, the beams cutting through the encroaching darkness. The surrounding landscape had changed, the dense forest giving way to rolling hills and open fields. They were approaching the outskirts of Frankfurt, the city lights visible in the distance. Charles knew they had to avoid the city itself, its streets likely teeming with German soldiers and checkpoints. Instead, he veered westward, following the plan he and Klaus had devised. The road ahead was lonely, the silence of the night broken only by the occasional cry of a distant animal or the rustling of leaves in the wind. Charles's eyes scanned the darkness for any sign of movement, his nerves on edge as they pressed on. The pressure of the mission was immense, with every decision and every turn crucial to their success. He couldn't afford to make a mistake.

Hours passed in a blur of dark roads and cautious driving. The moon rose high in the sky, casting a pale light over the landscape. Charles's mind raced with thoughts of the Maginot Line, the formidable barrier that lay ahead. He knew that crossing into France would be their greatest challenge yet, but he didn't have a Plan B.

Chapter Nine

The Perilous Crossing

Charles sat in the driver's seat, his hands resting on the steering wheel, his knuckles white from gripping it too hard. The car's engine hummed softly, a steady reassurance in the night's stillness. They had driven for hours, navigating through the dark German countryside with nothing more than Klaus's makeshift map and Charles's memory to guide them. And now, as he brought the car to a stop on a quiet country road, Charles found himself in a state of disbelief. They had made it this far without encountering a single German patrol or checkpoint. Not a single tricky situation.

"Unbelievable," he muttered under his breath. Max, seated beside him, cocked his head as if detecting the worry in his voice. Ahead of them, the road continued for a short distance before it disappeared into a vast, barren field. But it wasn't the field that caught Charles's attention. It was the enormous concrete structure looming in the distance—a monolithic fortress that seemed to rise out of the earth itself. The structure was part of the Maginot Line, one of the massive fortifications built just a few miles apart by the French after the First World War. It was a sight that would have filled most men with awe, but to Charles, it felt like the last obstacle in a nightmare that had no end. The structure was formidable – a giant concrete dome topped with a gunturret, slits cut into its walls like the cold eyes of some ancient beast. It seemed to stare back at Charles menacingly, daring him to approach. The surrounding ground had been cleared of any vegetation, leaving the land barren and desolate. There was no cover, nothing to obscure the approach of anyone foolish enough to cross the field. Charles swallowed hard. He had known this moment was coming, but now that it was here, he felt a chill run down his spine. They had made it to the French border, but now they faced a new and very real danger. The Maginot Line was not just a defensive structure; it was a fortress manned by soldiers trained to shoot first and ask questions later.

"There's no time to sit here and stare," Charles said, more to himself than to Max. He had to do something, and he had to do it now. The information he carried was too important to delay any longer. He turned off the engine and opened the car door, stepping out into the cool night air. Max followed him, his tail wagging slightly, though his eyes were alert and cautious. Charles took a deep breath, looking around. The quiet country road was deserted, and the only sound was the gentle rustling of the wind through the grass. It was eerily peaceful. Charles knew that as soon as he left the relative safety of the car, he and Max would be exposed. The French soldiers inside the fortification would spot them immediately. But he reasoned that a lone man walking across an empty field with a dog at his side wouldn't be mistaken for a German soldier. If he walked slowly, hands raised, they should be able to see that he was unarmed and no threat. "Come on, Max," Charles said quietly, more to reassure himself than the dog. He began to walk towards the Maginot Line, his steps slow and deliberate. Max trotted beside him, staying close to his leg. The field was wide and open and the distance to the fortress greater than he had expected. Every step felt like an eternity, each one taking him closer to an uncertain fate.

As he walked, Charles could hear faint voices coming from the other side of the structure. He strained to listen, trying to make out what they were saying, but his knowledge of French was minimal. The words were jumbled and distant, carried on the wind like a half-remembered melody. One word, however, seemed to stand out among the others. "A rat."

Charles frowned, trying to make sense of it. Had he heard correctly? Why would they be talking about a rat? It made little sense. He shook his head, focusing on the task at hand. There was no time to worry about strange phrases now. As they continued across the field, Charles suddenly noticed a movement near the fortress. Several figures appeared, silhouetted against the dim light. French soldiers, rifles in hand, emerged from behind the concrete walls and moved towards him, their voices growing louder and more urgent. "Arrêt, arrêt, arrêt!" they shouted, their words sharp and commanding. Charles froze in his tracks. He didn't need to understand French to know what they were saying. Stop. The soldiers were motioning for him to halt immediately; their rifles were trained on him and Max.

"Mines!" one of the soldiers barked, his voice laced with urgency. Charles glanced around, confusion washing over him. Then he saw it—a large sign posted at the edge of the field. The words were in French, but the meaning was clear even to him. "Champ de mines." His blood ran cold as the realisation struck him. He had walked straight into a minefield. The ground beneath his feet was a deadly trap, and he was right in the middle of it. Max, oblivious to the danger, looked up at him with trusting eyes.

Slowly, carefully, Charles knelt down and scooped Max into his arms, cradling the dog against his chest. How could he have been so careless? So focused on reaching the Maginot Line, he hadn't even noticed the signs warning of mines. From his exposed position, Charles conveyed to the soldiers that he was British and unarmed. He raised one hand, still holding Max with the other. The soldiers exchanged glances, their expressions a mix of disbelief and confusion. One of them, a young man with dark hair and a stern face, stepped forward. He spoke rapidly in French, but Charles could only catch a few words. Something about a foreigner and being unarmed. Finally, the soldiers seemed to reach a consensus. The young man called out to someone behind the fortress walls, and a moment later, another soldier emerged. This one was older, with a grizzled face and a thick moustache. He looked Charles up and down, then spoke in halting English.

"You... British?"

"Yes," Charles replied, his voice shaky but firm. "I'm British, and I need to speak to your commanding officer. It's urgent." The older soldier frowned, clearly suspicious. He looked at the minefield surrounding them, then back at Charles. "How did you..." "Stupid mistake," Charles interrupted, not wanting to waste time on explanations. "But I have information—important information—that your commander needs to hear. Please, you have to get me out of here." The soldier hesitated, then nodded. He shouted instructions to the others, and within moments, one of the soldiers produced a map—an old, worn piece of paper that had been folded and unfolded countless times. The soldier studied it intently, then began to issue directions to Charles in a calm, measured tone.

"Forward," the soldier said, pointing ahead. "Slowly." Charles took a deep breath and began to move, following the soldier's instructions to the letter. He stepped carefully, one foot in front of the other, trying not to think about the deadly explosives hidden beneath the soil. "To the left," the soldier called out, and Charles adjusted his course accordingly. Each step felt like a gamble, but he had no choice. Max remained still in his arms, his body warm against Charles's chest. The dog seemed to sense the seriousness of the moment, his usual energy giving way to a calm alertness. "To the right," the soldier instructed, and Charles shifted again, his movements slow and deliberate. The fortress grew nearer with each step. His pulse hammered as he pressed forward. But he kept moving, following the soldier's directions with unwavering focus. Finally, after what felt like an eternity, he reached the edge of the minefield. The soldiers rushed forward, helping Charles over the last few feet of cleared ground. He set Max down gently, the dog immediately shaking himself off and wagging his tail as if nothing had happened. Charles, on the other hand, felt as though he might collapse from the sheer relief of having made it through alive. But the respite was short-lived. The moment they were clear of the minefield, the soldiers closed in around Charles, their rifles still at the ready. The older soldier, the one who had spoken English, gestured

THE PERILOUS CROSSING   141

to the entrance of the fortress. "You will come with us," he said, his tone leaving no room for argument. Charles nodded, knowing he had little choice. They led him through a narrow corridor carved into the concrete, the walls cold and damp. The air inside the fortress was heavy with the scent of oil and metal, a sharp difference from the fresh air outside. The soldiers marched him through a series of passageways, their footsteps echoing off the concrete floors.

At last, they reached a small room at the heart of the fortress. It was sparsely furnished, with only a wooden table and a few chairs. A French commander sat behind the table, a stern-looking man with a square jaw and piercing eyes. He glanced up as Charles was brought in, his expression one of annoyance rather than curiosity. "Who is this?" the commander demanded in French, his tone sharp. The older soldier briefly explained the situation, his words rapid and clipped. The commander listened, his eyes narrowing as he took in the details. When the soldier finished, the commander turned his gaze on Charles, his expression unreadable. "You claim to be British," the commander said in heavily accented English. "And you say you have information for us. Is that correct?" "Yes, sir," Charles replied, trying to keep his voice steady. "The German army is planning to invade Belgium and France through the Ardennes Forest. They're bypassing the Maginot Line entirely, and they'll be there soon. You need to alert your superiors and the British government immediately." The commander's eyes flickered with something—surprise, perhaps, or disbelief. He leaned back in his chair, studying Charles for a long moment. "That is a very bold claim," the commander said slowly. "And you expect me to believe this, coming from a man who walked into a minefield?"

Charles felt a flash of frustration but forced himself to remain calm. "I know it sounds incredible, but it's the truth. The Germans are moving faster than anyone expected, and if we don't act now, they'll trap the British and French forces in northern France. This could be our only chance to stop them." The commander's expression hardened, scepticism evident in his eyes. "How do I know you're not a spy? A German trying to sow confusion and panic?" Charles shook his head, desperation creeping into his voice. "You have to believe me. I'm not a spy. I'm just trying to save lives. Please, you need to warn them before it's too late." The commander stared at Charles for what felt like an eternity, his gaze cold and unyielding. Then, without a word, he motioned to the soldiers standing nearby. They moved forward, seizing Charles by the arms. "Take him to the holding cell," the commander ordered. "We'll decide what to do with him later."

Charles struggled against their grip, but it was no use. They were stronger, and he was exhausted. As they dragged him away, he felt a crushing sense of defeat. He had come so far, risked everything to get this information to the French, and now it seemed that all his efforts were in vain. Max barked, straining against the length of rope one of the soldiers had attached to him, but there was nothing the dog could do. Charles looked back at the commander one last time, hoping to see some sign of doubt, some sign that his words had made an impact. But the commander's face was impassive, his eyes hard as stone. As the door to the holding cell slammed shut behind him, Charles was left alone with Max in the cold, dark room. His mind raced, trying to come up with a new plan, some way to convince the French of the danger that was bearing down on them. But as the reality of his situation sank in, he knew that time was running out. The Germans were coming, and unless he could find a way to escape and get the warning to the right people, everything would be lost.

Chapter Ten
An Ominous Reckoning

General DuBois sat in silence, staring intently at the telephone on his desk, uncertainty etched across his face. The receiver sat motionless on the desk, a decision waiting to be made that could change the course of the war—or confirm its inevitable path. He drummed his fingers on the table, the soft taps the only sound in the quiet, dimly lit bunker. The French General was a man of experience, one who had seen the ravages of war before. But this—this was different. The stakes were higher, the enemy more cunning, and the situation more precarious. Reluctantly, DuBois reached for the receiver, lifting it to his ear with a sigh. He dialled the number to his superiors, his heart heavy with the burden of the information he was about to relay. Finally, a voice crackled through the receiver. "General DuBois? This is Command. What do you have for us?" DuBois hesitated for only a moment before speaking. "We've received... troubling intelligence, sir. There's reason to believe that the German forces are not planning a direct assault on the Maginot Line but a sweeping manoeuvre through the Ardennes Forest. I've dispatched a reconnaissance aircraft to confirm."

The silence on the other end of the line was palpable. "And?" the voice on the other end finally demanded. "The plane is in the air now. We'll know more shortly." Without another word, DuBois hung up the phone. The spotter plane, a small and nimble aircraft, had been sent from an airfield in Northern France. It climbed quickly into the sky, the roar of its engines echoing across the landscape as it headed towards the Ardennes forest.

Above the thick canopy of trees, the plane soared higher, the pilot scanning the ground below for any signs of the German forces. The dense forest, with its ancient trees and rugged terrain, stretched out in all directions like a vast green ocean. For a moment, it seemed peaceful, serene even. But as the plane flew closer to the edge of the forest, the scene below began to change. Beneath the canopy, shadows moved—unnatural and deliberate. The pilot squinted, adjusting the plane's altitude to get a better look. As he broke through a thin layer of cloud, the sight that greeted him was unmistakable and terrifying. Spread out across the edge of the forest was a massive German force, thousands of troops, and countless tanks and vehicles, all poised to strike. The Germans, aware of the spotter plane above, scrambled to conceal their positions. Camouflage netting was hastily thrown over tanks, and soldiers ducked under the cover of trees. But it was too late. The pilot had already seen enough. The aircraft banked sharply, turning back to the airfield with all the speed it could muster. The pilot's hands shook as they relayed the details of the massive German build-up to the command centre upon landing. Within minutes, the information was transmitted to the French high command and then forwarded to Westminster.

Back in the heart of France, where diplomats and military leaders had gathered, the news spread like wildfire. Phones rang, papers shuffled, and tense conversations filled the halls. The implications of the report were staggering. The Germans were bypassing the formidable Maginot Line, ready to strike deep into Belgium and France. But the reaction was not one of alarm but of scepticism.

Across the Channel, in the corridors of Westminster, British officials received the news with a mixture of disbelief and dismissiveness. The French diplomats were equally dismissive. They made a perfunctory phone call back to the French government, advising them to remain calm. After all, the idea that the Germans could simply drive through the dense and rugged Ardennes Forest seemed preposterous.

Meanwhile, in the bunker deep within the Maginot Line, General DuBois sat alone in his office, staring at the large map of the French-German border that hung on the wall. His eyes traced the thick line of fortifications, the pride of France, designed to stop any German advance. But his gaze kept drifting north, to the Ardennes where the defence was thin and the terrain was thought to be impassable. His thoughts were interrupted by a knock at the door. It was one of his officers, his face serious. "General, Mr. Sterling, is here as you requested." DuBois nodded and motioned for them to bring him in. Charles entered the room, Max by his side, looking tired and apprehensive. DuBois didn't stand to greet him; instead, he waved him over to the map. "Good news and bad news, Mr Sterling," the general began, his voice flat and devoid of any warmth. "The good news is that your story checks out. Our reconnaissance has confirmed a massive German force gathering on the edge of the Ardennes. They're preparing to drive straight through it, just as you warned." Charles felt a brief surge of relief, but it was quickly extinguished by the grim expression on DuBois's face. "The bad news," DuBois continued, "is that neither of our governments believes it. They're adamant that the German Panzers and troops cannot just drive straight through the forest. They think this is some kind of ruse or that the intelligence is exaggerated."

Charles stared at the general in disbelief. "I've seen it with my own eyes. How can they ignore that?" DuBois sighed, rubbing his temples as if trying to ward off a headache. "You're not the only one who's frustrated, Mr. Sterling. But these decisions are made far above our heads. Here we are, ten thousand French troops in a bunker, miles from the action, defending our country from a British diplomat and his dog!" Max, sensing the apprehension, barked once, his tail wagging slightly as if to break the ice. But the mood in the room was too heavy for even Max to lighten. "There's further news," DuBois continued. "London wants you back. They've ordered us to deliver you to Dunkirk."

"Dunkirk?" Charles echoed, incredulous. "Why there of all places?" "Because London thinks this is a walk in the park," DuBois replied, his voice dripping with sarcasm. "They insist on Dunkirk because there are plenty of Allied troops there. They could have chosen any other fishing port in the north of France, but no—they've chosen the one place where the storm is about to break."

Charles felt a cold knot of fear form in his stomach. He had been so focused on getting the information to the French that he hadn't fully considered what would happen next. Heading to Dunkirk in the middle of a full-scale invasion sounded like a suicide mission.

DuBois stood up, walking over to the map on the wall. He traced a line from the Ardennes to Dunkirk with his finger, his expression dark. "The Germans will hit hard and fast, cutting through Belgium and racing to the coast. If they succeed, Dunkirk will be cut off from the rest of France, and the British Expeditionary Force will be trapped." He turned back to Charles, his eyes filled with a grim resolve. "I think we both know this is a ridiculous idea. But orders are orders. A boat will be sent for you in two days. We have no choice but to deliver you to Dunkirk." Charles nodded, though every instinct in his body told him to run in the opposite direction. But he knew there was no escaping this. He had to see this through. "Come," DuBois said, his tone softening slightly. "You'll need to get moving."

With that, the general led Charles and Max out of the office and into the labyrinthine corridors of the underground fortress. The deeper they went, the more oppressive the atmosphere became. The walls seemed to close in; the air growing colder and more stale. They passed by offices where soldiers and officers worked furiously, poring over maps and reports. Dormitories lined the corridors, filled with rows of bunks where the soldiers tried to catch some sleep amid the constant hum of activity. Supplies were stacked high in storerooms, enough to keep the fortress running for months, even if war consumed the world above. As they walked, Charles couldn't help but feel a sense of dread. The Maginot Line, for all its strength and security, was a monument to a past war—a war fought with different tactics and different enemies. Now, it felt like a prison, a place where men were buried alive while the real battle raged elsewhere.

They passed a large hospital, its sterile halls eerily quiet. The thought of what might happen if the Germans broke through the Ardennes and this place became a refuge for the wounded was too horrible to dwell on. Finally, they reached a set of escalators that descended into the bowels of the earth. The sound of machinery echoed through the cavernous space as they stepped onto the escalator and began their descent. It carried them down to an underground station, a vast subterranean hub where soldiers moved about with purpose, their faces set with determination.

They boarded a light railway carriage, joining several other troops who were being transported to different parts of the bunker. As the train hummed to life and began to move, Charles looked around at the faces of the men beside him. There was a quiet resignation in their eyes, a realisation that they were far from where they were needed most. One-third of the French army was dug in here, deep underground at the wrong end of the country. Immobile and cut off from the rest of the world, they were helpless to defend their nation when it would be most needed. And in a matter of days—perhaps even hours—everything could change.

As the train rattled through the dark tunnels, Charles tried to steel himself for what lay ahead. He was heading to Dunkirk, to the front lines of a war that was about to explode with unimaginable ferocity. And as the echoes of the train reverberated through the underground warren, he couldn't shake the feeling that he was descending not just into the depths of the earth but into the heart of a disaster from which there might be no return.

Chapter Eleven

Betrayal at Longuyon

"End of the line!" shouted a young French soldier, his voice echoing through the cold metal confines of the miniature train. The screech of the brakes filled the narrow station, reverberating off the curved walls of the underground bunker. Charles stirred from his seat, rubbing his eyes, and looked over at his faithful companion, Max, who sat at his feet, staring up at him with curious eyes. The two men accompanying them, French soldiers Alain and Philippe, were already rising, stretching their legs after the cramped journey. Charles followed the soldiers as they disembarked from the train. The small platform was a flurry of activity, with soldiers rushing past and the distant murmur of orders being exchanged. Max jumped down from the train with a graceful bound, shaking off the dust as he waited for Charles to catch up. "Come on, Max," Charles muttered, running his hand through the dog's smooth fur. "Let's see what comes next." The underground station had been stifling, a relic of the First World War, repurposed into a military outpost. Charles was grateful to leave its shadowy depths behind as they began ascending a flight of stone stairs that wound upwards. His legs were heavy, fatigued by days of travel and sleepless nights. The last time he had a proper rest seemed like a lifetime ago.

Emerging into the open air, the evening light was fading over the French countryside, casting long shadows across the rolling hills. The contrast from the dim, suffocating bunker was startling. The air was crisp, carrying with it the scent of damp earth and fresh leaves. It felt refreshing—almost too peaceful, given how close they were to the German border. Alain, the more talkative of the two escorts, waved towards a small wooden hut stationed just beyond the platform. He motioned for Charles and Max to follow while Philippe remained quiet, his face set in a permanent scowl. The two soldiers disappeared inside the hut, leaving Charles standing outside with Max at his side. The dog's ears perked up at every distant sound; his sharp instincts were never dulled by fatigue or distraction. Within minutes, Alain and Philippe re-emerged, a set of keys in hand. Alain twirled the keys in the air with a casual flick of his wrist and gestured towards a military vehicle parked nearby. The vehicle—a dusty, olive-green Citroën Traction Avant—was a sturdy machine, well-suited for the rough terrain they would undoubtedly face. "Voilà, our chariot for the evening," Alain said with a slight grin. He approached Charles, holding out the keys. "I think we should be on a first-name basis, don't you, Mr. Sterling?" Alain asked, his tone light yet cordial. Charles nodded, shaking the soldier's hand firmly. "Charles," he replied, offering his first real smile since the journey began. "And I'm Alain," the soldier said, his handshake firm but friendly. "That's Philippe," he added, nodding towards the other soldier, who gave a quick, almost imperceptible nod in return. Philippe's demeanour was more reserved, his English far less fluent than Alain's, but his eyes were sharp, always scanning the horizon for any sign of trouble.

As the introductions concluded, Alain leaned in slightly, his expression growing a touch more serious. "We weren't exactly thrilled about being sent to babysit you," he admitted, his eyes meeting Charles's with a hint of apology. "But the monotony of life inside that bunker takes it out of everyone. I think we were all ready for a change of scenery." Charles chuckled softly. He couldn't blame them for their hesitation. He wasn't here to be babysat, but it was clear that Alain and Philippe saw him as a responsibility, one they had not necessarily asked for. "The feeling's mutual," Charles replied, shrugging slightly. "I'm not exactly thrilled to need an escort, but I suppose it's better than the alternative." Alain's expression softened, and he nodded in agreement. "At least we'll have some interesting stories to tell after this." With that, they piled into the vehicle. Alain took the wheel. With Philippe in the passenger seat and Charles in the back, Max nestled beside him. As they pulled away from the bunker, the engine hummed steadily, the headlights cutting through the growing darkness that enveloped the countryside.

The plan, as Alain had explained earlier, was simple: they would drive for a couple of hours, following the route of the French border with Germany, and then stop for the night at a small guest house that the military had connections with. The journey was straightforward, but something warned Charles that even the simplest plans could unravel, especially with war drawing so near. Charles leaned back in his seat, his eyes half-closed, trying to relax, but the exhaustion gripping his limbs did little to calm the knot of anxiety tightening in his chest. It had been nearly two days since he'd last slept properly, and the toll was starting to show. Max rested his head on Charles's lap, sensing his master's unease. Charles absent-mindedly stroked the dog's ears, drawing comfort from the simple, grounding presence of his loyal companion. Max had been with him through thick and thin, from diplomatic receptions to Embassy garden parties, and Charles trusted him more than most people. The dog was more than just a pet; he was a partner, a confidant in moments when his duties felt like too much.

The French countryside stretched out around them in all directions, bathed in the soft glow of twilight. Fields of wheat swayed gently in the breeze, and the occasional farmhouse appeared on the horizon, its windows glowing warmly as the families inside prepared for the night. The peacefulness of the scene belied the growing unease that gripped Europe. The border was less than a few dozen miles away, and beyond it, Germany stirred with preparations of its own—preparations that threatened to tear the continent apart once again. For the first hour, the drive passed in silence, save for the low hum of the engine and the occasional creak of the vehicle's suspension as they navigated the narrow country roads. Alain focused on the road ahead, his hands steady on the wheel, while Philippe kept his gaze fixed on the horizon, ever watchful. As the truck rolled into the small French town of Longuyon, the setting sun cast long shadows over the cobblestone streets. The town, nestled near the Belgian border, had a timeless quality, with its stone buildings and narrow alleys that seemed untouched by the modern world. The air was cool and fresh, a welcome change from the oppressive, stagnant atmosphere of the underground bunkers they had left behind. Charles felt a slight sense of relief as they approached the *Hôtel de Lorraine* their refuge for the night. The hotel was a modest but sturdy building, its stone façade showing signs of age and wear from years of exposure to the elements. The window shutters, though functional, were faded and chipped, hinting at a time when a fresh coat of paint was long overdue. The overall structure conveyed a sense of resilience, fitting for a place that had weathered many seasons and the tumult of history. The dim light spilling from its windows gave the place an inviting warmth, unlike the cold uncertainty that lay beyond the town's borders.

Alain and Philippe guided the truck to a stop in front of the hotel. They moved with the confidence of men who knew this place well. As they entered the hotel, it was clear that they were not strangers here. The lobby of the *Lorraine* was quaint, with a polished wooden counter and a small seating area by the fire. The smell of burning wood mixed with the faint scent of lavender, creating a cosy, homely atmosphere. Henri, the hotel's owner, was a burly man with a thick moustache and a jovial demeanour. He greeted Alain and Philippe with a broad smile, his eyes twinkling with recognition. "Ah, mes amis!" Henri exclaimed, his voice booming in the small space. "You've returned! And with a guest, I see." He glanced at Charles, his smile never wavering. Alain returned the smile, shaking Henri's hand firmly. "Yes, Henri. This is Charles. We're here on important business and will need rooms for the night." Henri nodded, already reaching for the keys behind the counter. "Of course, of course. But first, a nightcap, eh?" He winked, knowing well the habits of the soldiers who frequented his establishment. Phillippe, who had been unusually quiet during the journey, managed a small smile as he took his key. "A nightcap sounds perfect," he said, his voice betraying a hint of weariness. Henri pretended to roll his eyes, a playful gesture that was part of his routine. "You soldiers and your drink," he said with mock exasperation, though it was clear he was more than happy to oblige. With a theatrical sigh, he descended into the cellar, returning moments later with a dusty bottle of brandy. The bottle's label was faded, and the glass had a cloudy, aged look, but the liquid inside gleamed a rich amber, promising warmth and comfort.

As Henri placed the bottle on the table by the fire, he also brought out a platter of bread and cheese. The four men settled into the chairs by the hearth, the fire crackling softly as it cast flickering shadows on the walls. The evening was mild, but the fire added a sense of cosiness that they all seemed to need – a small reprieve from the harsh realities that awaited them. Henri poured the brandy into small glasses, the rich aroma filling the air as they raised their drinks in a silent toast. The first sip was strong, the warmth of the alcohol spreading through their bodies, easing the unease that had built up during the long journey. Charles leaned back in his chair, trying to relax but finding it difficult to shake off the discomfort that had settled over him. The brandy slightly dulled the edge of his anxiety. It did little, though, to dispel the dark thoughts that lingered. Alain, sensing the atmosphere, tried to lighten the mood. "So, Charles," he said with a grin, "have you ever tasted brandy like this before? Henri's got the best in all of Lorraine." Charles forced a smile, grateful for the distraction. "It's excellent," he replied, taking another sip. "I could get used to it."

Philippe remained quiet, staring into his glass, his expression unreadable. Charles noticed but said nothing, attributing it to the strain of their mission. Alain, however, was more observant and gave Philippe a sidelong glance, his brow furrowed in concern. The night wore on, the brandy slowly disappearing as they spoke in low voices about everything and nothing, each man trying to mask his fears with casual conversation. The anticipation of what the next few days would hold hung over them, unspoken but palpable. As the clock struck midnight, the fire had burnt down to glowing embers, and the room was filled with a comfortable silence. Henri, seeing the weariness on their faces, finally stood up, stretching his arms with a yawn. "Time to get some rest, gentlemen," he said. "Tomorrow will be here soon enough."

The men nodded in agreement, their fatigue catching up with them. Alain clapped Charles on the back as they made their way to their rooms. "Get some sleep," he said. "We'll need our wits about us tomorrow." Charles nodded, exhaustion creeping in, making it harder to stay alert. He opened the door to his room, Max padding quietly at his heels. The room was small but clean, with a single bed, a wooden chair, and a window that looked out over the quiet town square. Charles sat on the edge of the bed, removing his shoes and jacket. Max curled up in the chair by the window, his eyes half-closed but still alert. As Charles lay back on the bed, he stared at the ceiling, his mind racing despite his physical exhaustion. The route that lay ahead was a dangerous one, and the uncertainty of it all gnawed at him. But eventually, the warmth of the brandy and the comfort of the bed began to take effect, and his thoughts grew hazy. He closed his eyes, letting sleep slowly overtake him.

A sudden, frantic yelp shattered the stillness of the night. Charles jolted awake, a surge of adrenaline coursing through him as he sat up disoriented. It took him a moment to realise that it was Max barking, the dog's deep, urgent growls filling the room. "Max, quiet!" Charles hissed, his voice barely above a whisper. But Max continued to bark, his body tense, his gaze fixed on the door. Charles's pulse quickened. What could have set

Max off like this? He listened carefully, and then he heard it—a soft creak, the sound of someone moving outside his door. Before he could react, the door slowly creaked open, revealing Philippe standing in the doorway. The young soldier's face was pale, his eyes wide with fear and something else—something darker. In his trembling hand, he held a pistol; the barrel pointed directly at Charles.

Charles froze, his mind struggling to process what he was seeing. "Phillippe...?" he began, his voice barely audible. But Philippe didn't respond. His gaze flicked to Max, whose barking had intensified. The dog's sharp, insistent barks seemed to rattle Phillippe, his hand shaking more visibly as he aimed the gun at Max. A surge of dread gripped him as he realised what was about to happen. "Phillippe, don't!" he shouted, but the young man was beyond reasoning.

Phillippe's finger tightened on the trigger, desperation etched on his face. But before he could fire, the door behind him swung open with a loud crash, knocking him off balance. The gun went off, the shot echoing through the room as the bullet shattered the window, sending shards of glass raining down. Henri, the hotel owner, stood behind the door, holding an old blunderbuss rifle that looked like it hadn't been used in decades. His hands were trembling, but his eyes were fierce as he levelled the ancient weapon at Phillippe. The sudden chaos gave Charles the opportunity he needed. Without a second thought, he leaped from the bed, tackling Philippe to the ground. The two men crashed to the floor, grappling with each other as the pistol skidded out of Phillippe's hand and under the bed. Max barked furiously, circling the struggling men, his instincts driving him to protect his master. Henri, still holding the blunderbuss, hovered uncertainly, the unwieldy weapon too dangerous to use in such close quarters. Philippe fought like a man possessed, his strength fuelled by desperation and fear. He landed a hard punch to

Charles's side, causing him to grunt in pain, but Charles held on, using his weight to pin Philippe to the ground. "Henri, get help!" Charles shouted, struggling to keep Phillippe's flailing arms under control. But before Henri could move, the door burst open again, and Alain stormed into the room, his own pistol drawn. "Stop!" Alain bellowed, his voice cutting through the chaos. He quickly assessed the situation, his eyes narrowing as he saw Philippe pinned beneath Charles. "Get off him, Charles," Alain ordered, his tone firm but calm. "I'll handle this."

Charles hesitated for a moment, his breath coming in ragged gasps, but then he slowly released his grip on Philippe, stepping back with his hands raised. Alain kept his pistol trained on Philippe, his expression a mix of anger and disbelief. "What the hell were you doing, Philippe?" Alain demanded, his voice low and dangerous. "Why did you do this?"

Philippe, still lying on the floor, didn't answer immediately. His chest heaved as he struggled to catch his breath, his eyes darting between Alain and Charles, then to the gun lying just out of reach. For a long, tense moment, the room was silent except for Max's low growls and the sound of everyone's heavy breathing. Then, finally, Philippe spoke, his voice thick with barely contained rage.

"France is weak and corrupt. The Republic is falling apart. Someone has to step up, to save us from the chaos. Doriot, 'La Cagoule'... they're the ones with the vision, the ones who understand what must be done."

Charles felt a cold chill run down his spine as Philippe's words hit him. "You've sided with the Nazis?" Charles said, his voice low and steady, the accusation clear in every word. Philippe's eyes filled with a burning conviction rather than guilt. "You don't understand," he said, his voice steadying. "Doriot sees what needs to happen. We need strength and order. The Germans—they're not the enemy. The real threat is the communists, all the vermin who are tearing our country apart from the inside. If you had seen what I've seen, you'd know this is the only way forward." Alain's grip on his pistol tightened, his jaw clenching in anger. "You were supposed to protect your country, Philippe," he said, his voice trembling with barely controlled rage. "You betrayed us all."

Philippe sat up, wiping the blood from his mouth. "No. You don't see it yet, but I'm trying to save us. France can't survive in this mess. The Germans will bring a new order, and we'll be part of it. I joined Doriot because he understands—'La Cagoule' know what needs to be done. We'll root out the weakness, the rot, and rebuild something pure." Charles took a step back, shaking his head. "You're delusional. You're selling out your own people for—what? Nazi lies?" Philippe's face hardened. "Not lies. Survival. This is the future, Charles. Better to be on the winning side than left to die in the ashes of a broken republic."

Henri, who had been standing frozen with the blunderbuss still in his hands, finally found his voice. "What do we do now?" he asked, his voice tinged with fear. Alain glanced at Charles. "We tie him up," Alain said, his tone hardening. "And then we call the police. They'll deal with him."

As Alain moved forward, Philippe gave a last defiant glare. "You'll see. When the Germans win, you'll wish you had listened. France will rise again—stronger than ever." Alain said nothing as he bound Philippe's hands, but the grim silence that followed was enough to confirm the finality of their decision.

Once Philippe was secured, Alain put his pistol away and turned to Henri. "Get the police on the phone," he instructed. "Tell them we have a prisoner who needs to be taken into custody immediately." Henri nodded and quickly left the room, the sound of his footsteps fading as he hurried down the stairs to the lobby. Charles wiped the sweat from his brow as he looked at Phillippe, who lay on the floor, defeated and broken. Alain stood beside Charles, his expression softening as he placed a hand on his friend's shoulder. "Are you okay?" he asked quietly.

Charles nodded, though he still felt a lingering unease. "I'm fine," he replied, though his voice lacked conviction. "I just... I never expected this." Alain sighed, shaking his head. "Me neither," he said. "But this war... it changes people. It makes them do things they'd never imagine."

They sat in silence for a moment. Max, sensing that the danger had passed, finally stopped growling and moved to Charles's side, nuzzling his leg for comfort. Charles reached down to pat the dog's head, grateful for his presence. "Thank you, Max" he said softly. "You saved us tonight." Max wagged his tail, his large, expressive eyes reflecting a loyalty and understanding that was beyond words.

A few minutes later, Henri returned and reported the police were on their way. "They'll be here soon," he said, his voice unsteady. "They said to keep him secured until they arrive." Within minutes, the sound of a vehicle pulling up outside broke the silence, and moments later, two uniformed police officers entered the hotel. They were led upstairs to Phillippe, who offered no resistance as they escorted him out of the building and into the back of the police car.

As the car drove away, its rear lights disappearing into the night, Charles felt an overwhelming sense of exhaustion. He turned to Alain, who looked just as weary, and gave him a tired smile. The full impact of what had just occurred started to settle in. They had narrowly avoided disaster, but the cost had been high. A friend had become an enemy, and the line between right and wrong had blurred in the harsh light of war. When they reached the lobby, they found Henri pouring himself a stiff drink, his hands still shaking. He offered the bottle to Charles and Alain, who both accepted gratefully. They drank in silence, the warmth of the brandy doing little to ease the cold knot of dread in their stomachs. "We should get some sleep," Charles said, though he knew sleep would not come easily after what they had just been through. Alain nodded in agreement. "Yes," he said quietly. "Tomorrow will be another long day." With that, they bid Henri goodnight and made their way back to their rooms. Charles entered his room, the shattered window now covered with a blanket that Henri had hastily tacked up. Max followed him inside, settling back into the chair by the window. But for now, he had survived another day. He lay back on the bed, his eyes closing as he allowed the exhaustion to finally overtake him. And as he drifted back to sleep, Max kept watch, ever vigilant by his side.

Chapter Twelve
GHOSTS IN THE MIST

The early morning air was crisp, carrying the scent of dew as Charles and Alain exchanged a silent look. Philippe was left behind, his fate uncertain, and the burden of that decision lingered in their minds. But there was no time for regret. The mission ahead demanded their complete focus.

"We need to keep moving," Charles said, breaking the tense silence that had settled over the car. His voice was calm, but there was an edge to it—a reminder of the urgency that drove them forward. Alain nodded, his hands gripping the steering wheel with a steady resolve. "Agreed. Are you good to drive after that brandy?" Charles offered a slight smile, more of a grimace than a gesture of amusement. "I didn't have much. We can take turns, but for now, let's just focus on getting to Dunkirk." They had bid a hasty farewell to Henri, their contact in Longuyon, who stood at the edge of the small town as they drove away. Henri's face was lined with worry, his broad shoulders hunched against the morning chill. He had seen many men come and go, and he knew better than most the dangers they faced. His parting words had been brief – to stay safe, though both Charles and Alain knew that safety was a relative term in times like these.

In the back seat, Max was curled into a tight ball. As they left Longuyon behind, the surrounding landscape was bathed in the soft glow of the rising sun. The rolling hills and scattered farms were a picture of tranquillity, but Charles knew better than to trust appearances. War had a way of creeping into even the most peaceful of places, and they were deep in the heart of a country on the brink of catastrophe. Nearly an hour had passed since they had set off when Alain suddenly slowed the car. Charles, who had been lost in thought, looked up, instantly alert. Ahead of them, something large and white hung from a tree, its ghostly form fluttering in the light breeze. "Is that a sheet?" Charles asked, squinting to get a better look. "No," Alain replied, his voice tight with suspicion. "It's a parachute." The car rolled to a stop on the gravel road, and for a moment, neither man moved. They stared at the parachute, which hung limply from the tree, as if contemplating its strange presence in this remote area. Max raised his head from his spot in the back seat, his ears perked up in curiosity. His dark eyes followed the direction of their gaze, but he made no sound, sensing the unease that had suddenly filled the car. "We should check it out," Charles suggested, though he was already reaching for the door handle. His instincts told him that this was more than just a random discovery. Alain nodded, and the two men stepped out of the car, their shoes crunching on the gravel as they approached the parachute. The morning air was still, and the only sound was the rustling of leaves as a light breeze swept through the trees.

As they neared the tree, a rustling sound from the nearby hedgerow caught their attention. Alain tensed, his hand instinctively moving towards the pistol at his side. Charles stopped in his tracks, his eyes scanning the area for any sign of movement.

Suddenly, a figure stumbled out from the hedgerow, nearly collapsing onto the road in front of them. It was a woman, her clothes torn and dirty, her face smeared with blood. She held a gun in her hand, though it wavered unsteadily as she tried to keep it pointed in their direction.

"Sorry," the woman said in a thick, accented French, her voice barely more than a whisper. "J'ai besoin de votre voiture." Alain's eyes widened in surprise as he realised her accent was not French—it was English, though heavily accented. Charles, sensing the danger, remained still, his diplomat's mind already calculating the risks and potential outcomes. The woman's grip on the gun faltered, and she took a shaky step further forward. "I need your... help," she said again, her voice growing weaker. Then, as if her body could no longer sustain her will, she collapsed to the ground, the gun slipping from her grasp. Without a moment's hesitation, both men rushed to her side. Alain carefully picked up the pistol, ensuring it was no longer a threat, while Charles knelt beside the woman, quickly assessing her condition. "She's badly hurt," Alain said, his voice laced with concern. He glanced at the parachute hanging overhead and the broken suitcase lying beneath it. The contents—a jumble of wires and shattered electronics—were scattered across the ground. Charles studied the remnants of the equipment. "This was some kind of reconnaissance mission," he said. "We need to get her to a doctor," "What about the parachute?" Alain asked, casting a wary glance at the telltale sign of the woman's arrival. Charles shook his head. "Leave it. The first French woman who sees it will turn it into five silk dresses before evening." Alain allowed himself a brief smile at the remark, though the situation was anything but amusing. Together, they carefully lifted the unconscious woman and carried her to the car. Max watched them intently. His body tensed as if sensing the urgency of the moment. Charles settled the woman in the back seat, taking care to make her as comfortable as possible. Max, who had been occupying the back seat, reluctantly squeezed into the footwell, his expressive eyes showing a mixture of concern and displeasure. "We should reach Cambrai in about an hour," Alain said as he started the car. He glanced in the rearview mirror at the woman, her face pale and bloodied. "Let's hope she makes it."

The journey to Cambrai was tense and silent. The roads were eerily empty, the usual signs of life conspicuously absent. The further they drove, the more apparent it became that the town was bracing for something terrible. The population had fled westward, sensing the impending storm that would soon engulf them. As they approached the outskirts of Arras, the silence grew heavier, oppressive in its intensity. The town, once a vibrant centre of life and culture, now seemed to hold its breath, waiting for the inevitable onslaught.

Cambrai had been nearly destroyed in the First World War, its grand buildings reduced to rubble. The Battle of Cambrai was one of the first battles of the Great War in which tanks played a key role. The aftermath had left complete devastation, but through immense effort, it had been rebuilt and restored to its former glory. The town hall, a magnificent gothic structure, stood as a testament to that resilience. But now it seemed to tremble in the face of the advancing tide of war. Alain brought the car to a stop in front of the steps. The building's spire reached towards the sky, its intricate carvings and soaring arches rising above the surrounding buildings in the square. In the distance, faint plumes of smoke could be seen rising into the sky, accompanied by the distant rumble of cannon fire. The war was drawing nearer, its ominous presence impossible to ignore. They ran up the steps of the town hall, leaving the mystery parachute woman in the car. The grand doors stood before them, and as they pushed them open, the cavernous interior—a vast space of marble floors, high ceilings, and grand chandeliers that had once been the pride of the town greeted them.

But now, the hall was empty; the echoes of their footsteps were the only sound that filled the void. They moved through the empty corridors, looking for signs of life.

Chapter Thirteen

The Call for Help

The sound of a telephone ringing echoed through the empty corridors of the town hall in Cambrai. It startled Charles but he traced the sound to an office, where a nervous clerk stood clutching the receiver. The man hesitated, visibly anxious, before lowering the phone and turning to Charles with wide, uncertain eyes. "Puis-je....utiliser...votre...téléphone?" Charles asked in his best French. The clerk, eager to help, dialled local telephone exchange explaining who he was, the call was then routed to the National Exchange in Paris then transferred to the International Operator and then on to London. Charles' first call was to Neville Henderson, the British Ambassador to Germany. Charles had known Henderson for years; they had a strained professional relationship, but in times of crisis, they relied on each other. The phone rang several times before it was answered, and Charles was relieved to hear Henderson's familiar voice, though it was tinged with the weariness of recent events. "Sterling?" Henderson's voice was sharp, immediately recognising Charles's voice. "Yes, it's me," Charles replied. "I'm in Cambrai, in France, in the middle of something big. The Ardennes Plan—it's not just a rumour. It's happening, and I'm in the thick of it."

Henderson was silent for a moment, absorbing the gravity of Charles's words. When he spoke again, his tone was calm but resolute. "Yes, they don't believe it." "It's true, Mr. Henderson," Charles insisted, his voice edged with urgency. "They're advancing through the Ardennes forest as we speak—and with alarming speed."

The call ended abruptly, leaving Charles with a heightened sense of dread. Wasting no time, he quickly asked for another number, this time hoping for a voice that would provide him with a brief escape from the mounting chaos—his wife, Elizabeth. The phone rang several times, and as he waited, his pulse quickened. When the crackly line was finally answered, it wasn't Elizabeth's voice on the other end. To his surprise, someone else had picked up. "Daddy!" a small voice chirped, full of innocent excitement. It was Lucy, his three-year-old daughter. A pang of emotion hit Charles at the sound of her voice. "Lucy, darling, where's Mummy?" he asked, trying to keep his voice steady despite the overwhelming emotions coursing through him. Lucy babbled on, clearly delighted to hear from her father, but she was too young to understand the gravity of the situation. She handed the phone over to her mother, who sounded breathless as she greeted him. "Charles? Is that you? Oh my word, I thought you were...we thought....." Her voice stopped, unable to finish the sentence. "Yes, it's me," he replied, feeling a pang of guilt for the distress he knew he was causing. "I'm safe, for now. But things are moving quickly here. I just wanted to hear your voice, to know that you and the children are alright."

"We're fine," Elizabeth assured him, though he could hear the tremor in her voice. "But Charles, please... be careful." "I will," he promised, though they both knew it was a promise he might not be able to keep. The line went dead, and Charles took a moment to steady himself. He put down the receiver and left the office and hurried back to the woman they had rescued. Charles and Alain headed back to the car, but as they approached it, they saw that the back door was open and the woman was no longer inside. Charles rushed down the steps, his mind racing with a thousand possibilities. Had she been captured? Had she wandered off in a daze? But as he rounded the corner, he spotted her sitting on a bench near the car, Max by her side. She looked pale and shaken, but she was awake. "How are you?" Charles asked in English, dropping the pretence that she might not understand him. The woman looked up at him, her expression weary but defiant. "I've had better days," she replied, her voice tinged with a dry humour that belied her condition. Charles allowed himself a small smile. "I'm sure you have. We need to get you to a doctor."

Across the road, a small sign indicated the presence of a doctor's surgery. Wasting no more time, Charles helped the woman to her feet, and together with Alain and Max they made their way to the doctor's surgery. The surgery was small and dimly lit, but to their relief, Doctor Augustin was still there, though he looked as if he was on the verge of leaving. The doctor's eyes widened in surprise as they entered, but he quickly regained his composure and ushered them into the back room. "She's been through a lot," Charles explained as they sat the woman down. "Can you help her?" Doctor Augustin nodded, his expression serious. He set to work, examining her injuries with a practiced eye. Meanwhile, Charles, Alain, and Max waited in the small reception area, their eyes scanning the deserted square outside. After a few tense minutes, Doctor Augustin reappeared. "She'll be alright," he said, his voice reassuring. "A few bumps and bruises, a nasty knock to the head, but nothing life-threatening. She should rest for a while." Charles thanked the doctor, and they all returned to the consulting room, where the woman was now sitting up, looking much more alert. She had washed the blood from her hair and face, and despite her injuries, she managed a small smile.

Max jumped up onto the chair beside her, his tail wagging slightly as he nuzzled her hand. She stroked his head absentmindedly, her thoughts clearly elsewhere. "We need to know who you are," Charles said gently, not wanting to push her too hard but needing answers. "Why were you out there? " The woman looked at him for a long moment, as if weighing her options. Finally, she spoke, her voice steady despite the fatigue that lined her face. "My name is Charlotte. My mission was to gather intelligence on movements along the border and report back, but things... didn't go as planned." Before she could say more, the door to the surgery suddenly burst open with a loud crash. Someone or something had pushed open the surgery door with a mighty force. Doctor Augustine gestured with his index finger to his lips for silence. He left the consulting room and went down the short corridor to the reception. A German soldier appeared in the doorway, his uniform blackened with dust and his eyes wild with desperation.

The soldier grabbed Doctor Augustine by the lapel, shaking him roughly as he barked out a question in broken French. "Are you alone?" the soldier demanded, his voice harsh and guttural. Doctor Augustin nodded frantically, his eyes wide with fear. "Oui, oui," he stammered, trying to appease the soldier. But the soldier wasn't satisfied. He shoved the doctor aside, sending him sprawling onto the street outside. In the consulting room, Charles, Alain, and Charlotte exchanged a quick, tense glance. Alain reached for his gun, knowing they were moments away from a potentially deadly confrontation. Charlotte, still too weak to fight, felt a surge of frustration as she realised she no longer had her own weapon. She glanced around the room, desperate for something she could use to defend herself. Charles peered cautiously around the door frame, assessing the situation. The German soldier had left, but more would surely follow. He looked to his right and noticed the small corridor leading to a back door. It was their only chance. "We need to move, now," Charles whispered urgently. Alain nodded, his hand steady on his weapon. Charlotte struggled to her feet, and Max, ever alert, was by her side in an instant. They filed silently through the small corridor, Charles leading the way.

The back door opened into a small courtyard, enclosed on all sides by high walls. Disheartened, they filed back into the surgery and climbed the steps to the first-floor rooms. The distant rumble of tanks rolling into Cambrai was growing louder, the reality of the German advance becoming impossible to ignore.

Chapter Fourteen
FIRES IN THE SQUARE

FROM THE UPSTAIRS ROOM in Dr. Augustin's surgery, the trio had a chilling view of the city square below. Cambrai, once a bustling town, was now a stark tableau of occupation. The square was filling rapidly with German Panzer tanks and hordes of soldiers. Charles, Alain, Charlotte, and Max watched in tense silence, their hearts sinking as they realised that the Germans were not merely passing through. The soldiers began to settle in the square, their actions making it clear that they intended to stay. The initial shock of seeing the enemy forces up close gave way to a gnawing dread as they observed the soldiers' behaviour. Windows were smashed with careless brutality, and the distinctive pop of corks being pulled from looted bottles of wine echoed through the streets. Some of the few remaining French villagers were being herded up the steps of the town hall, their faces etched with fear. As the German soldiers filled the square, the sense of menace grew. A few of them leaned against the church walls, their rifles slung carelessly over their shoulders as they drifted off to sleep, but the real terror lay in the sporadic bursts of machine gun fire that shattered the early evening stillness. Each staccato volley was a reminder of the violence that could erupt at any moment. "How long can we stay hidden?" Charlotte whispered, her voice tinged with the same fear that gripped them all. Charles didn't answer. There was no need; they all knew that their time was running out.

Suddenly, the sound of the surgery door opening downstairs snapped them out of their thoughts. The ominous noise of things being smashed and overturned echoed up the staircase. More Germans were inside the building, searching for anything of value—pharmaceuticals, supplies, anything that might ease their weariness or satisfy their greed. Charles, Alain, and Charlotte remained perfectly still, not daring to breathe as the intruders ransacked the rooms below. After what felt like an eternity, the crashing sounds subsided, and the soldiers left, their search having yielded nothing of interest. The trio allowed themselves a moment of relief, but it was short-lived. The night outside was growing darker, and with it came a rising sense of danger.

Fires began to flicker in the square as the Germans, drunk on stolen wine and fatigue, lit bonfires to stave off the encroaching darkness. The once-organised soldiers were becoming increasingly unruly, smashing more windows, raiding more cellars, and even turning on each other in drunken brawls. Their lack of discipline made them unpredictable and more dangerous than ever, but it also presented an opportunity. "They're losing focus," Alain murmured, peering through the narrow gap in the curtains. "If we're going to escape, it has to be now." Charlotte nodded in agreement, her mind already racing through possible escape routes. "We can't go back to the van," she said. "It's too risky. They'll hear the engine the moment we start it." Charles glanced around the small room, his eyes settling on a narrow wardrobe in the corner. He walked over and opened it, revealing a spare set of civilian clothes that Dr. Augustin had kept in there. "Here," he said, handing the clothes to Alain. "You need to change out of your uniform." Alain took the clothes silently, quickly changing from his soldier's uniform into civilian attire. While it would help him blend in if they were spotted in the distance, everyone understood the severe consequences if he were caught by the Germans dressed this way.

Once Alain was dressed, they descended the stairs as quietly as they could, their footsteps barely making a sound on the creaky wooden steps. They knew they had to avoid detection at all costs; one wrong move could mean their deaths. In the small courtyard behind the surgery, they faced their next challenge: a high wall that enclosed the yard. Beyond it lay the darkened streets of Cambrai, and with them, the hope of freedom. Charles examined the wall, estimating its height and the best way to scale it. He dragged two chairs from the consulting room into the yard, placing one under the wall and then leaning over to position the second chair on the other side. "Can you make it?" Charles asked Charlotte, his voice low but urgent. Charlotte glanced up at the wall, her expression determined. "Got no choice," she replied, her tone leaving no room for doubt. With a quick nod, Charles helped Charlotte onto the first chair. She balanced herself carefully, then reached for the top of the wall. Alain moved in to support her from behind, giving her a boost as she pulled herself up. She paused at the top for a moment, catching her breath before swinging her legs over and dropping down onto the chair on the other side. Next came Alain, who made quick work of the climb. He paused only to take Max from Charles, passing the dog over the wall with surprising ease. Max, ever the loyal companion, remained calm as he was lifted over the wall. Charles was the last to go. He pulled himself up onto the wall, his muscles straining as he hoisted his body over. As he dropped down on the other side, he landed lightly, adrenaline giving him a burst of energy.

They paused for a moment in the shadows of the narrow alley beyond the wall, catching their breath and steadying their nerves. The sound of

German voices and the crackling of fires filled the air, but they were well hidden in the dark, their presence unnoticed.

Moving swiftly and silently, they began to navigate the labyrinth of backstreets that crisscrossed Cambrai. The streets deserted, save for the distant rumble of tanks and the occasional shout of a soldier heading to the square.

They stuck to the shadows, their progress slow but steady. Every step brought them closer to the edge of the town, to the possibility of escape. They knew they had to reach the outskirts before dawn, before the Germans began their patrols in earnest. They pressed on, driven by the knowledge that their survival depended on it. At last, they reached the edge of the town. Before them lay the open fields that surrounded Cambrai, stretching out into the night like a vast, dark ocean. Beyond the fields lay safety, or at least the hope of it. Charles crouched low, peering out at the open expanse. "We'll have to run for it," he whispered. "Stick close together, and don't stop for anything. Alain and Charlotte nodded, fully aware of the seriousness of what lay ahead. They all knew that this was their best—and perhaps only—chance to escape. Without another word, they broke cover, sprinting across the field as fast as their legs would carry them. Charlotte hobbling as best as she could. The ground was uneven, the tall grass whipping at their faces as they ran, but they didn't dare slow down.

Behind them, the town of Cambrai was a smouldering ruin, the fires in the square casting an eerie glow over the horizon. But there was no time to look back. All that mattered now was putting as much distance between themselves and the Germans as possible. They ran until their lungs burnt, and their legs felt like lead, the adrenaline that had fuelled their escape beginning to wane. Despite that, they kept going, driven by the primal instinct to survive. Finally, after what felt like an eternity, they reached the cover of a small grove of trees on the far side of the field. They collapsed to the ground, gasping for breath, their bodies trembling with exhaustion and relief. Max, ever faithful, circled around them, his tongue lolling out as he panted heavily. He nudged Charlotte with his nose, as if to check on her, and she smiled weakly, reaching out to stroke him. "We made it," Alain said between gasps, his voice tinged with disbelief. "For now," Charles replied, his eyes scanning the horizon. "But we're not safe yet. We need to keep moving." Charlotte nodded, though she was clearly exhausted. "Where will we go?" Charles considered their options. The roads would be dangerous, but they couldn't stay out in the open for long. They needed to find shelter, somewhere they could rest and regroup before deciding their next move. The others agreed, and after a brief rest, they set off again, moving more slowly now as the initial burst of adrenaline faded. The night was cool and quiet, the stars overhead offering little comfort as they trudged through the fields.

It was a long and arduous journey, but eventually they reached the outskirts of a village. The houses were dark, the streets deserted, but it felt like a sanctuary compared to the chaos they had left behind.

They found an abandoned barn on the edge of the village, its doors slightly ajar. It wasn't much, but it would provide shelter for the night. They slipped inside, grateful for the cover it offered, and settled down in the hayloft, where they could rest without fear of being discovered. As they lay there in the darkness, the events of the day began to catch up with them. The fear and the sheer terror of their narrow escape—it all came crashing down, leaving them drained and hollow.

Max curled up next to Charlotte, his warm body a small comfort in the cold night. She closed her eyes, trying to block out the images that kept replaying in her mind—the tanks, the soldiers, the fires. But sleep was elusive, and she could tell from the sound of Charles and Alain's breathing that they were equally restless. They had escaped Cambrai, but the war was far from over. Ahead lay more dangers, more challenges, and the uncertain future of a country in turmoil. But for now, they had each other. And that, at this moment of respite, was enough.

Chapter Fifteen

A PATH LESS TAKEN

THE TRIO AND MAX huddled in a weathered barn on the outskirts of Cambrai, surrounded by the rolling fields of northern France. Inside, the air was thick with dust and the lingering scent of hay. Outside, the world was descending into chaos, but here, within the wooden walls of their temporary sanctuary, Charles, Alain, and Charlotte were suspended in a brief moment of calm. Across the English Channel, a massive evacuation effort was swiftly taking shape. Winston Churchill, finally accepting that Charles had been right all along, now faced the brutal truth that the British had been completely caught off guard by the sheer force of the German blitzkrieg sweeping across Europe. The relentless speed and precision of the German advance had shattered Allied defences, leaving British and Allied forces on the verge of encirclement. Nearly half a million troops were now stranded on the beaches around Dunkirk, vulnerable and exposed.

With the situation growing increasingly dire, Churchill confronted the reality of catastrophic losses if immediate action wasn't taken. In an extraordinary move, he ordered the mobilisation of every available vessel—fishing boats, pleasure yachts, ferries, and even lifeboats—anything that could navigate the treacherous waters. The operation, later codenamed "Dynamo," was a desperate gamble. Yet in that moment of crisis, it was the only hope to save an army standing at the edge of annihilation. This ragtag flotilla was tasked with the perilous mission of rescuing the stranded soldiers from the beaches of Dunkirk. It was a desperate and dangerous gambit, one that would go down in history as the "Miracle of Dunkirk."

But for Charles, hunkered down miles from the coast, the notion of a boat waiting for him at Dunkirk seemed laughable. The distance from Cambrai to Dunkirk was considerable – 2 to 3 days' march under normal circumstances, but these were far from normal times. The path was fraught with danger, littered with German patrols, bomb craters, and the lingering scent of defeat. Charles's body ached from the relentless pace of their retreat, and he could see the strain etched on Alain's and Charlotte's faces as well. Yet they all understood that there was no turning back. Alain, the stoic French soldier, was torn between his duty to rejoin his unit and his loyalty to the companions who had become like family in the midst of the chaos. Charlotte, ever resourceful and determined, had her own mission, one that was crucial to intelligence gathering, but her radio equipment had been destroyed. Their objectives were disparate, but their survival was intertwined. For now, they would remain together. Charles stepped towards the barn door, the creaking wood breaking the heavy silence.

He squinted against the early morning light and saw a small group of what looked like British soldiers making their way towards Cambrai. Their uniforms were ragged and their faces smeared with dirt and exhaustion. It was clear that these men, like so many others, had been scattered by the chaos of the German advance. "Shouting to them would be suicide," Charles muttered, more to himself than to his companions. The trio remained in the shadows of the barn, waiting to see if the soldiers would pass by or seek refuge within the same dilapidated structure. As the soldiers drew closer, their movements became cautious. They spread out, rifles at the ready, scanning the surroundings with the wariness of men who had seen too much. One soldier, barely more than a boy, crept towards the barn door and slowly peered inside. "If this is supposed to be a surprise operation, you're all dead," Charles called out, his voice cutting through the air. The young soldier froze, wide-eyed with shock, as his comrades quickly pointed their rifles at the barn, their confusion palpable. "Don't worry! We're British!" Charles added, stepping into the dim light with his hands raised. The soldiers hesitated, but seeing Charles's raised hands and weary expression, they gradually lowered their weapons.

Slowly, Charlotte, Alain, and Max, who had stuck by their side through thick and thin, emerged from the shadows. The soldiers, recognising the fatigue and determination in the trio's faces, began to relax. They were young—barely out of their teens—and the haunted look in their eyes spoke of the horrors they had witnessed. "There's three of us here," Charles began, "and you're heading straight into the belly of the beast. Cambrai is crawling with Germans." The soldiers exchanged uneasy glances. They were a ragtag group, having become separated from their units. With no clear orders and no safe haven in sight, they had banded together in the hope that Dunkirk would be their salvation.

"We have a problem," Charles said, in an understated way. He quickly outlined the dire situation—the overwhelming German presence in Cambrai, the near-impossible task of reaching Dunkirk through enemy territory, and the sheer hopelessness of finding a boat in the midst of the chaos. One of the soldiers who seemed to have taken on the role of leader despite his youth, spoke up. "We were ordered to Dunkirk. They said the Navy would get us out." "Fat chance of that," Alain interjected, his English tinged with a strong French accent. "There are ten thousand drunk and angry Germans between here and Dunkirk. You'll never make it."

The soldiers' faces fell, their hopes visibly crushed. The dream of Dunkirk, once a beacon of hope, now seemed more like a distant mirage. "We're not going to Dunkirk," Charles stated firmly, taking control of the situation. "The only option I see is to go further down the coast. We might have a chance at Dieppe." "Dieppe?" one of the soldiers echoed, his voice tinged with uncertainty. "Yes," Alain chimed in. "It's further down the coast. We might find a boat there." The soldiers exchanged uncertain glances, weighing the options. Dieppe was a long shot, but it was better than marching straight into the teeth of the German defences at Dunkirk. After a brief discussion, they all agreed—their best chance was to head for Dieppe. The decision made, they began to move out, sticking to the fields and avoiding the main roads. The group of nine—Charles, Alain, Charlotte, Max, and the five British soldiers—moved quickly but cautiously, their footsteps muffled by the soft earth. The journey to Dieppe was fraught with danger.

Dieppe was more than a week's walk away, and with the threat of German patrols and Stuka dive-bombers, they couldn't afford to be careless. The countryside, normally peaceful and serene, was now a landscape of fear. Every rustle of leaves, every distant sound, set their nerves on edge.

As they walked along the country roads, they encountered occasional groups of French civilians. The fortunate ones rode in horse-drawn carts, carrying their worldly possessions, while others walked on foot, burdened with whatever they could manage. All were heading to what they believed was the safety of western France.

By mid-afternoon they approached a crossroads where they saw an army truck half-submerged in a ditch. Scattered around it were empty crates and supplies, hastily abandoned by whoever had been driving it. The sight of the truck sparked a flicker of hope—if they could get it running, it would cut their journey time drastically. Alain was the first to approach the truck, his soldier's instincts kicking in. He climbed into the driver's seat and tried the ignition. The engine coughed and sputtered, but didn't catch. Undeterred, Alain tried again. Once, twice—on the third try, the engine roared to life with a shuddering groan. "Get the wheels out of the ditch!" Charles shouted, and the group sprang into action. The British soldiers, though young and inexperienced, threw their weight against the side of the truck, straining to push it back onto the road. With a great heave, the truck finally lurched free, its wheels finding purchase on solid ground. There was a palpable sense of relief as they climbed into the truck, their backs to Cambrai and, hopefully, the German army. The journey to Dieppe, while still fraught with danger, suddenly seemed more manageable. The truck rumbled down the road, its engine growling like a caged beast, carrying them away from the heart of the conflict.

As they drove through the French countryside, the mood in the truck was tense but cautiously optimistic. The soldiers, still young enough to believe in luck, exchanged nervous grins and hopeful glances. But beneath the surface, they were all too aware of the dangers that still lay ahead. The truck jolted and swayed as it sped along the narrow roads, its tyres kicking up dust in the dim light of dawn. The countryside was eerily quiet; the people they did pass walked in silence. They passed through abandoned villages and empty fields. Alain, his hands gripping the steering wheel tightly, kept his eyes on the road ahead. He knew the risks they were taking—one wrong turn, one moment of inattention, and they could end up in a German checkpoint or under the sights of a Stuka. But the alternative—walking, exposed, and vulnerable—was even more dangerous. In the back of the truck, Charles and Charlotte sat side by side, their minds racing with thoughts of what lay ahead. Dieppe was still a long way off, and the road between them and the coast was anything but safe. But for now, they were moving, and that was what mattered. The British soldiers, huddled together in the cramped space, whispered among themselves, their voices barely audible over the roar of the engine. They spoke of home, of the families they had left behind, and of the uncertain future that awaited them. It was a fragile camaraderie, born out of shared fear and the desperate hope of survival.

As the evening sun began to set, casting long shadows across the landscape, the truck rumbled on, each mile bringing them closer to Dieppe and the uncertain promise of escape. The truck's fuel gauge hovered perilously close to empty as they neared a small village, its stone houses huddled together like sheep against the cold. They decided to stop and scavenge for fuel, knowing that without it, their journey would come to an abrupt and dangerous halt. Alain pulled the truck to a stop just outside the village, and the group disembarked, fanning out to search for anything that could keep them moving. The village was eerily silent; its streets deserted. They moved cautiously, checking each building for supplies. Charles and Charlotte entered a small garage, its doors hanging askew on rusted hinges. Inside, they found a few jerry cans of petrol, just enough to refill the truck's tank. They worked quickly, filling the truck.

As they refuelled, the sound of distant engines reached their ears, growing louder by the second. Alain squinted slightly, studying the distant horizon. "Germans," he muttered, his voice tense. "We need to move, now." They hurriedly finished refuelling and piled back into the truck, the sense of urgency palpable. Alain floored the accelerator, and the truck roared back to life, speeding away from the village just as the first German vehicles came into view.

The truck careened down the narrow roads, Alain pushing the vehicle to its limits. The German patrol, faster and better equipped, closed the distance with alarming speed. The soldiers in the back of the truck gripped their rifles, ready for a fight they knew they couldn't win. As they raced through the countryside, the sound of gunfire echoed in the distance. Alain swerved the truck onto a narrow dirt road, hoping to lose the Germans in the maze of rural paths. The truck bounced and jolted over the rough terrain, the passengers clinging to whatever they could hold onto. The German patrol didn't give up easily. They pursued relentlessly, their vehicles tearing up the dirt road in a cloud of dust and smoke. But Alain knew these roads better than they did—he had grown up in this region, and his knowledge of the terrain was their only advantage. As they rounded a sharp bend, Alain spotted a narrow bridge up ahead, barely wide enough for the truck to cross. He put his foot down, aiming for the bridge. The truck hurtled across the rickety structure, the wooden planks creaking ominously under its weight. Just as they reached the other side, Alain slammed on the brakes, skidding the truck to a stop. Everyone jumped out and began dismantling the bridge as quickly as they could, pulling up planks and tossing them into the rushing river below. Within minutes, the bridge was impassable, a mere skeleton of wood stretching across the water. They drove on as the German patrol screeched to a halt on the opposite bank, their vehicles unable to follow. They drew their rifles and began shooting, but the truck and its occupants were quickly out of harm's way. The close call had shaken them, but it also steeled their resolve.

After a few more hours on the road, they reached the outskirts of Dieppe and decided to catch some sleep in the truck before the day broke. Dieppe, once a bustling port town, was now eerily quiet. The harbour, normally filled with fishing boats and cargo ships, was empty. The docks were deserted, the buildings silent. The group disembarked from the truck, their eyes scanning the town for any sign of life—or danger.

Chapter Sixteen

CROSSING THE DIVIDE

Morning broke over Dieppe, stretching shadows across the cobblestone streets and the quiet harbour. The distant roar of Stukas punctuated the uneasy silence. These feared German dive-bombers, flying from bases near the border, circled like vultures over the northern coast of France. From Le Havre to Dunkirk, ready to unleash devastation at any moment. Occasionally, a plane would streak across the sky, a lone sentinel in a deadly game of cat and mouse. In the distance, the horizon was darkened by smoke, the harbinger of the destruction ravaging the coast.

At the harbour in Dieppe, the sweeping curve of the coast and the 90 miles in between masked the true scale of the mission unfolding. A massive flotilla of nearly 900 small boats had taken to the waters of the English Channel, a desperate attempt to rescue the thousands of soldiers trapped by the German advance. The skippers of these vessels, many of whom had been enjoying the simple comforts of their morning routines just hours before, now found themselves thrust into the chaos of war, unarmed and vulnerable. They had answered the call to save their fellow countrymen, setting aside their fears and doubts as they embarked on what could only be described as a mission of madness and courage. Yet, despite the overwhelming odds, there was a sliver of hope. The German army, having relentlessly marched through the Ardennes, was now beginning to show signs of exhaustion. Fuelled by amphetamines to maintain their relentless pace, the troops were starting to feel the dangerous effects of their overexertion. Days of near-constant infighting, combined with a lack of sleep and proper nourishment, had taken their toll. The once-efficient war machine was now sputtering, its gears grinding under the strain. Ill-discipline and confusion were beginning to spread through the ranks, and the lack of direct orders from the high command only exacerbated the situation. This lapse in German efficiency, however brief, was buying the Allies precious time to evacuate.

The British army truck rumbled to a stop at the quayside, its passengers disembarking quickly, their faces set with determination. Charles Sterling, Charlotte, Max, and a handful of young English soldiers stepped onto the dock, their eyes scanning the scene before them. The harbour was quiet, but beneath the surface, there was a palpable sense of dread. Civilians and local fishermen moved with a nervous energy, acutely aware that the window for escape was closing rapidly.

The group approached several fishermen, "We need a boat," Charles said, his voice firm. "And a skipper who knows these waters." but their pleas for help were met with cold stares and indifferent shrugs. Emotion or desperation did not easily sway these men, hardened by years of battling the treacherous waters of the Channel. They had their families to think of and their homes to protect. The sea was dangerous enough without adding the threat of enemy aircraft and gunfire. Even Alain, found his efforts rebuffed. His rapid, pleading fell on deaf ears. The fishermen had made up their minds—they would not risk their lives and livelihoods on what they saw as a fool's errand. Frustration began to mount in the group.

Every moment wasted was a moment closer to disaster. Charles clenched his fists in frustration, trying to keep his composure.

As hope began to wane, a young man in his late-twenties, who had been watching the scene unfold from the shadows, stepped forward. His name was Jules, and though his youthful face bore the marks of a life spent at sea, there was a fire in his eyes that spoke of courage and determination. He had been a fisherman all his life, his veins filled with the salt of the Channel. The sea was his territory, and while he was aware of the dangers, he couldn't stand idly by while others were in danger. "Over here," Jules called out, his voice carrying over the din of the harbour. The group turned to see him standing by a small fishing boat, weathered by years of hard work but still sturdy. "I'll take you across." Relief washed over the group as they hurried towards the boat. It was not large, but it was seaworthy, and that was enough. In times like these, there was no room for second-guessing or doubts. On the quayside, they gathered to make their final plans. Charlotte, ever the realist, recognised the limitations they faced. Without a Morse radio transmitter, her mission—to coordinate intelligence efforts and facilitate communication between the French and the British command—would be severely hampered. The British couldn't risk parachuting in equipment until the situation in France stabilised, which could take weeks, if not months. She would need to return to England to regroup and rearm with the necessary tools.

Alain, however, was torn by a different set of obligations. His heart was with his country, his unit stationed near Strasbourg, preparing for what would likely be a last stand against the advancing Germans. The thought of abandoning his comrades, of fleeing to England while they faced the enemy alone, was unbearable. He knew that the situation was hopeless and that France was on the brink of collapse, but duty and honour compelled him to return. "Come with us, Alain," Charles urged, seeing the conflict in his friend's eyes. "You've done enough here. England could use men like you." Alain shook his head, his expression resolute. "My place is with my brothers, Charles. France needs every man it has right now, no matter how dire the situation. I can't abandon them." Charles understood Alain's decision, though it pained him to see his friend walk into what seemed like certain death. There was no changing his mind; Alain's loyalty to his country was unshakeable.

Finally, they shook hands, their grip firm and filled with the unspoken words of friendship and respect. "Goodbye, my friend," Alain said quietly, his voice tinged with sorrow. "Good luck, Alain," Charles replied, his voice thick with emotion. "May we meet again in better times." With that, Alain turned and climbed back into the truck, its engine sputtering to life. He cast one last look at his companions before driving off, the vehicle disappearing into the distant landscape. It was a bitter farewell, but there was no time to dwell on it. The boat was ready, and they needed to move quickly.

Jules, already at the helm, motioned for them to board. Charles helped Charlotte and Max into the boat, then climbed in himself. The young English soldiers, their faces pale but determined, followed suit. They were a small, disparate group, bound together by the common goal of survival. As Jules steered the boat away from the quay, the enormity of their situation became apparent. The waters of the English Channel stretched out before them, deceptively calm under the grey, overcast sky. The small engine hummed steadily as they cut through the waves, heading into the unknown.

The crossing was thick with foreboding. Each person on board was lost in their own thoughts, gazing out at the horizon, torn between hope and fear. The sea, which had always been a source of livelihood and sustenance for men like Jules, was now a battleground. Charles kept a vigilant watch on the skies, his eyes scanning for any sign of enemy planes. Every shadow, every speck in the distance, sent a jolt of fear through him. The Spitfires, though valiant in their defence, were stretched thin, and the Stukas were relentless in their pursuit of any vessel that dared to cross the Channel. But fortune seemed to favour them. Jules remained focused on the task at hand, his hands steady on the wheel. He knew these waters intimately, each wave and current familiar to him. The threat from above was real, but he felt a sense of calm, trusting in his knowledge of the sea to guide them safely to the other side. He glanced back at his passengers, seeing the fear and determination etched into their faces.

Chapter Seventeen

A Haunting Horizon

As the small boat entered the vast expanse of the English Channel, the distant roar of war seemed to follow them. Charles turned to the young skipper, , and with a weary but sincere tone, expressed his heartfelt gratitude. "Thank you," he said. Jules, several years younger than Charles, acknowledged the thanks with a nod, his eyes focused on the horizon ahead. The sea was deceptively calm, unlike the chaos they had left behind in France. The boat's engine droned steadily, a monotonous hum that, for a moment, seemed to drown out the memories of explosions and gunfire. The faint outline of the French coast was fading behind them, and the group of soldiers allowed themselves a fleeting moment of relief. They had escaped. But as they ventured further into the Channel, the war's reminders were inescapable.

About an hour into the journey something unusual caught their attention. A small object bobbing up and down in the water, almost indistinguishable against the choppy waves. Jules squinted into the distance, his experienced eyes recognising the shape before anyone else did. "It's a lifeboat," he said, his voice tense with urgency. Charles and the others strained to see. As they drew closer, the outline of a wooden dinghy became clear, rising and falling with the rhythm of the sea.

A few figures in the boat started waving frantically, their voices carrying faintly over the water. "Help!" they shouted, their cries tinged with desperation and exhaustion. The scene grew more alarming as Jules noticed something else—the dark, viscous slick that surrounded the lifeboat. It spread across the water like a blackened shroud, a mix of oil and diesel that clung to the surface, a remnant of the ongoing battle. Jules quickly acted, his hand reaching for the throttle to cut the engine. The boat coasted to a stop, and the engine silenced as they drifted into the slick. The thick, oily substance adhered to the sides of their boat, sticking like tar, and a heavy silence fell over the group. The lifeboat and its passengers were embedded in the mess, and without the engine, they were now at the mercy of the slow, treacherous drift. The young skipper's face hardened with determination as he assessed the situation. "We need to get them aboard," he said, his voice steady. With no engine running, the only option was to use whatever strength they had left to manoeuvre closer. The soldiers, despite their fatigue, rallied together, grabbing oars and using their hands to steer the fishing boat closer to the lifeboat.

As they neared the lifeboat, the reality of the survivors' condition became clear. There were three men in the boat, all of them barely conscious, their bodies covered from head to toe in the thick, black oil. They were injured; their faces pale and gaunt from exhaustion and exposure. They had escaped from a ship that had been bombed near Dunkirk and had been adrift for nearly two days, battling the sea and the elements with no food, no water, and little hope. Their eyes, hollow with exhaustion, conveyed their desperation as they looked up at their rescuers. With tremendous effort, the soldiers aboard Jules' boat reached down to pull them up, their hands slipping on the oily surface of the lifeboat. One by one, the three survivors were hauled onto the fishing boat. Each rescue was an agonising process, as the men were almost dead weight, too weak to assist in their own salvation. The air was thick with the stench of oil and sweat, and the groans of the injured men filled the silence left by the engine. Charles and his comrades worked silently, their faces set with grim determination as they pulled the last survivor aboard. Once on the deck, the rescued men lay sprawled out, gasping for breath. Their bodies trembled with the effort of staying alive, and their clothes were soaked through with oil, sticking to their skin like a second, suffocating layer. Their eyes were bloodshot, and their faces smeared with dirt and oil.

They were alive, but only just. Jules took a moment to catch his breath, leaning against the rail as he surveyed the scene. It was then that one of the soldiers noticed something that had been hidden in the lifeboat's shadows—a fourth figure, lying motionless at the bottom of the boat. His face was turned away, and his body was unnaturally still. "There's another one," the soldier called out, his voice breaking the heavy silence. Charles stepped forward, peering into the lifeboat. The man was clearly dead, his body twisted in an unnatural position. His face was partially submerged in the oily water that had pooled in the bottom of the boat, and his skin had taken on a waxy, pallid hue. A sombre discussion followed. The question of what to do with the dead man lingered in the air. Each person grappled with the implications of the decision, aware that the choice they made would carry significant consequences. Some men suggested a burial at sea, a final, respectful farewell to a fallen comrade. But others, their voices thick with emotion, argued that he deserved to be returned to his homeland, to be buried on English soil, where his family might find some measure of peace. In the end, the decision was made to bring him back with them. It was not a decision made lightly, but it was one that felt right, even in the face of the overwhelming tragedy that surrounded them. Jules moved quickly to secure a rope to the lifeboat, his hands working methodically despite the shaking that had set in. He tied the dinghy to the stern of the fishing boat, preparing to tow it behind them.

The oil slick clung to everything it touched, and as Jules tightened the knots, his hands came away slick and black, the substance sticking to his skin. He wiped his hands on his trousers, leaving dark smears. The lifeboat, with its dead passenger, bobbed gently in the water, now tethered to their own vessel. Just as the rope was secured, a low, ominous sound broke through the stillness. The unmistakable drone of aircraft engines filled the air. Stukas. The dreaded German dive bombers that had wreaked havoc on the beaches of Dunkirk and the ships attempting to flee. The sound was growing louder, more distinct, as the planes approached. Instinctively, the men on the boat ducked, their eyes scanning the sky for the source of the noise. The planes appeared in the distance, their dark silhouettes cutting through the hazy sky. Jules felt his stomach twist in fear, every muscle in his body tensing as the Stukas roared overhead. For a terrifying moment, it seemed as if they were headed straight for the boat. But by some miracle, the planes did not turn towards them. Instead, they continued on their path, their engines roaring as they flew towards Dunkirk, where the battle still raged. The men on the boat watched in tense silence as the planes disappeared into the distance, the noise fading into the background hum of the war. The relief was palpable, though no one dared to speak it aloud. They had been spared, at least for now. The Channel, though it represented a path to freedom, was still a battlefield.

With the immediate danger passed and the boat out of the oil slick, Jules returned to his task, guiding the boat with its bedraggled passengers towards the safety of the South Coast of England. The journey was long and arduous, the boat moving slowly through the water, the lifeboat dragging behind them like a heavy burden. The survivors lay huddled together on the deck, their bodies trembling with cold and fatigue. They had no energy left to speak, their eyes staring blankly at the sky, as if searching for some sign of hope. Charles and the other soldiers did what they could to make them comfortable, offering water and whatever scraps of food they had left. But it was clear that these men had been through an ordeal that no amount of kindness could erase.

As the hours passed, the coast of England slowly came into view, a thin line on the horizon that gradually grew more distinct. The sight of land brought a surge of relief, a promise of safety that had seemed so distant just hours before. But even as they drew closer, the toll of their journey was evident in the air around them. Jules guided the boat towards a small harbour, the familiar coastline a balm to his frayed nerves. The closer they got, the more the tension began to ease, though the memories of what they had seen and endured would not fade so easily. The war was still raging, but for now, they had escaped its immediate grasp.

The fishing boat glided slowly towards the quayside of a deserted British seaside town. The light casting a soft glow over the still waters, and the sound of seagulls echoed across the harbour, their cries the only noise in the quiet dawn. As the boat drew closer, Jules carefully guided it to the dock, his hands steady on the wheel. With a final, quiet cough, the engine sputtered to a stop, and the boat came to rest against the wooden quay. Jules remained at the helm for a moment, his gaze fixed on the horizon, before he turned to face his passengers. Their journey had been long and fraught with danger, but now, at last, they were safe—or as safe as one could be in a country at war. "Alright, everyone," Jules said softly, his voice cutting through the stillness. "We've made it." There was a brief moment of silence as his words sank in. The boat's passengers exchanged glances, the relief in their eyes tempered by the exhaustion etched into their faces. The horrors they had left behind in France clung to them, but for now, they allowed themselves a moment of respite. Jules moved to the side of the boat, where a small, battered wooden dinghy floated in the water, tethered to the fishing vessel. Inside, covered by a dirty tarpaulin, lay the body of a man who had not survived the ordeal. He was not a soldier, just a normal civilian caught up in the chaos of a surprise evacuation. In the end, he had paid the ultimate price. With a solemn expression, Jules pulled the dinghy closer and adjusted the tarpaulin, making sure the man's body was respectfully covered. There was no time for ceremony, no chance for a proper farewell. The man's death was just one more tragedy in a war that had already claimed too many lives. Jules untied the dinghy from his boat and secured it to a rusted iron ring on the quayside. He glanced up at Charles, who stood nearby, his face lined with concern. "We'll call an ambulance and an undertaker as soon as we can," Charles said quietly, more to reassure himself than anything else. Jules nodded, grateful that someone else would take responsibility for the deceased.

First, Charlotte stepped out of the boat, her movements careful and deliberate. One soldier leaned over and gently lifted Max, passing him to Charles, who took the dog into his arms. Max's eyes, normally bright and curious, were now wide with exhaustion, but there was a glimmer of hope in them—a silent understanding that they were safe now. Charles followed

Charlotte out of the boat. Behind him, the three rescued evacuees and the three remaining soldiers clambered out of the boat one by one, each of them worn down but relieved to be on solid ground again.

It was 7:00 in the morning, and the first signs of life were stirring. People on their way to work or out for an early walk with their dogs began to notice the group gathered at the quayside. They paused, their curiosity piqued by the sight of these ragged strangers who had appeared out of nowhere. The war, it seemed, had come to their doorstep. They approached cautiously at first, unsure of what to make of the scene before them. But as they drew closer, their fears of a possible German landing began to fade. These were not invaders; they were survivors. Their clothes were torn and dirty, their faces streaked with oil and grime, and the haunted look in their eyes told a story of unimaginable hardship. Among the onlookers, a shopkeeper emerged from a nearby store. He was an older man, his face lined with the wisdom of years, and he carried with him a tray of chipped mugs and an urn of steaming tea. Without a word, he approached the group and began handing out mugs, filling each one with the hot, comforting brew. "You look like you could use this," the shopkeeper said kindly, his voice carrying the warmth of someone who had seen his share of troubled times.

Charles accepted a mug, the warmth of the tea seeping into his cold, stiff fingers. He took a sip, the hot liquid soothing his parched throat and bringing a moment of comfort in an otherwise chaotic world. Around him, the others did the same, their tense shoulders slowly relaxing as they felt the first glimmers of safety and hospitality. Max, nestled securely beside Charles, looked up at the shopkeeper with tired eyes. The old man smiled at the whippet, a smile that spoke of understanding and empathy. "You'll be alright now," he said gently, reaching out to scratch Max behind the ears.

The police arrived soon after, their initial wariness giving way to a more measured approach as they assessed the situation. The lead officer, a man with a firm but fair demeanour, quickly realised that these were not enemy combatants but civilians and soldiers who had escaped with their lives. Charles explained their situation as best as he could, and the officer listened intently, his expression growing more sombre with each word. Once the officer was satisfied with the explanation, he directed his men to help the survivors. Blankets were brought, and a drum of diesel was soon found for Jules to refuel. After only a short time on English soil, Jules prepared to set off back into the channel. He gave a final wave to the group as he turned the boat around, setting off to confront the uncertainty awaiting him in his home country.

As the group began to move away from the quay, Charles took one last look at the sea. The boat that had carried them to safety was now out of sight, but the memory of that perilous journey would stay with him forever. He thought of Jules, the young skipper who had risked his life to bring them home, and he silently wished him well.

After a moment of reflection, Charles stepped away from the group. He asked the shopkeeper if he had a telephone and was directed to a small room behind the counter. His hand trembled as he dialled his home number.

The phone rang, and he felt the burdens of the past days begin to ease as he heard her voice. "Charles! Thank God you're safe!" Elizabeth exclaimed, relief flooding through her words. "I'm back, love. I'm with Max," he reassured her, his heart swelling at the thought of their family reunited. "We're in Hastings for the night. I'll be home soon." "Thank goodness. The children have been so worried. I'll tell them you're safe. How is Max?" "Exhausted, but happy to be back. I'll make sure he gets a good rest. How are you all?" "We're fine, just relieved. I can't wait to see you."

After reassuring Elizabeth, Charles placed a second call to Westminster. He needed to report back to give them the news that he had returned safely. The line rang until a familiar voice answered. "Charles! It's good to hear from you. How did it go?" "Difficult, but we made it back," Charles replied. He recounted the details of their escape. The voice on the other end listened intently, offering support and understanding. Once he hung up, Charles felt a sense of closure wash over him. Although he was safe, the war was far from over.

Chapter Eighteen

EPILOGUE: AFTER THE STORM

THE LOCAL AUTHORITIES HAD arranged for them to stay in Hastings for a couple of days, providing rooms at the White Rock Hotel. It was a small comfort, but after the harrowing ordeal they had faced, it felt like a gesture of kindness amid the chaos of war.

The next morning, as the sun streamed through the hotel windows, the survivors gathered for breakfast in the hotel's dining room. The atmosphere was subdued, filled with an unspoken camaraderie born from shared trauma. They exchanged stories of their experiences, and for a moment, the thought of the war lifted as they found solace in each other's company. When the time came for goodbyes, the mood shifted. A truck had been sent to pick up the soldiers; they would be granted some leave after a thorough debriefing. Charlotte had been granted dispensation to stay in Hastings a little longer to recover from her ordeal. "Take care of yourselves," she said, her voice steady despite the emotion. "I hope to see you all again when this is over."

Charles felt a pang of sadness at parting ways with her. She had been a source of strength during their escape. "You too, Charlotte. Rest well, and we'll meet again," he promised, trying to instill a sense of hope. With the farewells behind them, Charles received his travel arrangements. A first-class train ticket had been provided for him, along with a new set of clothes that felt strange and foreign against his tired skin. He felt a renewed sense of dignity as he changed, the fresh garments a reminder of the life that awaited him in London. Max, always by his side, seemed to sense the shift in their circumstances. He stood alert, tail wagging, eager to embark on the next leg of their journey. Charles smiled at his loyal companion, grateful for the comfort Max provided during such tumultuous times.

A taxi arrived to take them to the train station, the driver friendly and chatty as they made their way through the sleepy streets of Hastings. The town had a serene beauty, the seaside air filled with the scent of salt and the sound of distant waves crashing against the shore. As they approached the station, Charles felt a mix of emotions wash over him—relief, gratitude, and a lingering sadness for those they had left behind.

At the station, Charles purchased some snacks for the journey and waited on the platform, Max by his side, looking up at him with expectant eyes. When the train arrived, the rhythmic clatter of wheels on tracks filled the air, and the conductor waved them aboard. Charles settled into his seat, the plush fabric a welcome change from the roughness of the last few days. Max curled up beside him, resting his head on Charles's lap, content to be homeward bound.

As the train pulled away from the station, Charles gazed out the window, watching the scenery change from the seaside views of Hastings to the rolling hills of the countryside. It was a beautiful morning, and although the shadows of war still hung overhead, he felt a flicker of hope ignite within him. He thought of Elizabeth and the children waiting for him at home, and the warmth of their embrace filled him with determination. He would share the stories of their escape, the bravery of those he had met, and the bond that had formed between them in the face of adversity.

The train chugged onwards, the world outside a blur of colours, and as they moved closer to London, Charles knew that despite the uncertainties that lay ahead, he was ready to face whatever came next.

THE END

MAX: THE HEAT *OF* THE COLD WAR

Contents

1. Beneath the Red Banner — 207
2. Family Threads — 211
3. Turning Pages — 216
4. Waves and Skyscrapers — 224
5. Into the Shadows — 231
6. Castro's Catch — 241
7. The Long Road North — 252
8. Cranes Over London — 257
9. Footsteps in the Gallery — 262
10. A Life of Books and Tea — 268

Chapter One

BENEATH THE RED BANNER

OXFORD UNIVERSITY, 1961. THE COMMON room buzzed with the murmur of anticipation, packed to the rafters with students, some seated on worn leather chairs, others standing shoulder to shoulder. All eyes were fixed on the makeshift stage, where two men—Edward Sterling and Guy McClean—stood locked in debate, their voices rising above the scattered hum of whispered conversations. The late afternoon sunlight poured through the tall windows, casting long shadows across the polished wood floor.

"Communism, in its essence, demands that we tear down the walls of inequality," Guy proclaimed, his voice sharp and commanding, cutting through the air like a blade. "A system where the worker isn't exploited for the benefit of the wealthy few! Where capitalists no longer oppress the masses!" Edward stood tall, his expression calm but eyes burning with passion. "And yet, in practice, it has only replaced one form of oppression with another. You can talk about equality all you like, Guy, but where is the freedom in a regime that silences its own people?" Guy smirked, his tone unwavering. "Freedom? You mean the so-called 'freedom' we're offered by capitalist societies? The freedom to starve, the freedom to be unemployed, while the rich line their pockets? Communism offers real freedom—freedom from the chains of class!"

"The chains of class? Or the chains of dictatorship?" Edward's retort was sharp, cutting through the room. "Communist regimes strangle freedom of speech, of thought, of culture! You defend the ideology, but what about the thousands who have been silenced, imprisoned, or worse, under Communist rule?"

The room tensed as their voices grew louder, the ideological gulf between them widening with each passing sentence. Faces in the crowd were rapt, some nodding in agreement with Edward, others murmuring their support for Guy. "Look around you, Sterling," Guy shot back, his eyes gleaming with conviction. "The right-wing extremists, the Nazis—what did they thrive on? Division, fear, hatred. Communism unites; it lifts people up." "And yet, both systems end in totalitarianism," Edward countered, leaning forward slightly, the intensity of his gaze locking on Guy. "Yes, we both agree that Nazism is a plague, but you can't ignore the fact that the pursuit of a utopia under Communism has brought about just as much suffering. You can't cherry-pick the ideology." Guy's smile faltered, replaced by something darker. "You don't understand it, Edward. You cling to a crumbling system—a Labour Party that tries to please both sides while failing to make real, systemic change. Gaitskell's Labour is weak. Too afraid to take the necessary steps." "Necessary steps?" Edward's tone sharpened. "What are you advocating for? A revolution drenched in blood? Sacrificing freedom on the altar of equality?" Tension crackled between them, thickening the air in the room. There was something in the way Guy defended Communism so fiercely, so unwaveringly—something that made Edward's gut churn with suspicion. His eyes narrowed as he noted the precise phrasing of Guy's arguments and the way he seemed to know more than he let on, as if he was defending more than just an ideology. Was there something else behind Guy's fervour?

A round of applause erupted, breaking the silence that had settled after the heated exchange. The audience was engaged, energised by the debate, clapping loudly in appreciation of the intellectual spectacle. Both men nodded in acknowledgment, though the applause did little to ease the lingering animosity between them. After the debate, Edward retreated to a quiet corner of the common room, Max by his side, the whippet's watchful eyes following the movement around them. Edward sat with a few friends, their conversation turning to lighter topics as they sipped tea, but his mind lingered on the exchange with Guy. Max, ever attuned to his master, nuzzled Edward's hand, offering silent comfort. Edward scratched behind the dog's ears, but his thoughts remained unsettled. Guy's words replayed in his head, and with each repetition, Edward's distrust deepened.

Later that evening, Edward found himself walking along the river, the cool breeze rustling the autumn leaves. Max trotted beside him, his paws padding lightly on the stone path. The evening sky dimmed as the light began to fade, casting a golden glow over the water. As he rounded a bend, Edward's gaze landed on a familiar figure seated on a bench—Guy McClean. He wasn't alone. Seated next to him was a man, broad-shouldered and dressed in a dark overcoat, his voice low and thick with a faint Eastern European accent. Edward's steps slowed, his instincts prickling. Guy looked up as Edward approached, offering a half smile. "Sterling. Didn't expect to see you out here." "Just getting some air," Edward replied casually, though his attention was fixed on the man beside Guy. "This is Anton," Guy said, gesturing vaguely. "He's an Eastern Studies tutor, from one of the colleges on the other side of town." Anton nodded, his blue eyes sharp, assessing. "Good to meet you." Edward smiled politely, though the unease in his chest tightened. "A pleasure." He shook the man's hand, noting the firmness of his grip and the way his gaze lingered just a moment too long. Max, sensing Edward's discomfort, stood a little closer to his master. "Well, I'll leave you two to it," Edward said after a brief civil exchange. As he walked away, the hairs on the back of his neck bristled. Something wasn't right. Guy's introduction had been too vague, too dismissive. "Stay close, Max," Edward muttered under his breath, glancing back over his shoulder. His mind raced, piecing together the fragments of suspicion that had been gathering since the debate. Guy's words, his choice of company—it all felt wrong, like pieces of a puzzle he hadn't yet fully assembled. Max trotted silently beside him, ever watchful, as they walked back.

Chapter Two

FAMILY THREADS

The following day, Edward sat comfortably in the corner of his college room, a warm cup of fragrant tea cradled in his hands. By his feet, Max, his sleek and graceful whippet, lay sprawled out in a patch of sunlight. The intricate patterns on the delicate china cup caught Edward's attention as he traced them absent-mindedly with his fingers. His gaze drifted out the window, taking in the manicured lawns and grand architecture of Trinity College. Lost in thought, Edward often found himself drawn back to his family's history. Memories not entirely his own but cherished, all the same, shaping him into the person he was today.

Born in the autumn of 1941, Edward was the youngest child of Charles Sterling, a man whose quiet, unassuming demeanour belied the daring nature of his escape from Germany that same year. The tale was a legend in the Sterling household, spoken of with hushed reverence. Charles had fled Berlin under the cover of night, with only his faithful whippet, Max, for company. They had slipped through the cracks of a city, tightening its grip under Nazi control. For Edward, born the following year, the story was both a shadow and a foundation—something that lingered in the background of his childhood, defining his family's resilience but never quite his own.

Their mother, Elizabeth, had been evacuated from Berlin in 1939, with his older siblings Lucy and Peter not knowing where Charles was. In the chaos, they were bundled onto a train and sent first to Switzerland. There was nobody to ring as every British person scrambled to get this last train. In her haste, she had left Max with their neighbours before heading to the station. Assuming they would never see him again. They could only leave with what they carried, and anything that didn't accompany them on the train, 'somehow' got lost.

When Charles had been appointed to the position in Berlin, they had rented their own house out. By sheer chance, their tenants had fled England, fearing invasion, and sought refuge in America.

Unlike many returning expats, Margaret, Lucy, and Peter were lucky to be able to walk back into their own home almost straight away. Throughout those long weeks when Charles was missing and believed dead, Elizabeth experienced unspeakable anguish and fear. And when he finally managed to make a call from Cambrai Town Hall in France, her joy knew no bounds.

Edward's elder siblings, Lucy and Peter, had been toddlers at the time of the escape. Lucy, with her pragmatic mind, claimed to remember nothing of their early life in Germany before the war. Peter, ever the adventurer, claimed only flashes—a sense of the tall buildings, the distant sound of a train, the rush of their departure with their mother. What they both shared, however, was a deep respect for their father's courage and a certain expectation that they, too, would carry the torch of adventure and service.

Peter had taken their father's legacy to heart, determined to follow in his footsteps. With unwavering determination, he entered the civil service and let his career take him across the globe. From the Philippines to Laos and now Hong Kong, Peter found himself working at Government House, immersed in the inner workings of politics and power. His letters home were filled with tales of exotic lands, political intrigues, and the ever-present buzz of life in faraway places. He thrived in this unpredictable world, relishing in the chaos and complexity that surrounded him. While Edward admired his brother's courage and adventurous spirit, he couldn't quite envision himself living such a transient life, always on the move and never truly having a place to call home.

The oldest sibling, Lucy, had chosen a unique path for herself. She had recently started her position as a biology professor at Edinburgh University. While her life in academia appeared to be stable, there was still a hint of their father's brazen spirit within her. Lucy was relentless in her quest for knowledge, immersing herself in her research with the same fervour that Peter once used to conquer foreign lands. However, unlike her father's grand adventures abroad, Lucy's endeavours took place in the controlled environment of a laboratory, where she delved into the secrets of science and discovery.

And then there was Edward, the youngest and most introspective of them all. Unlike his siblings, whose sense of adventure was loud and bold, Edward's thirst for exploration was more subtle and contained within the pages of books or the rich exchanges of debate. While their father, Charles, encouraged all his children to seize the world as an opportunity, Edward's ambitions always turned inward. He relished in the structured elegance of a well-crafted argument and felt invigorated by the thrill of uncovering new ideas rather than new places. His heart belonged to Oxford, with its ancient walls steeped in history and its halls filled with heated debates. The rhythm of academic life suited him perfectly, allowing him to thrive within its structured environment.

Max awoke from his slumber and lifted his head, sniffing the air for any traces of a familiar scent. Edward looked down at him with a warm smile. Max was not just any dog - he was the beloved grandson of Charles's original Max, who had bravely made the perilous journey alongside his owner from Berlin. It was a fitting tribute to their family's past, and Max's quiet loyalty bound Edward to his ancestors in more ways than one. Despite the strict rules at the college, Max had become an honorary member of Trinity in the hearts of all who knew him.

The arrangement had been orchestrated in a cunning manner by Granville, the wily college porter. Having known Charles during his days at Oxford, when he and Max would sneak through the gates together, Granville saw an opportunity to continue their companionship. So when Edward arrived at Trinity with Max in tow, the porter eagerly offered – more like insisted – that the dog should stay on campus, as if history were repeating itself. And so it did, with Max happily basking in the warmth of the Porter's Lodge while Edward attended lectures. It was a well-oiled system that brought joy not only to Edward, but also to Max, who relished in his daily rounds of the college grounds just as much as his owner did.

But it wasn't just Max who kept Edward grounded here in Oxford. Alice was another anchor. A year younger and studying at Somerville College, she had a way of seeing the world that complemented Edward's own—bright, thoughtful, with a quiet confidence that challenged him. Their time together was an escape from the pressures of academia, a reprieve from the constant debates about politics and philosophy that dominated his life. With her, there was laughter, warmth, and a sense of shared understanding that Edward hadn't quite realised he needed.

The wind shifted outside, rustling the leaves of the trees that lined the college grounds. Edward's mind drifted back to his family again—Peter, somewhere in Hong Kong, Lucy in her lab, and their father, still urging them all towards boldness, towards something more. He wondered if his own path was bold enough, if the debates and books he surrounded himself with could ever compare to the adventure of escaping across a continent or building a life in distant lands.

Max yawned and stretched, settling back into a comfortable sprawl. Edward reached down, scratching the dog's head. There was comfort in the routine, in knowing where you belonged. For now, Oxford was enough—its ancient walls, the scent of old books, and the thrill of intellectual challenge. The adventure, Edward supposed, would find him in its own time.

Chapter Three

Turning Pages

A warm glow spread across the old stone buildings of Oxford as the evening deepened. Edward's gown rustled softly in the breeze as he stood in the courtyard, his family gathered nearby, a picture of quiet pride. Charles and Elizabeth, his mother and father, exchanged smiles, their eyes reflecting the long years of dedication that had brought their youngest child to this moment. Lucy, his sister, stood off to the side, her lecturer's eye assessing the ceremony with familiarity, while Alice held Max's lead, the whippet sitting dutifully by her feet.

Edward had graduated. The final chapter of his academic journey closing as the future stretched out before him, wide and uncertain. They moved from the ceremony to a small gathering at a nearby café, where Charles finally posed the question that had been hanging over Edward for months. "So, Edward," Charles said, leaning forward, eyes sharp. "What's next for you? Any plans for the future?"

Edward shifted in his seat, glancing briefly at Alice before answering. "Nothing fixed, really. I'll stay in Oxford for another year while Alice finishes her degree. Beyond that... well, I haven't thought much further than that." Charles' brow furrowed, though he said nothing more. His father's silence spoke louder than any words could. Edward didn't know how to explain that, for him, staying still for a while felt like enough. He was content here, with Alice, with Max, with the quiet rhythm of his life. The grand adventure his father had always encouraged seemed distant and unnecessary.

The following week, as he strolled through town with Max, something caught Edward's eye – a small card pinned to the window of a local bookshop: 'Help Wanted'. He wandered inside. The scent of old leather and dust filled his senses. Behind the counter sat an old man, a retired university lecturer by the name of Mr. Hawthorne. His eyes, hidden behind thick glasses, flicked up from a book when Edward entered. The shop had seen better days. The shelves were crowded, books haphazardly stacked, dust thick on the edges of every surface. Mr. Hawthorne greeted him with a distant warmth. He'd run the bookshop for 20 years and was ready to retire, but couldn't bear to leave entirely.

"I'm not much of a businessman," Mr. Hawthorne admitted, his voice trailing off as he returned to his book. "I've spent more time reading than selling." Edward, sensing the opportunity, offered to take over the running of the shop for a few days each week. Max, as always, at his side. Hawthorne agreed, almost relieved, and the arrangement fell into place quickly.

As the weeks passed, Edward set to work transforming the dusty old shop. He tidied the shelves, carefully dusting off years of neglect. Customers trickled in, more out of curiosity than anything else, but soon they came for another reason—Max. The whippet, curled up by the counter or greeting customers with a gentle nuzzle, became something of a local celebrity. Visitors brought treats; children stopped by just to see him. The shop, once nearly forgotten, gained new life.

Christmas came swiftly, and with it, Peter's return from Hong Kong. The family gathered around the dinner table with the smell of roast and mulled wine filling the air. It was festive and warm, but the conversation inevitably turned back to Edward's future. "What will you do with your degree?" Charles asked again, a bit more insistently this time.

Peter, ever the adventurer, chimed in with enthusiasm. "You should travel, Edward. See the world while you're young. You've been cooped up in Oxford too long." Edward smiled faintly but shook his head. "I'm happy here, for now. I'll wait for Alice to finish her course, then we'll see what comes next." Charles frowned, clearly unconvinced. "Your education shouldn't be wasted in a bookshop, Edward. You've worked too hard for a wage that won't sustain you." Elizabeth and Lucy exchanged glances. Lucy's voice was calm but firm. "Leave him be, Father. Edward will find his way when he's ready." Elizabeth nodded. "He's happy, Charles. Isn't that what matters most?" The conversation shifted after that, but the undercurrent remained. Edward knew his father meant well, but the quiet life he had found in the bookshop felt like enough – for now.

As the final days of 1961 drifted into the new year, Edward found himself back in Oxford, Max trotting beside him as he opened the shop each morning. Life settled into a peaceful routine. That is, until Guy McClean wandered in one brisk afternoon. "Morning, Edward," Guy said smoothly, his eyes glancing around the shop, taking in the neatly stacked shelves and the faint dust motes still swirling in the afternoon light. His presence was unexpected, and Edward felt an instant tension settle in the room. "Guy," Edward greeted, his voice steady but cautious. Max, sensing something, shifted his position near Edward's feet, watching the visitor with curious, alert eyes. Guy didn't seem in any rush to leave. He walked slowly along the aisles, picking up a book now and then, flipping through its pages without much focus. There was a certain casualness about him that didn't match the intensity of his gaze when he looked up. Edward noticed the slight smirk that played on his lips, as if the real conversation lay just beneath the surface of pleasantries. "Quite the cosy place you've found yourself in," Guy remarked, placing a book back on the shelf. "Not exactly what I'd have expected for you." "I like it here," Edward said simply, watching as Guy moved closer to the counter, his fingers brushing along the spines of the books. "And Max enjoys it too."

Guy smiled faintly, his eyes flicking down to the whippet. "I can see that. But don't you ever think there's... more out there?" Edward caught the subtle edge in Guy's voice, the hint of a challenge. Before he could respond, Guy's eyes shifted to the window. Edward followed his gaze, noticing a man standing outside. His figure was familiar, though Edward couldn't quite place where he'd seen him before. He thought back to that strange evening after the debate, when Guy had met with a man with a thick Eastern European accent. Was this the same person? The resemblance was unsettling, but he couldn't be sure. Guy lingered a moment longer, then gave a small nod. "I'll leave you to it, Edward. Just thought I'd stop by." As he left, Edward's eyes remained on the man outside. The two exchanged a brief glance before walking away together, their figures soon disappearing down the street. The whole encounter left Edward with a knot of unease. There was something more behind Guy's visit, something unspoken yet undeniable. He just couldn't figure out what.

The next day, Edward was quietly working in the bookshop, stacking a fresh pile of books on the counter, when the telephone rang from the corner of the room. The unexpected sound broke the calm, making Max stir slightly from his nap near the door. Edward wiped his hands on a cloth and walked over to the receiver. "Oxford Books," he said, his voice steady. "Edward," came the familiar voice on the other end. It was his father, Charles, sounding calm, almost casual. "I've found something that might interest you—a position in Washington, D.C. at the British Embassy." Edward paused for a moment, processing the words. "Washington?"

"Yes," Charles replied, his tone conversational. "Junior administrative clerk. Nothing too strenuous, but I think it's something you might want to consider. Thought I'd let you know." Edward glanced around the shop, the news settling over him. "Washington... it's a bit sudden, isn't it?" Charles chuckled softly. "It's not a rush, Edward. Take your time. But it's a good opportunity—something worth thinking over."

The conversation ended without fanfare, leaving Edward thoughtful but not pressured. Later, as the evening wore on and the fire crackled in the hearth, Edward shared the details with Alice. "It seems my father has found me a job," Edward said, leaning back in his chair, his tone more reflective than concerned. "In Washington." Alice looked up, surprised. "Washington? What sort of job?" "Junior administrative clerk. Something quiet, I suppose," Edward replied, shrugging. "It was... unexpected, but he didn't push. Just mentioned it." They sat in silence for a while, the glow of the fire casting shadows on the walls. There was no urgency in Charles' call, but the idea of Washington lingered, quietly reshaping the future Edward and Alice had imagined.

The days that followed were filled with quiet reflection as Edward pondered the job offer. He enjoyed his life in Oxford—the familiar routine of running the bookshop, spending time with Alice, the comfort of Max always by his side, the ease of wandering the ancient streets—but he knew things were changing. Alice would be finishing her degree soon, and with her own ambitions blossoming, she would want more. More than the cosy life of Oxford, more than part-time work in a dusty old shop.

There was a pull at Edward, a quiet tug that had been growing over the past few days. It wasn't just about the job in Washington—it was the sense that America itself was on the edge of something significant. His father, Charles, had always encouraged him to seek out bigger opportunities, to push beyond the safety of what he knew. While Edward had found contentment in Oxford, the idea of something new—something vast and unpredictable—was starting to tug at him in ways he hadn't anticipated.

The thought of Washington was hard to shake. Not just the job at the embassy, but the sense of the times. America was changing, and Edward could feel the energy even from across the Atlantic. The news trickling in from Cuba, though vague, carried a sense of urgency that hinted at larger events stirring just beneath the surface. The name of Fidel Castro appeared in the reports with increasing frequency, and rumours of rising tensions between the United States and the Soviet Union swirled, though no one seemed to know the specifics.

There was also the promise of something different, something exciting. John F. Kennedy captivated the world with his youthful optimism, leading America through a moment of change and challenge. Even from a distance, Edward sensed the shift. It wasn't just about international politics; it was about the country itself—something in the air as if America was questioning itself, deciding what kind of nation it would be. It felt far from the quiet streets of Oxford, but somehow Edward couldn't shake the feeling that it was all connected.

That evening, as Edward and Alice sat by the fire, he tried to express the growing sense that something was happening. "America... it feels like something's happening there. Something important."

Alice watched him carefully, her fingers absently tracing patterns along Max's fur. "Do you think you want to be part of it?" she asked. Edward shrugged, though the question lingered with him. "I don't know. It's more than just the job. It feels like... everything's at a crossroads there." Alice smiled faintly. "Do you think it's worth going? Being in the middle of all that?" Edward leaned back in his chair, staring at the flickering flames. "Maybe. Or maybe it's just a chance to see something bigger than what we know.".

Together, they began to form a plan. Edward would take the job in Washington, and with Max he would sail there, departing from Southampton in April for the six-day journey across the Atlantic. Alice would remain in Oxford, finishing her studies, saving up. She would join them in August, travelling by aeroplane – a quicker but far less romantic trip, she joked. They both knew the separation would be hard, but the future was calling, and for once, Edward felt ready to answer.

The following day, with a mixture of excitement and guilt, Edward approached Mr. Hawthorne to tell him about his plans. The bookshop owner was perched behind the counter as usual, surrounded by his beloved volumes, his reading glasses slipping down his nose as he looked up. "I've been offered a job," Edward began, his voice tentative. "In Washington. I'll be leaving in April." Mr. Hawthorne's reaction was immediate, though subtle—a tightening of the eyes, a small slump in his shoulders. He tried to hide his disappointment, but it was clear. Edward felt a pang of guilt as he continued, trying to soften the blow. "It's just for a year—a twelve-month vacancy. I'll be coming back."

They both knew the words felt hollow. The idea of Edward returning to the little bookshop after a year in Washington, after working in the heart of political power, seemed unlikely. Hawthorne knew it as well as Edward. With a long, measured sigh, the old man leaned back in his chair and took off his glasses. "I wish you the best, Edward," he said finally, his voice soft but sincere. "You've been good for this shop. I'll miss you." "I'll miss this place too," Edward replied, and he meant it. The shop had been his sanctuary during a time of uncertainty, a place where he could hide among the books, where life had felt calm and manageable. But as he stood there, in the quiet of the shop, with Max beside him and the world waiting beyond the doors, he knew things were about to change. "Max will miss it, too," Edward added, glancing down at the whippet, who was busy sniffing at a pile of newly delivered books. Hawthorne smiled at that, the first real smile since the conversation began. "Max has been the real draw," he said with a chuckle. "People will be disappointed to see him go."

The next few months would be a whirlwind, and soon enough, Oxford would be in his rearview. Washington beckoned, with all its possibilities, its unknowns, and, perhaps, its adventures. For now, there was still time, still space to breathe in the familiar, but the clock was ticking. As he left the shop, Edward felt the pull of the future stronger than ever. There was no going back now.

Chapter Four

WAVES AND SKYSCRAPERS

The bustling port of Southampton faded into the distance as the Queen Mary set sail, its mighty hull cutting through the cold waters of the English Channel. Edward stood on deck, his hand resting gently on Max's head. The crisp April breeze carried the scent of salt, mingling with the hum of conversations from excited passengers. For Edward, the departure was bittersweet—he was leaving behind the familiar streets of Oxford, the comfort of the bookshop, and the quiet life he'd built. But ahead lay something new, something thrilling: Washington.

The ship itself was a marvel. Even as a second-class passenger, Edward couldn't help but admire the grandeur of the Queen Mary. While the first-class areas were known for their opulence, second-class still offered its own comforts. The cabins were compact but well-appointed, with polished wood panelling, a small porthole that framed the endless blue sea, and neatly made bunk beds. It wasn't luxury, but it was more than enough for Edward and Max, who curled up contentedly on the floor near the door.

Life onboard for second-class passengers had its own rhythm. In the lounge, fellow travellers gathered to read, play cards, or simply stare out at the vast ocean. The Art Deco décor—rich wood, brass fixtures, and intricate details—spoke to an earlier time when sea travel was an event in itself. Edward spent his mornings walking the deck with Max, the dog trotting happily beside him as the ship cut through the waves. The Atlantic stretched endlessly in every direction, the horizon blurring into the sky.

The dining room was one of Edward's favourite parts of the journey. The large room was elegant, though less opulent than the first-class dining hall. Chandeliers, smaller but still sparkling, cast warm light over white tablecloths and polished silverware. The meals were plentiful—roast meats, steamed fish, and indulgent desserts like trifle and fruit tarts. Each evening, Edward would sit by the window, watching the darkening sea as waiters moved briskly between tables. Max, as usual, lay at his feet, drawing smiles from nearby passengers.

Despite the routine, Edward felt a growing sense of anticipation. The recent magazines available on board brought news of the world beyond the ship. He followed the story of John F. Kennedy's rise in American politics with keen interest, but other headlines troubled him. Just a year ago, the Bay of Pigs invasion had ended in disaster—a failed coup in Cuba that had left Washington humiliated. Now, news had broken that the conspirators had been sentenced to thirty years in Cuban prisons and Kennedy had been left humiliated. The atmosphere in Washington was sure to be tense. Charles, back in England, was unsettled by the news. He'd always hoped Edward would stay safe, away from the mounting tensions of the Cold War. But now, with the growing threat of nuclear conflict between the U.S. and the Soviet Union, Washington seemed perilously close to the front lines.

As Edward sat in the quiet of his cabin, he couldn't help but think of his father. Was this the right choice? Was he sailing into danger? He pictured Charles at home, likely pacing the study, pondering whether it had been wise to encourage Edward's move to the U.S. "Everything will be alright," Edward muttered to himself, echoing what he imagined Charles was telling himself back in England.

The sixth day dawned with a sense of excitement. Edward rose early and stood on deck as the first sight of New York came into view. The iconic silhouette of the Statue of Liberty rose from the mist, her torch held high, a symbol of hope and new beginnings. Ships with water cannons sprayed jubilant arcs of water into the sky, welcoming the Queen Mary into the bustling port.

The disembarkation process was a whirlwind of movement. Edward collected his luggage and guided Max through the throngs of passengers. The air was filled with the sound of shouts and laughter, the clamour of porters unloading bags, and the calls of customs officers. Everything felt new and alive, and for the first time, Edward felt a surge of excitement as the thrill of the adventure coursed through him.

They made their way to Penn Station, where Edward purchased a ticket for the short train ride to Washington, D.C. The station was grand, its high ceilings and marble floors bustling with travellers, each on their own journey. Outside, the streets of New York pulsed with energy. Skyscrapers stretched into the sky, casting long shadows over yellow taxis that darted through the streets. Max, ever observant, seemed slightly overwhelmed by the noise and chaos. His ears twitched at every honk and shout, and he pressed closer to Edward's side.

The train ride to Washington was a chance for Edward to finally relax. He watched the landscape change outside the window, the dense city giving way to rolling fields and small towns, before slowly returning to the outskirts of the nation's capital. The excitement of the journey built as they approached the city. The skyline of Washington wasn't as towering as New York's, but it was stately, the Capitol Building standing tall against the afternoon sky.

When they arrived at Union Station, a young man in a neatly pressed suit greeted them. "Mr. Sterling?" he asked, offering a warm smile. "Welcome to Washington. I'll take you to your flat." They drove through the leafy suburbs, past rows of stately homes and cherry trees just beginning to blossom. The city felt quieter than Edward had expected, more serene. It wasn't the chaotic rush of New York but something more measured, more dignified.

They pulled up in front of a small flat, its brick facade framed by overhanging trees. Edward stepped out of the car and stretched, feeling the strain of the long journey finally begin to fade. The flat was small but comfortable, with large windows that let in the afternoon light and a small garden in the back where Max could stretch his legs. It wasn't home, not yet, but it felt like the beginning of something good.

Max sniffed around the new space, his initial apprehension fading as he explored. Edward sat down on the small couch, taking it all in. After weeks of planning, after the long voyage across the Atlantic, he was finally here. Washington was at his doorstep, with all its possibilities, its dangers, and its allure.

Edward's first few weeks in Washington, D.C., were filled with a mix of adjustment, discovery, and anticipation. The long journey had felt like a buffer between his old life and the new one that awaited him on American soil. Now, as he settled into his small flat in the quiet, leafy neighbourhood, Edward felt both excitement and trepidation about what lay ahead.

His first day at the British Embassy was a whirlwind of introductions, paperwork, and formalities. The embassy building, a stately structure with high ceilings and polished wood floors, was bustling with activity as staff members moved swiftly between offices, exchanging reports and whispers about the world beyond the embassy walls. Edward's role as a junior administrative clerk seemed simple enough on the surface—organising files, typing correspondence, and attending briefings—but there was an undeniable undercurrent of unease that made everything feel more urgent. The Cold War was heating up, and Washington was at the centre of it all.

Max was by his side, of course, a familiar and comforting presence amidst all the newness. Though dogs weren't exactly standard company at the embassy, Max quickly became a fixture. Edward would often walk him through the embassy gardens during breaks, earning friendly smiles and the occasional nod from passing diplomats. The other staff had grown used to seeing Edward and Max together, and the dog's calm presence always seemed to put everyone at ease. His presence was more than just companionship—it made Edward feel grounded, a piece of home that had come with him across the Atlantic.

But no matter how much he immersed himself in his work or explored the vibrant city, there was a part of Edward that couldn't quite settle. Alice was still in Oxford, finishing her final year, and the distance between them felt more pronounced with each passing day. Edward wrote letters every evening, recounting the small details of his day, from the embassy's inner workings to his weekend walks with Max along the Potomac River. He longed for her company, but it felt like an eternity away. Max seemed to sense it too, often sitting by the window, his ears perked up as if expecting Alice to appear at any moment.

The political landscape in Washington was unlike anything Edward had ever experienced. The city hummed with a kind of energy that was both exhilarating and unnerving. Every day brought new headlines—rumours of Cuba, the ever-present strain between the U.S. and the USSR, and President Kennedy's speeches about defending freedom. There was a palpable sense that the world was teetering on the edge of something big, and the embassy staff were constantly on alert, ready for any new development.

Edward's work involved handling some confidential documents—reports on the escalating situation in Cuba, intelligence about Soviet activity in the Caribbean, and diplomatic communications between London and Washington. It wasn't long before he began to notice patterns in the reports, subtle shifts in language that hinted at growing unease between the superpowers. He found himself piecing together clues, trying to make sense of the broader picture. Even Max seemed more alert during their walks through the city, as if he too could sense the anxiety in the air.

As the weeks passed, Edward found moments of solace in exploring his new surroundings. He and Max would take long walks around the National Mall, passing the towering Washington Monument and the stately Lincoln Memorial. The city was a blend of history and modernity, with wide avenues lined with trees and grand buildings that whispered of power and influence. Yet, despite the grandeur, Edward couldn't shake the feeling that something was simmering just beneath the surface, waiting to erupt.

But the one constant thought that occupied his mind was Alice. Every time he passed a bustling café or wandered through one of the city's many parks, he imagined her there with him, sharing the experience. He could already picture the day she would arrive, the two of them exploring the city together, Max trotting happily beside them. Until then, his letters to her became his lifeline, a way to stay connected despite the miles between them.

By the end of his first month, Edward had settled into a routine. He had made a few acquaintances at the embassy—mostly other junior clerks and secretaries who, like him, were adjusting to the complexities of their new roles. But it was Max who had truly become the star of the embassy. People would stop by Edward's office just to see him and offer treats.

Edward often found himself thinking about his father and how he had hoped this job would be a stepping stone towards a career in diplomacy and international affairs for him. Charles had always wanted the best for his children and saw this position as an opportunity for him to make his mark in the world. For now, though, he would focus on his work – on keeping Max happy and on counting down the days until Alice's arrival.

Chapter Five
Into the Shadows

The cold breeze off the Potomac River made Edward pull his coat tighter as he walked briskly through the early morning fog towards the British Embassy in Washington. Max trotted beside him, his nails clicking against the wet pavement, ever alert to Edward's pace. It had been four months since Edward had stepped into the role of junior administrative clerk. Four months of meticulously filing reports, cross-referencing diplomatic documents, and gradually finding his place among the fast-paced workings of international politics. His determination to prove himself had only grown stronger, and the embassy's tightly wound rhythm of efficiency had pushed him to adapt quickly.

He sat at his desk and began working through the piles of documents that had accumulated over the past few days. His job today was organising intelligence reports, a task that, on the surface, appeared mundane. But as Edward sifted through the documents, he noticed odd discrepancies. Certain memos from the Americans didn't align with the British reports. Cuban officials appeared in two places at once, dates that didn't add up, and names that seemed to vanish in the shuffle of papers. He frowned, eyes flicking over the repeated mention of a supposed buildup of Soviet activity in Cuba. The inconsistencies were subtle, but they were there, and Edward's gut told him they weren't accidental. Before he could delve deeper, Mr. Chambers, his boss, stepped into the room. His voice cut through the air like a blade as he spoke directly to Edward, "Please come to my office." Edward swallowed and followed down the narrow hall to his office, Max quietly padding along. Inside, the air was thick with the smell of tobacco. Chambers shut the door behind them, the usual sharpness in his eyes now softened by something deeper – concern, perhaps.

"You've done well these last few months," Chambers began, his voice low. "But what we're about to discuss will take you far beyond filing papers."

Sensing the seriousness of what was about to come, Edward said nothing. Chambers leaned forward, his fingers drumming lightly on his desk. "You've likely seen the reports of Russian activity in Cuba. Washington's on edge. The Americans are already rattling sabres, and we believe there's more going on than either side is letting on." Edward had heard the whispers and caught the nervous glances exchanged in the embassy halls. But to hear it laid out so plainly still shook him. "We need someone on the ground in Cuba," Chambers continued. "Someone low-profile. Someone who speaks Spanish, someone who can blend in. And I believe you and your dog would fit the bill perfectly."

His mind reeling at the thought of being thrown into a potential international crisis in Cuba, Edward would never would have imagined this scenario. "I...I'm not sure what to say," He stammered, trying to process everything. "Why me?" "Because you are the least likely suspect," Chambers said matter-of-factly. "A man with a dog is the perfect disguise. You can blend in and gather information without drawing attention. Keep your ears open but don't speak unless spoken to. Avoid attracting attention to yourself. Stay informed but don't believe everything you read. Listen to what the ordinary Cubans are saying."

Edward was suddenly struck by the enormity of his assignment. He would be a spy on the ground in Cuba. A country heavily influenced by the Soviet Union and surrounded by whispers of nuclear weapons. This was not just a simple task; it was like walking straight into the jaws of a lion. Chambers scrutinised him with a calculating gaze, as if carefully weighing his readiness for the task at hand. "We leave nothing to chance, Sterling," he said sternly. "A boat will depart from Florida under the cloak of darkness. This is a covert operation, and you must evade both American and Cuban patrols. It is a dangerous mission, and your assistance will be minimal once you reach your destination."

Edward's mind raced with potential outcomes, each one fraught with peril. The thought of getting caught by authorities or having everything go wrong sent shivers down his spine. Yet, underneath the fear, a sense of duty burnt within him. He had longed to prove himself, to be a part of something larger than himself. "I'll do it," he said, his voice steady despite the whirlwind of thoughts inside him. Chambers nodded, not at all surprised. "Good. You'll leave in three days."

The trip to Florida started quietly. Edward sat in the front of the car with Max in the back, his ears occasionally perking up at the sound of other passing cars. They had left Washington early, the streets still quiet as they made their way south, avoiding attention.

Driving the car was Alejandra, a Cuban exile who had come to the U.S. with her family in 1953, fleeing Batista's regime. Her father, a prominent artist, had been targeted by Batista's forces, and the family had barely managed to escape. The following year, her father had secured a position as a Fine Art lecturer at Georgetown University in Washington. It had been a difficult transition for Alejandra, who was 15 at the time, but she had adapted. Now, years later, she worked at the British Embassy in Washington, just like Edward.

Edward didn't know her well, but he'd heard her story in passing. It wasn't until this mission came up that they found themselves working together. Alejandra had insisted on joining Edward for the drive to Florida, arguing that her fluency in Spanish and knowledge of the region might be beneficial. She had pressed Chambers for permission to accompany Edward all the way, but Chambers had been firm. Her presence in Cuba, where she might be recognised, could jeopardise everything. Her role was simple: get Edward and Max to Florida, then head back to Washington.

They kept a steady pace, the long stretches of road passing by in silence, broken occasionally by casual conversation. After a while Edward began open up expressing concerns about the mission. Although his Spanish was good, could he really pass as a Cuban? And what about Max? Did they even have dogs like him in Cuba? Alejandra reassured him that the more he relaxed, the more he would blend in. Before Castro's rise to power, many of Cuba's middle class had dogs. Now, many of them roamed the streets, abandoned during the *Vuelos de la Libertad,* the great exodus of professionals and business owners just a few years earlier. Max, though, would be seen as a *'perro afortunado'*—a lucky dog, one whose owner hadn't left him behind. Edward smiled at the thought of the new name

Alejandra's driving was smooth, and Edward appreciated the quiet efficiency with which she handled the car. The first part of the journey passed without incident, the landscape gradually changing from the bustling suburbs of Washington to the more rural expanses of Virginia and the Carolinas.

By early evening, they crossed into North Carolina, then onto Daytona Beach, where they had arranged to stop for the night. Two rooms had been pre-booked by the embassy at a small roadside motel. As they pulled into the car park, the low hum of the car engine faded, replaced by the quiet of the surrounding countryside. The neon sign flickered as they entered the motel's lobby to check in. The rooms were basic but clean, with small windows overlooking the car park and minimal furnishings. Edward let Max out to stretch his legs while Alejandra booked them in. The motel clerk barely glanced at them, handing over the keys with a disinterested nod. It was precisely the kind of unremarkable place they needed—no questions, no attention.

The next morning, they resumed their journey. The highway stretched out before them, the landscape slowly transforming as they entered Georgia, with its long, flat roads lined with trees and scattered farmhouses. Edward read the occasional headline from a discarded newspaper about rising tensions between the U.S. and Cuba, wondering what kind of situation they would find when they arrived.

As they neared Florida, the air grew warmer and the palm trees became more frequent. The trip had been uneventful, which was exactly what they had hoped for. Alejandra focused on the road, while Edward sat quietly, keeping an eye on the map and occasionally checking on Max, who had settled into a comfortable rhythm with the motion of the car. By late afternoon, they reached their destination. Alejandra pulled into a quiet car park near a rest area, the final meeting point before Edward and Max would continue alone. Alejandra parked the car, and they both stepped out, the humid Florida air hitting them immediately. Max sniffed around, his tail wagging slightly as he explored the new surroundings.

"Safe travels," Alejandra said. Edward nodded, appreciating her calm and straightforward demeanour. Without further words, they parted ways—Edward and Max ready to begin the next phase of their mission, while Alejandra prepared for the long drive back to Washington.

After Alejandra left, Edward and Max made their way down to the dock. The sun was beginning to dip below the horizon, casting an orange glow over the water. At the far end of the pier, Edward spotted the man they were supposed to meet—Tomás, a grizzled fisherman who had agreed to ferry them across to Cuba. He was in his fifties, with salt-and-pepper hair and a face weathered by years of sun and sea. His boat, though small, looked sturdy enough, its worn exterior hinting at years of reliable service.

Tomás gave a brief nod as Edward approached, his eyes narrowing as he sized him up. Max, ever alert, sniffed the air cautiously but seemed at ease with the man. "So, you're the one," Tomás said, his voice low and gruff. "I don't ask questions. For the right price, I'll take anyone anywhere." Edward nodded, appreciating the directness. He had been told that Tomás had no strong political allegiances—he wasn't interested in the revolution or the Cold War. To him, the sea was his only loyalty, and as long as the money was good, he would ferry anyone who needed it. "We'll keep it simple then," Edward replied. "In and out. Quick as we can." Tomás gave a crooked smile. "That's how I like it." He glanced at Max, who had now settled by Edward's side. "Good dog. Quiet, but I bet he's smart. He'll do fine out there." With that, Tomás motioned towards the boat. "Be ready to leave in a couple of hours."

As the boat pulled away from the docks, Edward glanced back at the lights of the Florida coast slowly disappearing into the night. Each swell of the sea heightened his sense of distance from home and brought him closer to stepping into a volatile situation. The waters were dark, and the moon, half-covered by clouds, cast an eerie glow over the horizon. Max lay still beside him, his eyes wide and watchful. One of Chambers' contacts had provided them with a map, marking the known patrol routes of both

U.S. and Cuban naval forces. They were to slip through the gaps, avoiding detection at all costs. Edward's palms were slick with sweat as he kept his eyes trained on the horizon, scanning for any sign of trouble.

Hours passed in tense silence. The boat crept forward, the low hum of its engine barely audible over the lapping of the waves. Edward thought of the reports he had read—rumours of Soviet missiles hidden in Cuban jungles, of military build-ups that no one could confirm. The fear of what they might find gnawed at him. Suddenly, the boat's captain gestured sharply, pointing off to the east. Edward squinted into the darkness and saw the faint silhouette of a Cuban patrol boat cutting through the water. They had to be invisible; they had to avoid even the slightest mistake. He crouched lower, pulling Max closer, his breath shallow and quiet.

The patrol boat passed without incident, its searchlight sweeping briefly across the water but never lingering. Edward exhaled slowly, his muscles relaxing for the first time in what felt like hours. But the danger was far from over.

As they neared the Cuban coast, Tomás gave Edward a curt nod. "This is where you get off," he muttered, his voice barely above a whisper. Edward pulled on his pack, checking the small amount of gear he'd been given—basic survival tools, some clothes, and a few other essentials. The sea had been calm for most of the night, the dark horizon blending into the inky water as Tomás skilfully guided the small boat across the Florida Straits. Edward kept his eyes on the distant silhouette of Cuba, barely visible against the pre-dawn sky. Max lay quietly by his feet, occasionally lifting his head as the boat rocked gently with the waves. The journey had been silent—no conversation needed, as they each kept to their tasks, focused on the mission ahead.

As the boat neared the Cuban coastline, the faint outline of Mariel came into view. It was 4:00 in the morning, and the harbour was deserted, its usual activity long since quietened by the late hour. Mariel was not a large port, but its isolated location and natural harbour made it ideal for such clandestine arrivals. The quay, dimly lit by a single flickering light, was lined with old fishing boats and cargo crates, but otherwise, it was still.

Tomás manoeuvred the boat alongside the quay with practiced ease, the engine's low hum disappearing as he cut the motor. The boat bumped gently against the wooden dock, and Tomás looked to Edward, gesturing for him to get moving.

Edward stood up carefully, lifting Max as they stepped off the boat. The quiet of the place was almost unnerving. Edward glanced around, ensuring there were no signs of life, before turning back to Tomás. The fisherman's expression was stern, his eyes narrowing as he spoke in a low voice, "Same time, same date, next week. Don't be late."

Edward nodded, understanding the unspoken warning. There would be no second chances in this. Max pressed close to Edward's leg as they both stepped onto the deserted quay. Tomás gave them one last look, his weathered hand gripping the boat's side, before he pushed off into the darkness. The boat slipped back into the water, its silhouette disappearing as quickly as it had come, leaving Edward and Max standing alone at the edge of the harbour.

The mission had begun.

The days that followed were a rush of cautious movements and constant watchfulness. Edward manoeuvred through the bustling streets of Havana, doing his best to blend in with the lively atmosphere as if he were a native.

Max stayed by his side, drawing smiles and curious glances from locals, further cementing their cover. But beneath the lively surface, Edward could detect the anxiety simmering. Armed soldiers patrolled the streets, their presence a clear sign of the political unrest gripping the island.

Edward's job was straightforward - listen to gossip, read the news, and stay aware of what people were discussing. But every discussion seemed risky; every encounter held the possibility of being caught. The Americans had been right about one thing: something was happening in Cuba. The Soviets weren't being transparent, and the Cubans were caught in the middle of the growing storm.

One evening, as they approached the quayside, Edward's attention was drawn to the water. There, just off the shore, in the dark silhouette of an old, rusting boat, he spotted movement. At first, it was subtle—figures against the backdrop of the sea, slipping quietly along the edges of the pier. He squinted, trying to make out the shapes barely visible in the faint moonlight. There were three, maybe four of them, and they were doing something in the water. Not unloading cargo, not working the boat as sailors would. This was something different, something secretive.

The figures crouched low, occasionally pausing, as if to check their surroundings before continuing with whatever they were up to. Edward felt the chill run down his spine. He and Max ducked into the shadows, careful not to draw attention.

The soft splash of water, the quiet murmur of voices carried on the breeze, and the unmistakable urgency of their movements told Edward this was more than just late-night repairs on a forgotten vessel. His instincts sharpened. These men weren't supposed to be here. He watched as they moved between the boat and the water, their actions quick, deliberate, and shrouded in secrecy.

What were they doing out there, in the dead of night?

Edward crouched behind a crate near the edge of the pier, trying to get a better look. They were too close, and whatever was happening here, it was something they weren't supposed to see. He leaned down, whispering softly to the dog, reassuring him as they stayed hidden in the dark. Edward's pulse raced. This wasn't in the reports. And whatever they were witnessing wasn't meant to be seen by outsiders. He couldn't yet make sense of what they were doing, but one thing was clear: this was dangerous. Far more dangerous than he had anticipated.

Chapter Six
Castro's Catch

The following morning, Edward and Max made their way back to the quay, the site of the previous night's strange events. Today, though, a large crowd had gathered, buzzing with excitement. Edward pushed his way through the onlookers, trying to get a better view, while Max sniffed eagerly at the ground, occasionally glancing up at his companion for direction. The memories of last night's secret actions lingered in Edward's thoughts, but today the dock was bustling for an entirely different purpose. "Castro's here!" someone in the crowd murmured. Fidel Castro, Cuba's enigmatic leader, had arrived for his morning routine—one of his famed public appearances, this time to scuba dive. It was a populist gesture, a way to connect with his people, to show himself as both a revolutionary and a man of the people.

Edward watched from his viewpoint as Castro emerged from the water, still dripping and proudly holding up a string of freshly caught fish. The crowd erupted into cheers, swept up by the leader's charismatic aura as he generously shared the fish with those around him, as if it were a grand feast. Edward couldn't help but observe closely, taking in every detail of the Cuban leader's performance - his way of speaking, his gestures, and how effortlessly he moved among the people. It was more than just a simple morning dive; it was a display of control, presence, and power. And the biblical symbolism behind sharing his catch with his followers was not lost on Edward.

Suddenly, Max began barking. The sharp, excited sound cut through the cheers, causing heads to turn. Edward quickly tried to calm him, but it was too late—Castro's security detail, immediately on alert, swept in, surrounding Castro and scanning the crowd for any threat. Edward steadied himself, careful not to make any sudden moves, hoping Max's outburst hadn't drawn attention.

But Max wasn't barking without reason. His nose led him to the edge of the quay, pulling Edward toward something hidden beneath the surface. One of Castro's guards approached cautiously, eyes locked on Max. When the dog barked again, the guard peered over the side and froze. There, attached to the underside of the quay, was something metallic—something sinister.

A bomb.

"¡Bomba!" the guard yelled, setting off a whirlwind of activity. In an instant, Castro was rushed away, thrown into a waiting Jeep that screeched off into the distance. The crowd, once vibrant and celebratory, scattered in chaos, people pushing and shoving to escape the quay. Whistles blew, and Edward barely had time to react before the explosion ripped through the air. He hit the ground, pulling Max down with him as debris rained around them.

Edward lay on the ground, gasping for air as the chaos unfolded around him. The bomb had exploded right in front of him, mere meters away, and he could feel the heat from the blast on his skin. He struggled to stand, his ears still ringing and his vision blurred. He looked around, trying to make sense of what was happening. The once crowded quay was now a scene of devastation. The sea was filled with debris.

Max let out a sharp bark and tugged at Edward's sleeve, signalling him to hurry. With a jolt, Edward remembered his purpose for being here and forced himself not to panic. They swiftly left the docks and returned to their hotel just as the blaring sirens of ambulances rushing towards the scene could be heard in the distance.

Edward stumbled into the hotel room, unnoticed by the receptionist, who was engrossed in conversation with a couple of guests. His mind was still buzzing from the explosion as he closed the door behind him, grateful for the finality of the latch clicking. He paused for a moment, catching his breath. Max, still alert but quiet, stood by his side, his brown eyes watching Edward intently, as if gauging the level of danger that remained. Edward leaned against the dresser, peeling off his jacket with stiff, deliberate motions, feeling the strain of the morning settle deep in his bones. It wasn't until he faced the mirror that he realised how much the day had taken out of him.

The reflection that greeted him was haggard. Dust smeared across his face, cuts, and bruises marked his arms and hands. He hadn't noticed them in the chaos, adrenaline masking the pain, but now the dull ache began to set in. His shirt was torn, and his hair was dishevelled from the blast. He gently probed the worst of the cuts on his forearm, wincing slightly as he did. Nothing was deep, but they were enough to remind him of how close they'd come.

With a sigh, Edward moved to the bathroom, turning on the taps in the old, chipped bathtub. As the steam rose, filling the small room he let himself sink into the bath, the warmth soothing the tightness in his muscles. Max curled up on the floor nearby, never straying far. Edward closed his eyes for a moment, allowing himself the luxury of simply letting go. Yet the question lingered in his mind—who could have been responsible for planting the bomb? It must have been due to the suspicious activity he had witnessed the previous night. Could it be the work of CIA operatives? Had they secretly landed assassins in Havana? Edward was well aware of the CIA's deep involvement in Cuban politics, but the notion that they would go to such extreme measures to target Castro in a public and risky manner seemed far-fetched, even for them. But there were also other potential culprits to consider - internal Cuban dissidents or maybe even Soviet agents trying to create chaos. His thoughts raced, but no clear answers emerged.

After soaking for a while, Edward climbed out of the bath and dried off. The exhaustion of the morning hadn't left him, but sitting idle in the hotel room wasn't going to give him the answers he needed. He needed to get out, clear his head, and maybe overhear something useful. Pulling on a clean shirt, Edward fastened his watch around his wrist and called for Max. The whippet followed obediently as they stepped out into the afternoon streets of Havana.

They wandered through the narrow, sunlit streets, eventually finding their way to a small local market. Vendors called out, selling fresh fruits, meats, and handmade goods. The air was filled with the rich scent of cooked food and the lively sounds of casual bartering. Edward weaved through the crowd, his senses attuned to the rhythm of the city. Max trotted beside him, attracting the occasional smile from passersby.

They stopped at a café, sitting outside at one of the tables as Edward ordered lunch—a plate of rice, beans, and roasted pork. The flavours were rich, and though his mind was still restless, the food helped ground him. Max sat patiently by his feet, watching the bustling market but staying calm. The surrounding chatter was filled with the usual mix of gossip and local news, though today there was one story on everyone's lips: the explosion at the quay.

Edward listened carefully, picking up pieces of the conversations that floated around him. Some locals speculated wildly about who had been behind the attempt on Castro's life. Others claimed it was the work of exiled Cubans, while a few muttered about the CIA. None of it was useful, just the usual rumour mill spinning out of control. The explosion was big news, but it did nothing to help Edward in his mission. If anything, it had complicated things further. Havana was now on edge, and any movements he made would be under even more scrutiny.

He sipped his coffee, gazing out at the market but lost in thought. The whispers of the CIA's involvement gnawed at him, but without any concrete evidence, it was just speculation. Still, it was a reminder that this wasn't just a straightforward mission—there were layers of deception, and Edward was walking a fine line between gathering information and becoming a target himself.

After a few hours of wandering the market and café, Edward and Max made their way back to the hotel. The streets were quieter now, as if the city was catching its breath after the events of the morning. Edward couldn't shake the feeling that something bigger was brewing—something that would soon pull him deeper into Havana's web of intrigue. For now, all he could do was stay alert and hope that the next piece of the puzzle revealed itself before it was too late.

The next morning, a knock at the hotel door shattered the fragile sense of calm Edward had managed to build. His heart raced as he opened the door to find two men standing there, dressed in plain but unmistakably authoritative clothes. Secret police. The blood drained from Edward's face as they gestured for him to follow. He didn't have a choice.

They directed Edward and Max to the back seat of a waiting car and slowly made their way through the bustling streets of Havana. Passing through checkpoint after checkpoint, Edward felt a mounting unease, unsure where they were ultimately headed. After what felt like an eternity, they pulled up to a large, walled compound with a sign that sent chills down Edward's spine: *Punto Cero* - Castro's heavily guarded private residence. His stomach twisted with fear as he grasped the seriousness of the situation, knowing that entering the compound could mean facing real danger—or even death.

Security was in abundance. Soldiers stood to attention along the walls, closely observing as Edward and Max were escorted into the building. This wasn't a routine questioning; it was much more intimate than that. They walked through opulent corridors before arriving at a spacious chamber where Castro, donning his recognisable military uniform, was already seated. The man who had nearly met his demise just hours ago now appeared peaceful, as if nothing out of the ordinary had occurred.

To Edward's shock, Castro smiled. "You saved my life, but I know why you are here," he said in perfect, measured English. Edward was too stunned to speak. He hadn't expected Castro to know anything about him, let alone his mission. The Cuban leader stood, his eyes locking onto Edward's. Castro continued. "You're working for the British. You want to know what's happening between us and the Soviets. You're not the first." Edward felt his breath catch. How much did Castro know?

As Fidel Castro began speaking to Edward, his voice grew stronger, his words rising from a quiet conversation to something resembling a grand speech, as though he were addressing thousands of his supporters in a packed stadium.

"Look at them!" Castro began, his tone sharp and biting. "Kennedy and Khrushchev—so different, from opposite ends of the political spectrum, yet they are slaves to the same reality. They face the same pressures. Each man wants peace, but around them, their generals, their advisors, push for war! Kennedy, Khrushchev—they're trapped by the hawks who see only conflict!"

Castro paced, his hands gesturing wide, as if painting the scenario before Edward's eyes. "But I tell you this, Edward: a convoy of Soviet ships is on its way to Cuba as we speak. They carry weapons and power, a symbol of strength from the Soviet Union. Let me tell you the truth—the ships will stop. They will turn back just as they approach Cuba's shores. Why? Because this entire drama is pre-planned. Kennedy and Khrushchev—they know what they are doing. Kennedy will make a show of it, but in return, he will remove American missiles from Turkey. They will make it look like a stand-off, but it's all prearranged." He paused, his voice lowering for a moment before rising again. "You must tell your people in London to keep quiet, Edward. The British must not intervene. This is a game between two men who know what is at stake. We don't need more cooks in the kitchen."

Then, with a glint in his eye, Castro turned his attention to the Mafia. "And here, Kennedy and I—again, we are alike. We want them gone—the mob, the crime lords who infect our nations. I was successful in driving them out of Cuba. They ran casinos, exploited the poor and corrupted everything they touched. I sent them packing, Edward! Bobby Kennedy should take a page from my book. Maybe he'll have the same success. But you know, it's funny. I'm one step ahead of them, always one step ahead. The Mafia, the CIA—they have tried, and they will try again to kill me. But they will fail, as they failed yesterday with that bomb." His voice grew darker and more ominous as he leaned in closer to Edward. "Tell the Kennedys to be careful. There are many who want them gone. More powerful enemies than they realise. They should watch themselves because one day, the target will be on their back, not mine."

Castro stood tall again, looking out as if surveying the whole world. "Remember this, Edward. Those who seek power through violence often find themselves the victims of it. Let this be a warning to all who think they can rule the world with a clenched fist."

As Castro's intense speech wound down, his tone shifted, becoming more relaxed and even warm. "Edward," he said, offering a smile that almost seemed out of place after the gravity of their conversation. "I could offer you and Max a trip back to America aboard my yacht, *The Granma*. It's quite the experience."

Edward smiled politely but shook his head. "Thank you, but I think it's better if we stick to the original plan." Castro nodded, his smile remaining. "Very well. Then, allow me to offer something more comfortable for the remainder of your stay. You'll be my guest at the Hotel Nacional de Cuba. It's much more fitting for someone in your position. Consider it my gift." Edward hesitated for a moment, but given the circumstances, it was an offer he couldn't refuse.

Castro nodded thoughtfully, then gestured to the telephone on the desk. "Call your people, Mr. Sterling. Don't worry. The Americans think they've tapped every phone line on the island, but they only hear what we allow them to hear. I know your people must be worried. Reassure them—and remind them, there's no need to intervene."

Castro knelt down to Max and, reaching into his pocket, pulled out a small silver disc which had been engraved with a tocororo, bird the symbol of Cuba. "Freedom, Edward. The Bird of Freedom. This is a medal for Max. For his bravery. He should wear it on his collar with pride." And with that, Castro left the room.

Edward glanced at the telephone, his mind racing. He was touched by Castro's thoughtfulness, but how could Castro be so certain of British anxiety? The idea that the Cuban government might be eavesdropping on the British Embassy made him uneasy. For a moment, he hesitated to reach for the phone, unsure of who else might be listening. He picked up the receiver and relayed the message word for word to a surprised Mr. Chambers in Washington.

Returning to their small hotel, Edward and Max quickly gathered their few belongings before a government car whisked them through the busy streets of Havana, the tension from the previous day's events still palpable in the city.

Upon arrival, the opulence of the Hotel Nacional de Cuba immediately struck Edward. Perched on a hill overlooking the Malecón and the sparkling waters of the Gulf of Mexico, it was an iconic symbol of Havana's glamorous past. The whitewashed façade gleamed in the sunlight, while inside, rich marble floors and grand chandeliers greeted them. The grandeur of the hotel, with its high ceilings and ornate details, was a contrast to the simple life outside its walls.

During its heyday in the 1940s and 1950s, it had been the playground of the world's elite—Hollywood stars, politicians, and, most notably, members of the American Mafia. Infamous figures like Meyer Lansky and Lucky Luciano had once walked these halls, using the hotel as a hub for their operations when Havana was a playground for the rich and powerful. Those days were gone, thanks to Castro's expulsion of the Mafia from Cuba, but the hotel still carried the air of that lost opulence.

As they entered their luxurious room, Edward took in the view from the balcony. Below, the sprawling gardens of the hotel stretched out, dotted with palm trees and lounge chairs. Guests strolled leisurely through the well-manicured grounds, completely at ease. The serenity of the place seemed almost absurd given the high stakes of the political world just beyond the hotel's doors. Max padded around the room, his tail wagging as he explored the new space.

For the next few days, Edward and Max found themselves slipping into the easy rhythm of hotel life. They dined in the grand dining room, where chandeliers cast a soft glow over tables adorned with crisp white linens. The waiters, dressed immaculately, served meals of roast meats and tropical fruits with coffee that was rich and aromatic. Edward couldn't help but appreciate the beauty and comfort of it all—yet it felt wrong. While he sat in luxury – outside, he knew the streets of Havana were filled with people struggling under Castro's regime. He sympathised with the poor, the exploited—those who had suffered under Batista and now under Castro, whom he saw as just another corrupt ruler, albeit dressed in revolutionary rhetoric.

He and Max spent time wandering the grounds of the hotel, admiring the sweeping views of the sea and the lush gardens that surrounded them. Max, ever curious, chased the occasional lizard that darted across the path, while Edward found himself reflecting on the odd juxtaposition of their situation. Despite the surrounding beauty, Edward couldn't ignore the sense of isolation that came from the fact that no newspapers were available in the hotel, leaving him with little access to outside news and only Castro's cryptic words echoing in his mind. Inside the walls, life seemed perfect. The sun shone, the food was delicious, and there was nothing to suggest that the world was teetering on the edge of disaster. And yet, all around them, the Cuban Missile Crisis was unfolding exactly as Castro had said it would. President Kennedy had imposed a quarantine around the island, halting Soviet ships en route to Cuba. On October 24th, the world held its breath as the Soviet fleet, approaching the quarantine line, abruptly turned around. Edward and Max were blissfully unaware of just how close the world thought it had come to the brink of nuclear war. The world outside was tense, but within the hotel, Edward and Max were caught in a strange bubble of tranquillity.

Chapter Seven

THE LONG ROAD NORTH

EXACTLY ONE WEEK AFTER their arrival in Cuba, a jeep rolled up to the *Hotel Nacional* to collect Edward and Max. The driver, a quiet man in military fatigues, gave a curt nod, his face expressionless as they loaded their bags. The streets of Havana were unusually still in the early morning light, with the distant hum of the city muted and quiet. The of streetlamps was the only signs of life as they wound through the empty streets, heading towards the coast.

At Mariel, the harbour was bathed in the soft glow of the rising sun, and there, as expected, stood Tomás, waiting by his small boat. The water lapped gently at the dock as he gave a slight wave, his lined face revealing no emotion, just the steady patience of a man used to the sea. He expressed no surprise as Edward and Max arrived in a Jeep. The boat was ready, bobbing with the rhythm of the calm waves. With few words exchanged, Edward and Max climbed aboard.

As the engine sputtered to life, they drifted away from the island, the sight of Cuba growing smaller and smaller. Max sat quietly beside Edward, his alert eyes scanning the horizon, the medal Castro had given him still hanging from his neck, a symbol of their brief yet significant time in Havana. Edward stared ahead, his thoughts drifting like the boat through the still water. The last few days had been a delicate dance between diplomacy and danger, and now, as they left Cuba behind, the anxiety gradually began to fade into the endless sea.

The crossing was long, the sea stretching out in all directions. Edward tried to find comfort in the monotony, but his mind kept replaying the events of the past week. It had been a narrow escape from a place teetering on the brink of conflict. As the day wore on, the sun sank lower in the sky, casting a golden hue over the water, finally signalling the end of their journey.

When they reached the docks in Florida, the sun was already dipping beneath the horizon, casting long shadows across the wooden planks. Alejandra was waiting, her figure silhouetted against the fading light. Her face lit up with a mixture of relief and concern as she waved them over. Edward disembarked, nodding to Tomás, who, after receiving his payment, simply tipped his hat and set off back into the twilight.

As Alejandra drove them north to Washington, D.C., her mood grew more serious. She kept glancing in the rearview mirror, her lips tight with concern. "We're being followed," she muttered, barely loud enough for Edward to hear. He shifted in his seat, turning to glance behind them. Sure enough, a car had been trailing them for the last few miles, two indistinct figures visible through the windscreen. "They don't seem like fellow travellers," Edward said, his voice calm but cautious.

The car behind them stayed at a steady distance, never overtaking but never falling far behind. After another few tense miles, Alejandra turned off the main road and pulled into the car park of the same motel they had stayed in on their way down, just outside Daytona Beach. The car followed, parking near the main road.

Inside the motel, Edward and Alejandra checked in, trying to appear nonchalant despite the unease gnawing at them. Once inside, they briefly discussed their next move. "We could drive off in an hour," Edward suggested, his voice low. But Alejandra shook her head, her brow furrowed in thought. "If they're up to something, they could tamper with the car while we're inside. Better not risk it."

For the next hour, they waited, watching the shadows lengthen as the night deepened. Finally, Alejandra peeked through the curtains, her eyes scanning the car park. "They're gone," she whispered. The car that had been following them had vanished, though neither of them was certain if it was a coincidence or part of a larger plot. Exhausted and unsure, they retired for the night. Max remained at Edward's side, his ears alert, sensing the unease in the air.

The next morning, Edward inspected the car thoroughly. Nothing seemed out of place—no cuts on the brake lines, no signs of tampering—but the unease lingered. Alejandra, ever practical, suggested they leave the car behind and take a taxi into Daytona Beach, where they could catch a train back to Washington. After some deliberation, Edward agreed.

The taxi ride into Daytona Beach was uneventful, though the driver was more than happy to point out landmarks, talking excitedly about the upcoming Daytona 500 as they passed the boardwalk and the wide, sandy shores. The town was just waking up; beachgoers already setting up umbrellas and chairs in the early morning light.

When they arrived at the train station, it was bustling with the usual morning commuters. Alejandra purchased their tickets, and with a few hours to spare before the train, they wandered through the nearby Riverfront Shops, stopping for a quiet breakfast at a small café. The normality of it all felt strange, given the danger they had just escaped.

By the time they returned to the station, the sun was high in the sky, and the train was pulling into the platform. They boarded, settling into their seats as the train began its steady journey north. Max curled up beneath Edward's feet, his calm presence a balm after the week's tension. The train swayed gently as it moved through the countryside, the rhythmic clatter of the wheels on the track a soothing backdrop.

As the hours passed, the landscape shifted from the flat, sandy plains of Florida to the rolling hills and green fields of the southern states. Edward watched the scenery pass by, lost in thought. The train ride was long, but after the intensity of their time in Cuba, the quiet and uneventful journey was a relief. They were heading back to Washington, back to the familiar, but the events of the past week stayed with him, lingering like an unanswered question.

When they finally arrived at Union Station, it was late afternoon. The city was as busy as ever with the usual rush of travellers moving through the station with purpose. At the station's exit, Edward and Alejandra paused, sharing a tired but grateful look. "That was... something," Alejandra said with a wry smile, her eyes reflecting the exhaustion of the past few days.

"Eventful, to say the least – what shall we do about the car?" asked Edward.

"It'll probably be cheaper to leave it there, but don't worry, I'll get it collected and make sure Chambers doesn't see the cost." Alejandra laughed softly. "I'll see you on Monday, Edward. Have a good weekend." With that, they parted ways, each heading back to their lives.

Edward walked towards the exit, Max trotting beside him, his steps light and content. The Cuban medal clinked softly against Max's collar, a reminder of the unusual journey they had just completed. Edward knew the world was changing, shifting in ways he couldn't yet understand. But for now, he was home.

Chapter Eight
CRANES OVER LONDON

Alice arrived in Washington with a warmth that immediately eased the tension Edward and Max had been feeling for weeks. She laughed, calling them both heroes, though Edward felt far from it. Max, however, seemed to enjoy the praise, his Cuban medal prominently displayed in a photograph published by The Washington Post. Though the article celebrated Max's recognition, any real details of their activities remained firmly under wraps. Still, the appearance of Max in the paper made one thing clear—whoever was watching them wasn't done yet.

Edward had sensed it almost from the moment they stepped off the boat back in Florida. They never approached directly, but Edward felt their presence, their eyes on him, their footsteps echoing behind him in alleys and streets. And as the weeks passed, Edward became more convinced that the CIA had been behind the explosion in Havana and that they were monitoring him.

The sense of being watched lingered in everything he and Max did. Every stroll through Dupont Circle, every coffee at a quiet corner shop, felt like it was being monitored. The shadow of suspicion crept through their days, making what should have been a fascinating stay in Washington feel uncomfortable and claustrophobic. But Alice's arrival made things easier. With her beside him, Edward found it easier to shake off the sense of paranoia, even if only for a while.

Thanksgiving was a curious novelty for Edward, Alice, and Max. They gathered with their new friends at the Embassy, enjoying turkey and stuffing, sharing laughs, and trying to forget about the cold gaze of the CIA agents hovering nearby. Christmas was quieter, spent in their small flat in Washington. They exchanged gifts, sang carols, and even walked through the streets to see the city's festive lights. Max, of course, was the centre of attention wherever they went, his medal gleaming in the winter sun.

But as May approached, the sense of finality settled in. It was time to leave. Edward had mixed feelings—he had learnt so much during his time in America, but it was difficult to enjoy the last few months. Bidding farewell to his colleagues at the Embassy was bittersweet, though Alejandra's hug lingered a bit longer than the others. She had been a steady presence through all the uncertainty.

The train ride to New York was filled with quiet reflection. As the city's skyline appeared on the horizon, Edward couldn't help but think back on everything that had happened in the past twelve months. The memories felt tangled—danger, laughter, the thrill of espionage, and the strange feeling of always being watched. But now, it was all coming to an end. The Queen Mary awaited them at the docks, ready to take them across the Atlantic and back to England.

Twelve months had passed since Edward and Max first set off for their American adventure. Now, the familiar grey skies welcomed them as they arrived. They had both decided to spend some time in London. Both Edward and Alice needed jobs and felt that London would be the best place to base themselves. At least for a few months. Edward felt a mix of emotions—a sense of relief at being back on British soil yet a nagging unease lingered. The return to normality didn't feel as comforting as he had expected. Something was off.

For weeks, Edward had been plagued by the unsettling feeling of being watched in London too. Strangers seemed to linger too long at street corners, or their gazes would follow him for just a moment too long. There was no clear evidence, but the paranoia had crept into every corner of his life, its shadow growing longer with each passing day.

One rainy afternoon, as he sat leafing through an old newspaper in his living room, a headline caught his attention. He stopped mid-page and questioned out loud, "Guy McClean is now overseeing the royal collection of paintings at Buckingham Palace?" The name leapt off the page, immediately stirring old suspicions that had never quite died down. Could it really be true? Could Guy, the man who had argued so vehemently for a Communist state, now be so closely tied to the British establishment?

The longer Edward stared at the article, the more the uneasy pieces of the past began falling into place. He had never fully trusted Guy, and now the thought of him working so close to the heart of the British Establishment sent a cold chill through his spine.

Without hesitation, Edward reached for the phone and dialled his father, Charles. As the call connected, his voice trembled slightly. "...I'm not sure who to trust any more. Did you hear about Guy? He's at Buckingham Palace."

Charles listened carefully, his silence urging Edward to continue. But then, in the middle of the conversation, there it was—a faint click on the line. Edward froze. "Father..." he whispered. "I think the line's bugged."

They quickly agreed to meet in person the next day, choosing an open space where they could easily spot anyone with ill intentions. Edward hung up, the unsettling realisation settling in deeper. The game he thought he had left behind was far from over.

Richmond Park was nearly empty when Edward arrived, Max trotting quietly at his side. The early morning air was cool, a light mist clinging to the grass as they approached the old oak tree where Charles was waiting. As Edward sat down beside his father, the unease he had been carrying for months seemed to intensify. In an attempt lighten the air, Edward made a joke, speaking in a poor Russian accent, "Have you seen the cranes migrating south?" But Charles didn't smile. His expression remained serious as he looked at his son. "Don't play games, Edward. We can't just assume an old friend of yours has bad intentions because he held far-left views at university."

Charles leaned in, lowering his voice. "But you think you're being followed?"

Edward hesitated, the truth lingering on his tongue, waiting to be spoken. "Ever since... well, ever since that business with the Soviets last November," he said, deliberately vague, not wanting to reveal the full extent of his dealings in Cuba. His father, however, understood the broader implications.

Later that evening, as the rain came down, they found refuge in a small pub tucked away in a quiet corner of the city. Inside, the warmth and hum of conversation did little to settle Edward's nerves. His father had slipped outside, pulling up his collar as he went into a telephone booth just outside. Edward watched through the foggy window before his gaze turned to the inside of the pub. Was the man at the bar nursing his drink too long? Was the man in the corner really reading his newspaper?

Charles finished his call, his expression tight. He sat next to Edward, his face unreadable. "We are being watched," Charles confirmed in a low voice, glancing subtly at the man at the bar.

That night, as they drove through the rain-soaked streets heading north, the uncertainty of what lay ahead became harder to ignore. They were en route to see John Lockhart, one of Charles' old colleagues from MI5. John's house was a relic of the Cold War, filled with secrets. The heavy curtains and low light gave the impression of a man who had spent his life moving in shadows.

Lockhart poured them each a whisky as the three settled into deep leather chairs, the air thick with cigarette smoke. "Guy McClean's been working at the Courtauld Gallery," John began, his voice measured. "He's been cataloguing the collection for weeks now. We've had him under surveillance, but we haven't got enough to act on so far." Edward leaned forward, his brow furrowing. "I can approach him. Max and I... we could pay him a visit. See if he slips up." The suggestion lingered for a short while before Lockhart took a long drag of his cigarette, considering. "It's risky," he admitted, "but it might shake something loose. You should know, though—MI5's been watching you too, Edward." Edward stiffened. "What? Why?" Lockhart sighed, swirling the whisky in his glass. "The CIA flagged you. They've been spreading rumours that you'd turned – suggesting you might be working for the Communists after, well, thwarting one of their operations."

Lockhart gave a small, reassuring smile. "Don't worry. I'll clear it up. I'll call them off. But you'll need to be careful. We're not the only ones in the game."

Chapter Nine

FOOTSTEPS IN THE GALLERY

A FEW DAYS LATER, Edward, Alice, and Max stood in the courtyard of Somerset House, the autumn chill biting at their skin. Edward adjusted his jacket, taking a deep breath before heading into the Courtauld Gallery. Max's tail wagged idly as he sat beside Alice, both of them watching the steady flow of people passing by. Edward disappeared inside, his mind focused, his instincts alert.

The gallery was quiet, the soft shuffle of footsteps barely disturbing the silence. The air was thick with the scent of old paint and varnished wood, as though history itself had settled in the corners of the room. Edward's eyes scanned the walls, searching. Then he saw him—Guy McClean, standing alone in front of a large canvas, staring blankly at the artwork as though it could protect him.

Their eyes met. In an instant, Guy's face paled. He didn't hesitate. Without a word, he bolted, pushing through the gallery's heavy doors and into the corridors beyond. Edward lunged forward, the sound of his footsteps echoing through the gallery's hallowed halls. People turned in confusion, but he didn't stop. He burst through the door, out into the courtyard, just in time to see Guy leap onto a bicycle parked at the gate.

"Stop him!" Edward shouted as he sprinted towards the entrance.

Alice and Max stood frozen for a moment, their surprise evident. Then, as if by some divine stroke of luck, a taxi rolled up just in time. Edward yanked the door open, pulling Alice and Max inside. "Follow that bike!" he barked, his adrenaline kicking into high gear. The driver raised an eyebrow, but a grin spread across his face. "I've always wanted someone to say that," he muttered as the taxi roared to life, tires screeching as they tore off after Guy.

The streets of London were a maze, narrow, and winding. The rain slicked the roads, making the chase treacherous. Guy weaved in and out of traffic, his wheels kicking up water with every sharp turn. Edward leaned forward, watching the figure grow smaller as they sped through the rain-soaked city. The taxi's engine roared as they hurtled through the alleys, tires skidding around corners. The distance between them and Guy shortened, but he was quick—he knew the streets well.

Every sharp corner felt like it might be the last. They narrowly avoided pedestrians, dodged cars, and splashed through puddles, their sights set firmly on Guy. "Faster!" Edward urged, his voice tight with urgency.

The chase felt like it stretched for miles, their hearts pounding in their chests. Rain lashed at the windows, obscuring their view. Guy's silhouette appeared and disappeared in the mist, but Edward never lost him. They approached Hampstead Heath, the trees standing like shadowy figures in the distance. Guy darted off the main road and vanished into the park.

"This is as far as I go," the taxi driver called out as he pulled to a stop at the park's entrance. Edward nodded, shoving a handful of notes into the driver's hand. "Wait here."

He and Max jumped out, dashing into the open heath. Max's instincts kicked in immediately, his speed unmatched as he shot ahead of Edward, his powerful legs carrying him towards the fleeing figure. Guy was no match for Max's agility. Within moments, Max had caught up, barking furiously, circling Guy as he tried to pedal faster. Guy kicked out, trying to keep the dog at bay, but Max didn't back down. His barking echoed through the empty heath, drawing the attention of the few scattered walkers. But they were confused, unsure whether to intervene or stay back. Edward sprinted across the wet grass, his lungs burning with the effort. But by the time he reached Max, Guy was gone, having disappeared into the trees. Max sat, panting heavily, looking up at Edward with apologetic eyes. Breathless and soaked, Edward stood at the edge of the park, defeated. Guy had slipped through his fingers.

Later that night, back at John Lockhart's house, the tension was palpable. The rain that had been pounding the streets earlier had finally eased, leaving behind a damp stillness. Inside, the atmosphere remained thick with frustration and unease. John poured himself a stiff drink, the glass catching the dim light as he moved. His face was clouded with thought, lines etched by the strain of the situation.

"We had men watching his usual haunts," John muttered, pacing the room as his drink swirled in hand. "They were stationed at his flat for weeks. But we didn't expect a bloody bicycle chase," he said with a sharp edge of disbelief in his voice. "We didn't even know he had a bike." The unexpected nature of Guy's escape had caught everyone off guard.

Edward sat in one of the leather armchairs, rubbing his face in exhaustion. The sting of failure gnawed at him, the memory of losing Guy still fresh. "He was faster than I thought," Edward admitted, frustration simmering beneath his calm exterior. The missed opportunity weighed on him deeply. John stopped pacing and turned sharply to face Edward, his eyes dark with intensity. His voice dropped to a low, steady tone, heavy with everything left unsaid. "You don't know the half of it," he said grimly, swirling the last of his drink. He took a deep sip before continuing, his movements deliberate. "Guy McClean—he's not just another defector. He's gone rogue, yes, but his ambitions... they're on a different scale than anything we initially thought."

Walking over to the cluttered desk, John picked up a thick folder, the edges frayed from handling. He tossed it onto the table in front of Edward. "This is the full extent of what we know."

Edward's fingers trembled slightly as he flipped open the folder. Classified reports spilt out—names, photographs, a tangle of intelligence that painted a grim picture. His brow furrowed deeper with each page he read.

John continued, his words dropping like stones. "From within the heart of the British establishment, McClean has been quietly recruiting. Not just sympathisers—true believers in his radical, extremist views. He's been grooming them, possibly even experimenting with hypnosis, trying to get them to carry out the kind of acts he believes would impress the Soviet Union."

Edward looked up, his eyes narrowing as the full scale of the situation dawned on him. "And what's the end game here? What's he trying to do?"

John's voice darkened, his gaze growing colder. "McClean is trying to gain favour with the hardliners in the Kremlin—the ones who think Khrushchev's lost his nerve. He wants to make a splash, something so bold it'll force their hand. There's talk of a plan – something big. In July, Kennedy's set to give a speech in front of the Berlin Wall. McClean wanted to take him out. He was planning to station a marksman—someone in a tall building, perfectly positioned to assassinate him."

Edward's breath caught, his shock and anger barely contained. "That's insanity," he said, his voice barely a whisper as the enormity of the plot sank in. Then a thought struck him, and he remembered something Fidel Castro had said about Kennedy's enemies circling. "Who's the gunman?"

John's reply was cold. "A Frenchman named Lucien. He's involved with organised crime the drugs trade in Marseille. That's how McClean was going to pay him. We've already tipped off the CIA. I just hope they act on it. John McCone has a much closer relationship with Kennedy than Allen Dulles ever did. They can't afford to overlook this"

Edward grasped the seriousness of the situation, realising just how close the world had come to disaster. The information they had gathered had the potential to save lives—or cause significant harm.

As the weeks went by, an uneasy feeling continued to gnaw at Edward. Yet, the world carried on as if nothing had changed. The stillness around him felt almost unnerving. One cool morning, the phone rang, breaking the silence that had settled in Edward's mind. It was John Lockhart again. "Edward," John's voice was tight with urgency. "Pravda ran a story this morning. McClean—he made it. He's in Moscow. They're hailing him as a hero." Edward's heart sank, though he couldn't say he was surprised. "What does it say?" Lockhart read the article, his voice brimming with frustration. "The Soviets are celebrating him as a defector, saying he's a man of principle who outsmarted British intelligence. They're calling him a hero." "Of course they are," Edward muttered, bitterness rising in his throat. "They don't know the whole story."

McClean's triumph, however, would unravel faster than anyone could predict. Just two days later, the phone rang again—this time with an entirely different tone in John's voice. There was excitement in the air. "Edward, you're not going to believe this," John began. "Kennedy himself called Khrushchev after we fed the information to the CIA. They spoke directly, and now the Kremlin's turned on McClean. He's been arrested."

Edward felt a strange mix of relief and disbelief. "So, trying to impress the Kremlin backfired?" "Exactly," John replied, the satisfaction clear in his voice. "It seems McClean's plan to assassinate Kennedy in Berlin was too extreme, even for them. Khrushchev couldn't afford to let it happen. McClean's out of favour, and this time, there's no escape." Edward leaned back in his chair, the strain that had been pulling at him for weeks finally beginning to ease. The world might never know how close it had come to disaster, but for now, the immediate threat had been neutralised.

Guy McClean, who had held a prominent position within the British establishment, was now forced into a life of obscurity. No longer basking in the grandeur of Buckingham Palace, he resided in a cramped eighth-floor apartment in Moscow. It was a far cry from the luxurious lifestyle he once had. Though he had managed to escape the gulag, his current living conditions and constant surveillance were all he could hope for. He spent his final years drowning his sorrows in vodka. His lonely death went unnoticed for almost a month.

Chapter Ten

A LIFE OF BOOKS AND TEA

WEEKS PASSED AFTER THE chaos of the chase and the revelations about Guy McClean. Life slowly returned to a sense of normality for Edward, though his thoughts often drifted back to the web of espionage that had defined much of the past year. One morning, under the bright spring sky, Edward found himself standing beside Max in Whitehall at a ceremony to celebrate the bravery of ordinary British citizens. This time Max's medal was presented by the Deputy Prime Minister and was a perfect match to the Cuban honour he had received months before.

As they stood together, Edward felt proud, but his mind wandered to quieter things—Oxford, the places that felt like home. The thrill of intrigue had dulled, and something simpler now called to him. His thoughts often returned to the little bookshop where he had once found solace, where dust-covered volumes waited patiently for someone to care.

Soon after, Edward and Alice returned to Oxford for a day trip. The sight that greeted them outside the bookshop hit Edward harder than he expected: a "To Let" sign hung wearily in the window. Mr. Hawthorn had passed away a few months before, and the once-bustling shop had fallen silent. The books inside still lined the shelves, their pages gathering dust as though frozen in time, waiting for someone to breathe life back into them. Edward stood in front of the window for a long moment, his hand resting on Max's head. The dog seemed to sense his hesitation, his tail wagging softly. Alice, standing beside him, gently placed her hand on his arm.

"What do you think, Edward?" she asked quietly. "Should we reopen it?" Edward turned to her, a smile forming on his face. He glanced down at Max, whose eager expression seemed to mirror their own. "We will," he said, his voice firm with quiet determination. "We'll call it 'Hawthorn's Books', in his honour."

The reopening of the bookshop was a modest affair, but one that brought joy to the quiet streets of Oxford. The locals were thrilled to see the shop return, many of them wandering in, nostalgic smiles spreading across their faces as they browsed the shelves. 'Alice's Tearoom', set up next door, was an immediate success. The rich scent of freshly brewed tea and the warmth of baked scones filled the adjoining space, drifting through the archway into the shop. The two businesses complemented each other perfectly—a place for the mind to wander and a place for the soul to rest. Max, ever the centre of attention, took his usual spot by the window, watching the world go by, his medals taking pride of place in the bookshop. Children came to pet him, their parents eager to meet the dog who had earned such distinguished honours. But for Max, this was his peace, his reward for the journey that had brought him here.

As the weeks passed, Edward felt himself settling into the rhythm of the bookshop. He had made his decision—his future adventures would now be ones of the mind, within the pages of books, both reading and writing. The danger and excitement of espionage had served its purpose, but now he sought something quieter. As he often said to his father, Charles, when they discussed the twists of the past year, "One adventure is enough for a man and his whippet."

Charles and Elizabeth, who often visited the tearoom to enjoy a cup of Earl Grey, could not have agreed more. Watching his son, Alice, and Max thrive in this quieter life, he knew Edward had found his peace. The world outside might still be a place of uncertainty and shadows, but here, in this little corner of Oxford, Edward had carved out a sanctuary—a world of books, tea, and the simple joys of life.

One Friday evening towards the end of November, as Edward, Alice, and Max sat down by the fireside surrounded by the warm glow of lamplight, he reflected on how much had changed. Guy McClean was a shadow in a distant city now, the drama of the past finally behind him. Here, in the calm of his reopened shop, with Alice by his side and Max curled up contentedly at his feet, Edward knew that this truly was where he belonged. As they turned on the television set, the BBC Six O'Clock news was being broadcast to be followed by Points of View. Suddenly, all the programmes were interrupted by a newsflash from Dallas, Texas.

Printed in Great Britain
by Amazon